Penguin Books

Clock without Hands

Carson McCullers was born in Columbus,
Georgia, in 1917. She was a Guggenheim
Fellow from 1942 to 1943 and in 1946, and also
received an award from the American Academy
of Arts and Letters in 1945. She wrote *The
Heart is a Lonely Hunter* (1940), *Reflections in a
Golden Eye* (1941), *The Member of the Wedding*
(1946; this book won the New York Critics
Award in 1950 and was staged at the Royal
Court Theatre, London), *The Ballad of the Sad
Café* (1951), *The Square Root of Wonderful* (1958),
a play; *Clock Without Hands* (1961), and *Sweet as
a Pickle and Clean as a Pig* (1964). Many of her
books have been published in Penguins, the
latest of which is *The Mortgaged Heart*. Carson
McCullers was a Fellow of the American
Academy of Arts and Letters. She died in 1967.

Clock Without Hands

Carson McCullers

 Penguin Books

Penguin Books Ltd, Harmondsworth,
Middlesex, England
Penguin Books, 625 Madison Avenue,
New York, New York 10022, U.S.A.
Penguin Books Australia Ltd, Ringwood,
Victoria, Australia
Penguin Books Canada Ltd, 41 Steelcase Road West,
Markham, Ontario, Canada
Penguin Books (N.Z.) Ltd, 182–190 Wairau Road,
Auckland 10, New Zealand

First published in the U.S.A. 1961
Published in Great Britain by the Cresset Press 1961
Published in Penguin Books 1965
Reprinted 1977
Copyright © the Estate of Carson McCullers, 1961

Made and printed in Great Britain by
Richard Clay (The Chaucer Press) Ltd,
Bungay, Suffolk
Set in Monotype Baskerville

For Mary E. Mercer, M.D.

One

Death is always the same, but each man dies in his own way. For J.T. Malone it began in such a simple ordinary way that for a time he confused the end of life with the beginning of a new season. The winter of his fortieth year was an unusually cold one for the Southern town – with icy, pastel days and radiant nights. The spring came violently in middle March in that year of 1953, and Malone was lazy and peaked during those days of early blossoms and windy skies. He was a pharmacist and, diagnosing spring fever, he prescribed for himself a liver and iron tonic. Although he tired easily, he kept to his usual routine. He walked to work and his pharmacy was one of the first businesses open on the main street and he closed the store at six. He had dinner at a restaurant downtown and supper at home with his family. But his appetite was finicky and he lost weight steadily. When he changed from his winter suit to a light spring suit, the trousers hung in folds on his tall, wasted frame. His temples were shrunken so that the veins pulsed visibly when he chewed or swallowed and his Adam's apple struggled in his thin neck. But Malone saw no reason for alarm. His spring fever was unusually severe and he added to his tonic the old-fashioned course of sulphur and molasses – for when all was said and done the old remedies were the best. The thought must have solaced him for soon he felt a little better and started his annual vegetable garden. Then one day as he was compounding a prescription he swayed and fainted. He visited the doctor after this and there followed some tests at the City Hospital. Still he was not much worried; he had spring fever and the weakness of that complaint, and on a warm day he had fainted – a common, even natural thing. Malone had never considered his own death except in some twilight, unreckoned future, or in terms of life insurance. He was an ordinary, simple man and his own death was a phenomenon.

Dr Kenneth Hayden was a good customer and a friend who had his office on the floor above the pharmacy, and the day the reports were due on the tests Malone went upstairs at two o'clock. Once he was alone with the doctor he felt an undefinable menace. The doctor did not look directly at him so that his pale, familiar face seemed somehow eyeless. His voice as he greeted Malone was strangely formal. He sat silent at his desk and handled a paper knife, gazing intently at it as he passed it from hand to hand. The strange silence warned Malone and when he could stand it no longer he blurted:

'The reports came in – am I all right?'

The doctor avoided Malone's blue and anxious gaze, then uneasily his eyes passed to the open window and fixed there. 'We have checked carefully and there seems to be something unusual in the blood chemistry,' the doctor said finally in a soft and dragging voice.

A fly buzzed in the sterile, dreary room and there was the lingering smell of ether. Malone was now certain something serious was wrong and, unable to bear the silence or the doctor's unnatural voice, he began to chatter against the truth. 'I felt all along you would find a touch of anaemia. You know I was once a medical student and I wondered if my blood count was not too low.'

Dr Hayden looked down at the paper knife he was handling on the desk. His right eyelid twitched. 'In that case we can talk it over medically.' His voice lowered and he hurried the next words. 'The red blood cells have a count of only 2·15 million so we have an intercurrent anaemia. But that is not the important factor. The white blood cells are abnormally increased – the count is 208,000.' The doctor paused and touched his twitching eyelid. 'You probably understand what that means.'

Malone did not understand. Shock had bewildered him and the room seemed suddenly cold. He understood only that something strange and terrible was happening to him in the cold and swaying room. He was mesmerized by the paper knife that the doctor turned in his stubby, scrubbed fingers. A long dormant memory stirred so that he was aware of something shameful that had been forgotten, although the memory itself was still unclear. So he suffered a parallel distress – the fear and tension of the doctor's words and the mysterious and unremembered shame. The doctor's hands were white and hairy and Malone could not bear to watch them fooling with the knife, yet his attention was mysteriously compelled.

'I can't quite remember,' he said helplessly. 'It's been a long time and I didn't graduate from medical school.'

The doctor put aside the knife and handed him a thermometer. 'If you will just hold this underneath the tongue –' He glanced at his watch and walked over to the window where he stood looking out with his hands clasped behind him and his feet placed well apart.

'The slide shows a pathological increase in the white blood cells and intercurrent anaemia. There is a preponderance of leucocytes of a juvenile character. In short –' The doctor paused, re-clasped his hands and for a moment stood on tiptoe. 'The long and short of it is, we have here a case of leukemia.' Turning suddenly, he removed the thermometer and read it rapidly.

Malone sat taut and waiting, one leg wrapped around the other and his Adam's apple struggling in his frail throat. He said, 'I felt a little feverish, but I kept thinking it was just spring fever.'

'I'd like to examine you. If you will please take off your clothes and lie down a moment on the treatment table –'

Malone lay on the table, gaunt and pallid in his nakedness and ashamed.

'The spleen is much enlarged. Have you been troubled with any lumps or swellings?'

'No,' he said. 'I'm trying to think what I know about leukemia. I remember a little girl in the newspapers and the parents had her Christmas in September because she was expected soon to die.' Malone stared desperately at a crack in the plaster ceiling. From an adjacent office a child was crying and the voice, half strangled with terror and protest, seemed not to come from a distance, but to be part of his own agony when he asked: 'Am I going to die with this – leukemia?'

The answer was plain to Malone although the doctor did not speak. From the next room the child gave a long, raw shriek that lasted almost a full minute. When the examination was over, Malone sat trembling on the edge of the table, repulsed by his own weakness and distress. His narrow feet with the side callouses were particularly loathsome to him and he put on his grey socks first. The doctor was washing his hands at the corner wash-basin and for some reason this offended Malone. He dressed and returned to the chair by the desk. As he sat stroking his scant, coarse hair, his long upper lip set carefully against the tremulous lower one, his eyes febrile and terrified, Malone had already the meek and neuter look of an incurable.

The doctor had resumed his motions with the paper knife, and again Malone was fascinated and obscurely distressed; the movements of the hand and knife were a part of illness and a part of some mysterious and half-remembered shame. He swallowed and steadied his voice to speak.

'Well, how long do you give me, Doctor?'

For the first time the doctor met his gaze and looked at him steadily for some moments. Then his eyes passed on to the photograph of his wife and two small boys that faced him on his desk. 'We are both family men and if I were in your shoes, I know I would want the truth. I would get my affairs in order.'

Malone could scarcely speak, but when the words came they were loud and rasping: 'How long?'

The buzzing of a fly and the sound of traffic from the street seemed to accent the silence and the tension of the dreary room. 'I think we might count on a year or fifteen months – it's difficult to estimate exactly.' The doctor's white hands were covered with long black strands of hair and they fiddled ceaselessly with the ivory knife, and although the sight was somehow terrible to Malone, he could not take his attention away. He began to talk rapidly.

'It's a peculiar thing. Until this winter I had always carried plain, straight life insurance. But this winter I had it converted to the sort of policy that gives you retirement pay – you've noticed the ads in the magazines. Beginning at 65 you draw two hundred dollars a month all the rest of your life. It's funny to think of it now.' After a broken laugh, he added, 'The company will have to convert back to the way it was before – just plain life insurance. Metropolitan is a good company and I've carried life insurance for nearly twenty years – dropping a little during the depression and redeeming it when I was able. The ads for the retirement plan always pictured this middle-aged couple in a sunny climate – maybe Florida or California. But I and my wife had a different idea. We had planned on a little place in Vermont or Maine. Living this far South all your life you get pretty tired of sun and glare –'

Suddenly the screen of words collapsed and, unprotected before his fate, Malone wept. He covered his face with his broad acid-stained hands and fought to control his sobbing breath.

The doctor looked as though for guidance at the picture of his wife and carefully patted Malone's knee. 'Nothing in this day and age is hopeless. Every month science discovers a new weapon against disease. Maybe soon they will find a way to control diseased cells. And meanwhile, everything possible will be done to prolong life and make you comfortable. There is one good thing about this disease – if anything could be called good in this situation – there is not much pain involved. And we will try everything. I'd like you to check in at the City Hospital as soon as possible and we can give some transfusions and try X-rays. It might make you feel a whole lot better.'

Malone had controlled himself and patted his face with his handkerchief. Then he blew on his glasses, wiped them, and put them back on. 'Excuse me, I guess I'm weak and kind of unhinged. I can go to the hospital whenever you want me to.'

Malone entered the hospital early the next morning and remained there for three days. The first night he was given a sedative and dreamed about Dr Hayden's hands and the paper knife he handled at his desk. When he awoke he remembered the dormant shame that had troubled him the day before and he knew the source of the obscure distress he had felt in the doctor's office. Also he realized for the first time that Dr Hayden was a Jew. He recalled the memory that was so painful that forgetfulness was a necessity. The memory concerned the time when he had failed in medical school in his second year. It was a Northern school and there were in the class a lot of Jew grinds. They ran up the grade average so that an ordinary, average student had no fair chance. The Jew grinds had crowded J.T. Malone out of medical school and ruined his career as a doctor – so that he had to shift over to pharmacy. Across the aisle from him there had been a Jew called Levy who fiddled with a fine blade knife and distracted him from getting the good of the class lectures. A Jew grind who made A-plus and studied in the library every night until closing time. It seemed to Malone that also his eyelid twitched occasionally. The realization that Dr Hayden was a Jew seemed of such importance that Malone wondered how he could have ignored it for so long. Hayden was a good customer and a friend – they had worked in the same building for many years and saw each other daily. Why had he failed to notice? Maybe the doctor's given name had tricked him – Kenneth Hale. Malone said to himself he had no prejudice, but when Jews used the good old Anglo-Saxon, Southern names like that, he felt it was somehow wrong. He remembered that the Hayden children had hooked noses and he remembered once seeing the family on the steps of the synagogue on a Saturday. When Dr Hayden came on his rounds, Malone watched him with dread – although for years he had been a friend and customer. It was not so much that Kenneth Hale Hayden was a Jew, as the fact that he was living and would live on – he and his like – while J.T. Malone had an incurable disease and would die in a year or fifteen months. Malone wept sometimes when he was alone. He also slept a great deal and read a number of detective stories. When he was released from the hospital the spleen was much receded, although the white blood cells were little changed. He was unable to think about the months ahead or to imagine death.

Afterwards he was surrounded by a zone of loneliness, although his daily life was not much changed. He did not tell his wife about his trouble because of the intimacy that tragedy might have restored; the passions of marriage had long since winnowed to the preoccupations of parenthood. That year Ellen was a high school junior and Tommy was eight years old. Martha Malone was an energetic woman whose hair was turning grey – a good mother and also a contributor to the family finances. During the depression she had made cakes to order and at that time it had seemed to him right and proper. She continued the cake business after the pharmacy was out of debt and even supplied a number of drugstores with neatly wrapped sandwiches with her name printed on the band. She made good money and gave the children many advantages – and she even bought some Coca-Cola stock. Malone felt that was going too far; he was afraid it would be said that he was not a good provider and his pride was affronted. One thing he put his foot down on: he would not deliver and he forbade his children and his wife to deliver. Mrs Malone would drive to the customer and the servant – the Malone servants were always a little too young or too old and received less than the going wage – would scramble from the automobile with the cakes or sandwiches. Malone could not understand the change that had taken place in his wife. He had married a girl in a chiffon dress who had once fainted when a mouse ran over her shoe – and mysteriously she had become a grey-haired housewife with a business of her own and even some Coca-Cola stock. He lived now in a curious vacuum surrounded by the concerns of family life – the talk of high school proms, Tommy's violin recital, and a seven-tiered wedding cake – and the daily activities swirled around him as dead leaves ring the centre of a whirlpool, leaving him curiously untouched.

In spite of the weakness of his disease, Malone was restless. Often he would walk aimlessly around the streets of the town – down through the shambling, crowded slums around the cotton mill, or through the Negro sections, or the middle class streets of houses set in careful lawns. On these walks he had the bewildered look of an absent-minded person who seeks something but has already forgotten the thing that is lost. Often, without cause, he would reach out and touch some random object; he would veer from his route to touch a lamp post or place his hands against a brick wall. Then he would stand transfixed and abstracted. Again he would examine a green-leaved elm tree with morbid attention as he picked a flake of sooty bark. The lamp post, the wall, the tree would exist when he was dead and the thought was loathsome to Malone. There was a further confusion – he was unable to acknowledge the reality of approaching death, and the conflict led to a sense of ubiquitous unreality. Sometimes, and dimly, Malone felt he blundered among a world of incongruities in which there was no order or conceivable design.

Malone sought comfort in the church. When tormented by the unreality of both death and life, it helped him to know that the First Baptist Church was real enough. The largest church in town, taking up half a city block near the main street, the property on off-hand reckoning was worth about two million dollars. A church like that was bound to be real. The pillars of the church were men of substance and leading citizens. Butch Henderson, the realtor and one of the shrewdest traders in the town, was a deacon and never missed a service from one year to the next – and was Butch Henderson a likely man to waste his time and trouble on anything that was not as real as dirt? The other deacons were of the same calibre – the president of the Nylon Spinning Mill, a railroad trustee, the owner of the leading department store – all responsible and canny men of business whose judgement was foolproof. And they believed in the church and the hereafter beyond death. Even T.C. Wedwell, one of the founders of Coca-Cola and a multi-millionaire, had left the church $500,000 for the construction of the right wing. T.C.Wedwell had the uncanny foresight to put his faith in Coca-Cola – and T.C. Wedwell had believed in the church and the hereafter to the tune of half a million dollars bequeathal. He who had never made a bad investment had so invested in eternity. Finally, Fox Clane was a member. The old Judge and former congress-man – a glory to the State and the South – attended often when he was in town and blew his nose when his favourite hymns were sung. Fox Clane was a churchman and believer and Malone was willing to follow the old Judge in this as he had followed him in his politics. So Malone went faithfully to church.

One Sunday in early April Dr Watson delivered a sermon that impressed Malone deeply. He was a folksy preacher who often made comparisons to the business world or sports. The sermon this Sunday was about the salvation that draws the bead on death. The voice rang in the vaulted church and the stained glass windows cast a rich glow on the congregation. Malone sat stiff and listening and each moment he expected some personal revelation. But, although the sermon was long, death remained a mystery, and after the first elation he felt a little cheated when he left the church. How could you draw a bead on death? It was like aiming at the sky. Malone stared up at the blue, unclouded sky until his neck felt strained. Then he hurried towards the pharmacy.

That day Malone had an encounter that upset him strangely, although on the surface it was an ordinary happening. The business section was deserted, but he heard footsteps behind him and when he turned a corner the footsteps still followed. When he took a short-cut through an unpaved alley the steps no longer sounded, but he had the uneasy sense of being followed and glimpsed a shadow on the wall. He turned so suddenly that he collided with his follower. He was a coloured boy that Malone knew by sight and in his walks he seemed always to run across him. Or perhaps it was simply that he noticed the boy whenever he saw him because of his unnatural appearance. The boy was medium-sized with a muscular body and a face that was sullen in repose. Except for his eyes, he looked like any other coloured boy. But his eyes were bluish-grey, and set in the dark face they had a bleak, violent look. Once those eyes were seen, the rest of the body seemed also unusual and out of proportion. The arms were too long, the chest too broad – and the expression alternated from emotional sensitivity to deliberate sullenness. The impression on Malone was such that he did not think of him in harmless terms as a *coloured boy* – his mind automatically used the harsh term *bad nigger*, although the man was a stranger to him and as a rule he was lenient in such matters. When Malone turned and they collided, the nigger steadied himself but did not budge, and it was Malone who stepped back a pace. They stood in the narrow alley and stared at each other. The eyes of both were of the same grey-blue and at first it seemed a contest to out-stare each other. The eyes that looked at him were cold and blazing in the dark face – then it seemed to Malone that the blaze flickered and steadied to a look of eerie understanding. He felt that those strange eyes knew that he was soon to die. The emotion was so swift and shocking that Malone shuddered and turned away. The stare had not lasted more than a full minute and there was no seeming consequence – but Malone felt that something momentous and terrible had been accomplished. He walked unsteadily the remaining length of the alley and was relieved to find ordinary friendly faces at the end. He was relieved to get out of the alley and enter his safe, ordinary, familiar pharmacy.

The old Judge often stopped by the pharmacy to have a drink before Sunday dinner, and Malone was glad to see that he was there already, holding forth to a group of cronies who stood before the fountain counter. Malone greeted his customers absently but did not linger. The electric fans on the ceiling churned the mixed odours in the place – syrupy smells from the fountain with the bitter medicinal smells from the compounding section in the rear.

'Be with you in a minute, J.T.,' the old Judge interrupted himself to say as Malone passed on his way to the back room. He was an enormous man with a red face and a rough halo of yellow-white hair. He wore a rumpled linen white suit, a lavender shirt, and a tie adorned with a pearl stick pin and stained with a coffee spot. His left hand had been damaged by a stroke and he rested it cautiously on the counter edge. This hand was clean and slightly puffy from disuse – while the right one, which he used constantly as he talked, was dingy-nailed, and he wore a star sapphire on the ring finger. He was carrying an ebony cane with a silver crooked handle. The Judge finished his harangue against the Federal Government and joined Malone in the compounding section.

It was a very small room, separated from the rest of the store by a wall of medicine bottles. There was just enough room for a rocking chair and the prescription table. Malone had brought out a bottle of bourbon and unfolded a desk chair from a corner. The Judge crowded the room until he lowered himself carefully into the rocking chair. The smell of sweat from his huge body mingled with the smell of castor oil and disinfectant. The whisky splashed lightly against the bottom of their glasses when Malone poured.

'Nothing is so musical as the sound of pouring bourbon for the first drink on a Sunday morning. Not Bach or Schubert or any of those masters that my grandson plays –'

The Judge sang:

'Oh, whisky is the life of man – Oh, whisky! Oh, Johnny!'

He drank slowly, pausing after each swallow to move his tongue in his mouth and take a little after-swallow. Malone drank so quickly that the liquor seemed to blossom in his belly like a rose.

'J.T., have you ever stopped to consider that the South is in the vortex of a revolution almost as disastrous as the War Between the States?' Malone had not considered, but he turned his head to one side and nodded gravely as the Judge went on: 'The wind of revolution is rising to destroy the very foundations on which the South was built. The poll tax will soon be abolished and every ignorant Nigra can vote. Equal rights in education will be the next thing. Imagine a future where delicate little white girls must share their desks with coal black niggers in order to learn to read and write. A minimum-wage law, so outrageously high that it will be the death knell of the rural South, may be forced on us. Imagine paying a passel of worthless field hands by the hour. The Federal Housing Projects are already the ruination of the real estate investors. They call it slum clearance – but who makes the slums, I ask you? The people who live in slums make the slums themselves by their own improvidence. And mark my words, those same Federal apartment buildings – modern and Northern as they are – will be turned into a slum in ten years time.'

Malone listened with the trustful attentiveness that he had given the sermon at church. His friendship with the Judge was one of his great prides. He had known the Judge ever since he had come to Milan and had often hunted at his place during the hunting season – he was there the Saturday and Sunday before the death of the Judge's only son. But a special intimacy had flowered after the Judge's illness – when it seemed for a time that the old congressman was finished politically. Malone would visit the Judge on Sundays bringing a mess of turnip greens from his garden or a certain water-ground cornmeal that the Judge liked. Sometimes they would play poker – but usually the Judge would talk and Malone would listen. At these times Malone felt near the centre of power – almost as though he too was a congressman. When the Judge was up and around, he came often on Sunday to the pharmacy and they would drink together in the compounding room. If Malone ever had misgivings about the ideas of the old Judge, he smothered them immediately. For who was he to cavil with a congressman? And if the old Judge was not right, who could be right? And now that the old Judge was talking about running for Congress again, Malone felt that the responsibility would be where it ought to be and he was content.

With the second drink the Judge brought out his case of cigars and Malone prepared both of them because of the Judge's handicap. The smoke rose in straight lines to the low ceiling and broke there. The door to the street was open and a slice of sunlight made the smoke clouds opalescent.

'I have a serious request to ask you,' Malone said. 'I want to draw up my will.'

'Always glad to oblige you, J.T. Is there anything particular?'

'Oh, no, just the usual thing – but I want it done as soon as you can get around to it.' He added in a flat voice, 'The doctors say I don't have too long to live.'

The Judge stopped rocking and put down his glass. 'Why, what on earth! What's wrong with you, J.T.?'

Malone was speaking of his illness for the first time and the words somehow relieved him. 'Seems I have a blood disease.'

'A *blood* disease! Why, that's ridiculous – you have some of the best blood in this State. I well remember your father who had his wholesale pharmacy on the corner of Twelfth and Mulberry in Macon. And your mother I remember, too – she was a Wheelwright. You have the best blood in this State in your veins, J.T., and never forget that.'

Malone felt a little chill of pleasure and pride that passed almost immediately. 'The doctors –'

'Oh, doctors – with all due respect to the medical profession, I seldom believe a word they say. Never let them intimidate you. Some years ago when I had that little seizure, my doctor – Doc Tatum over at Flowering Branch – began this alarmist talk. No liquor or cigars or even cigarettes. Seemed like I had better learn to pick a harp or shovel coal.' The Judge's right hand plucked on imaginary strings and made a shovelling gesture. 'But I spoke up to Doc and followed my own instincts. Instincts, that's the only thing a man can follow. And here I am as hale and hearty as a man my age could wish to be. And poor Doc, the irony – I was a pall bearer at his funeral. The irony was that Doc was a confirmed teetotaller who never smoked – although he occasionally enjoyed a chew. A grand fellow and a glory to the medical profession, but like every man-jack of them, alarmist in judgement and fallible. Don't let them intimidate you, J.T.'

Malone was comforted, and as he began another drink he began to consider the possibility that Hayden and the other doctors had made a mistaken diagnosis. 'The slide showed it was leukemia. And the blood count showed a terrible increase in leucocytes.'

'Leucocytes?' asked the Judge. 'What are they?'

'White blood cells.'

'Never heard of them.'

'But they're there.'

The Judge massaged the silver handle of his cane. 'If it was your heart or liver or even your kidneys I could understand your alarm. But an insignificant disorder like too many leucocytes does seem a little far-fetched to me. Why I've lived for more than eighty years without ever considering if I have any of those leucocytes or not.' The Judge's fingers curved with a reflexive movement, and as he straightened them again, he looked at Malone with wondering blue eyes. 'All the same it's a fact that you look peaked these days. Liver is excellent for the blood. You ought to eat crisp fried calves' liver and beef liver smothered in onion sauce. It's both delicious and a natural cure. And sunlight is a blood moderator. I bet there's nothing wrong with you that sensible living and a spell of Milan summer won't cure.' The Judge lifted his glass. 'And this is the best tonic – stimulates the appetite and relaxes the nerves. J.T., you are just tense and intimidated.'

'Judge Clane.'

Grown Boy had entered the room and stood there waiting. He was the nephew of Verily the coloured woman who worked for the Judge, and he was a tall fat boy of sixteen who did not have his share of sense. He wore a light blue suit that was too tight for him and pointed tight shoes that made him walk in a gingerly crippled way. He had a cold and, although a handkerchief showed in his breast pocket, he wiped his running nose with the back of his hand.

'It's Sunday,' he said.

The Judge reached in his pocket and gave him a coin.

As Grown Boy limped eagerly towards the fountain, he called back in a sweet slow voice, 'Much obliged, Judge Clane.'

The Judge was looking at Malone with quick sad glances but when the pharmacist turned back to him he avoided his eyes and began to massage his cane again.

'Every hour – each living soul comes closer to death – but how often do we think of it? We sit here having our whisky and smoking our cigars and with each hour we approach our final end. Grown Boy eats his cone without ever wondering about anything. Here I sit, a ruin of an old man, and death has skirmished with me and the skirmish has ended in a stalemate. I am a stricken field on death's old battleground. For seventeen years since the death of my son, I have waited. "Oh, Death where is thy victory now?" The victory was won that Christmas afternoon when my son took his own life.'

'I have often thought of him,' Malone said. 'And grieved for you.'

'And why – why did he do it? A son of such beauty and such promise – not yet twenty-five and graduated *magna cum laude* at the University. He had already taken his law degree and a great career could have been open to him. And with a beautiful young wife and a baby already on the way. He was well-to-do – even rich – that was the zenith of my fortunes. For a graduation present I gave him Sereno for which I had paid forty thousand dollars the year before – almost a thousand acres of the best peach land. He was the son of a rich man, fortune's darling, blessed in all ways, at the threshold of a great career. That boy could have been President – he could have been anything he wanted. Why should he die?'

Malone said cautiously, 'Maybe it was a fit of melancholia.'

'The night he was born I saw a remarkable falling star. It was a bright night and the star made an arc in the January sky. Miss Missy had been eight hours in labour and I had been grovelling before the foot of her bed, praying and crying. Then Doc Tatum collared me and jerked me to the door saying, "Get out of here you obstreperous old blunderbuss – get drunk in the pantry or go out in the yard". And when I went out in the yard and looked at the sky, I saw the arc of that falling star and it was just then that Johnny, my son, was born.'

'No doubt it was prophetic,' Malone said.

'Later on I bustled into the kitchen – it was four o'clock – and fried Doc a brace of quail and cooked grits. I was always a great hand at frying quail.' The Judge paused and then said timidly, 'J.T., do you know something uncanny?'

Malone watched the sorrow on the Judge's face and did not answer.

'That Christmas we had quail for dinner instead of the usual turkey. Johnny, my son, had gone hunting the Sunday before. Ah, the patterns of life – both big and small.'

To comfort the Judge, Malone said: 'Maybe it was an accident. Maybe Johnny was cleaning his gun.'

'It wasn't his gun. It was my pistol.'

'I was hunting at Sereno that Sunday before Christmas. It was probably a fleeting depression.'

'Sometimes I think it was –' The Judge stopped, for if he had said another word he might have cried. Malone patted his arm and the Judge, controlling himself, started again. 'Sometimes I think it was to spite me.'

'Oh, no! Surely not, sir. It was some depression that no one could have seen or controlled.'

'Maybe,' said the Judge, 'but that very day we had been quarrelling.'

'What about it? Every family quarrels.'

'My son was trying to break an axiom.'

'Axiom? What kind of axiom?'

'It was about something inconsequential. It was a case about a black man it was my duty to sentence.'

'You are just blaming yourself needlessly,' Malone said.

'We were sitting at the table with coffee and cigars and French cognac – the ladies were in the parlour – and Johnny got more and more excited and finally he shouted something to me and rushed upstairs. We heard the shot a few minutes later.'

'He was always impetuous.'

'None of the young people these days seem to consult their elders. My son up and got married after a dance. He woke up his mother and me and said, "Mirabelle and I are married". They had eloped to a Justice of the Peace, mind you. It was a great grief to his mother – although later it was a blessing in disguise.'

'Your grandson is the image of his father,' Malone said.

'The living image. Have you ever seen two boys so shining?'

'It must be a great comfort to you.'

The Judge mouthed his cigar before he answered: 'Comfort – anxiety – he is all that is left.'

'Is he going to study for the law and enter politics?'

'No!' the Judge said violently. 'I don't want the boy in law or politics.'

'Jester is a boy who could make his career in anything,' Malone said.

'Death,' said the old Judge, 'is the great treachery. J.T., you feel the doctors believe you have a fatal disease. I don't think so. With all due respects to the medical profession, the doctors don't know what death is – who can know? Even Doc Tatum. I, an old man, have expected death for fifteen years. But death is too cunning. When you watch for it and finally face it, it never comes. It corners around sideways. It slays the unaware as often as it does the ones who watch for it. Oh, what, J.T.? What happened to my radiant son?'

'Fox,' Malone asked, 'Do you believe in the eternal life?'

'I do as far as I can encompass the thought of eternity. I know that my son will always live within me, and my grandson within him and within me. But what is eternity?'

'At church,' Malone said, 'Dr Watson preached a sermon on the salvation that draws a bead on death.'

'A pretty phrase – I wish I had said it. But no sense at all.' He added finally, 'No, I don't believe in eternity as far as religion goes. I believe in the things I know and the descendants who come after me. I believe in my forebears, too. Do you call that eternity?'

Malone asked suddenly, 'Have you ever seen a blue-eyed Nigra?'

'A Nigra with blue eyes you mean?'

Malone said, 'I don't mean the weak-eyed blue of old coloured people. I mean the grey-blue of a young coloured boy. There's one like that around this town and today he startled me.'

The Judge's eyes were like blue bubbles and he finished his drink before he spoke. 'I know the nigger you're thinking of.'

'Who is he?'

'He's just a nigger around the town who's of no interest to me. He gives massages and caters – a jack-of-all-trades. Also he is a well-trained singer.'

Malone said, 'I ran into him in an alley behind the store and he gave me such a shock.'

The Judge said, with an emphasis that seemed at the moment peculiar to Malone, 'Sherman Pew, that's the nigger's name, is of no interest to me. However, I'm thinking of taking him on as a houseboy because of the shortage of help.'

'I never saw such strange eyes,' Malone said.

'A woods colt,' the Judge said; 'something wrong between the sheets. He was left a foundling in the Holy Ascension Church.'

Malone felt that the Judge had left some tale untold but

far be it from him to pry into the manifold affairs of so great a man.

'Jester – speaking of the devil –'

John Jester Clane stood in the room with the sunlight from the street behind him. He was a slight limber boy of seventeen with auburn hair and a complexion so fair that the freckles on his upturned nose were like cinnamon sprinkled over cream. The glare brightened his red hair but his face was shadowed and he shielded his wine-brown eyes against the glare. He wore blue jeans and a striped jersey, the sleeves of which were pushed back to his delicate elbows.

'Down, Tige,' Jester said. The dog was a brindle boxer, the only one of its kind in town. And she was such a fierce looking brute that when Malone saw her on the street alone he was afraid of her.

'I soloed, Grandfather,' Jester said in a voice that was lifted with excitement. Then seeing Malone, he added politely, 'Hey, Mr Malone, how are you today?'

Tears of remembrance, pride and alcohol came to the Judge's weak eyes. 'Soloed did you, darling? How did it feel?'

Jester considered a moment. 'It didn't feel exactly like I had expected. I expected to feel lonely and somehow proud. But I guess I was just watching the instruments. I guess I just felt – responsible.'

'Imagine, J.T.,' the Judge said, 'a few months ago this little rapscallion just announced to me that he was taking flying lessons at the airport. He'd saved his own money and already made the arrangements for the course. But with not so much as by-my-leave. Just announced, "Grandfather, I am taking flying lessons".' The Judge stroked Jester's thigh. 'Didn't you, Lambones?'

The boy drew up one long leg against another. 'It's nothing to it. Everybody ought to be able to fly.'

'What authority prompts the young folk these days to act on such unheard of decisions? It was never so in my day or yours, J.T. Can't you see now why I am so afraid?'

The Judge's voice was grieving, and Jester deftly removed his drink and hid it on a corner shelf. Malone noticed this and was offended on the Judge's behalf.

24

'It's dinner time, Grandfather. The car is just down the street.'

The Judge rose ponderously with his cane and the dog started to the door. 'Whenever you're ready, Lambones.' At the door he turned to Malone. 'Don't let the doctors intimidate you, J.T. Death is the great gamer with a sleeve of tricks. You and I will maybe die together while following the funeral of a twelve-year-old girl.' He pressed his cheek to Malone and crossed the threshold to the street.

Malone went to the front of the place to lock the main door and there he overheard a conversation. 'Grandfather, I hate to say this but I do wish you wouldn't call me "Lambones" or "darling" in front of strangers.'

At that moment Malone hated Jester. He was hurt at the term 'stranger', and the glow that had warmed his spirit in the presence of the Judge was darkened instantly. In the old days, hospitality had lain in the genius of making everyone, even the commonest constituents at a barbecue, feel that they belonged. But nowadays the genius of hospitality had disappeared and there was only isolation. It was Jester who was a 'stranger' – he had never been like a Milan boy. He was arrogant and at the same time over-polite. There was something hidden about the boy and his softness, his brightness seemed somehow dangerous – it was as though he resembled a silk-sheathed knife.

The Judge did not seem to hear his words. 'Poor J.T.,' he said as the door of the car was opened, 'it's such a shocking thing.'

Malone quickly locked the front door and returned to the compounding room.

He was alone. He sat in the rocking chair with the compounding pestle in his hands. The pestle was grey and smooth with use. He had bought it with the other fixtures of the pharmacy when he had opened his business twenty years ago. It had belonged to Mr Greenlove – when had he last remembered him? – and at his death the estate sold the property. How long had Mr Greenlove worked with this pestle? And who had used it before him? . . . The pestle was old, old and indestructible. Malone wondered if it wasn't a relic from Indian times. Ancient as it was, how long would it still last? The stone mocked Malone.

He shivered. It was as though a draught had chilled him, although he noticed that the cigar smoke was undisturbed. As he thought of the old Judge a mood of elegy softened his fear. He remembered Johnny Clane and the old days at Sereno. He was no stranger – many a time he had been a guest at Sereno during the hunting season – and once he had even spent the night there. He had slept in a big four-poster bed with Johnny and at five in the morning they had gone down to the kitchen, and he still remembered the smell of fish roe and hot biscuits and the wet dog smell as they breakfasted before the hunt. Yes, many a time he had hunted with Johnny Clane and had been invited to Sereno, and he was there the Sunday before the Christmas Johnny died. And Miss Missy would sometimes go there, although it was mainly a hunting place for boys and men. And the Judge, when he shot badly, which was nearly all the time, would complain that there was so much sky and so few birds. Always there was a mystery about Sereno even in those days – but was it the mystery of luxury that a boy born poor will always feel? As Malone remembered the old days and thought of the Judge now – in his wisdom and fame and inconsolable grief – his heart sang with love as grave and sombre as the organ music in the church.

As he stared at the pestle his eyes were brilliant with fever and fear and, transfixed, he did not notice that from the basement underneath the store there was a knocking sound. Before this spring he had always held to a basic rhythm about life and death – the bible rhythm of the three score years and ten. But now he dwelt on the inexplicable deaths. He thought of children, exact and delicate as jewels in their white satin coffins. And that pretty singing teacher who swallowed a bone at a fish fry and died within the hour. And Johnny Clane, and the Milan boys who died during the first war and the last. And how many others? How? Why? He was aware of the knocking sound in the basement. It was a rat – last week a rat had overturned a bottle of asafetida and for days the stench was so terrible that his porter refused to work in the basement. There was no rhythm in death – only the rhythm of the rat, and the

26

stench of corruption. And the pretty singing teacher, the blond young flesh of Johnny Clane – the jewel-like children – all ended in the liquefying corpse and coffin stench. He looked at the pestle with a sick surprise for only the stone remained.

There was a footstep on the threshold and Malone was so suddenly unnerved that he dropped the pestle. The blue-eyed nigger stood before him, holding in his hand something that glinted in the sun. Again he stared into those blazing eyes and again he felt that look of eerie understanding and sensed that those eyes knew that he was soon to die.

'I found this just outside the door,' the nigger said.

Malone's vision was dimmed by shock and for a moment he thought it was the paper knife of Dr Hayden – then he saw it was a bunch of keys on a silver ring.

'They're not mine,' Malone said.

'I noticed Judge Clane and his boy was here. Maybe they're theirs.' The nigger dropped the keys on the table. Then he picked up the pestle and handed it to Malone.

'Much obliged,' he said. 'I'll inquire about the keys.'

The boy went away and Malone watched him jay-walk across the street. He was cold with loathing and hatred.

As he sat holding the pestle there was in him enough composure to wonder at those alien emotions that had veered so violently in his once mild heart. He was split between love and hatred – but what he loved and what he hated was unclear. For the first time he *knew* that death was near him. But the terror that choked him was not caused by the knowledge of his own death. The terror concerned some mysterious drama that was going on – although what the drama was about Malone did not know. The terror questioned what would happen in those months – how long? – that glared upon his numbered days. He was a man watching a clock without hands.

There was the rhythm of the rat. 'Father, Father, help me,' Malone said aloud. But his father had been dead for these long years. When the telephone rang Malone told his wife for the first time that he was sick and asked her to drive to the pharmacy and take him home. Then he sat stroking the stone pestle as a sort of comfort as he waited.

Two

The Judge kept the old-fashioned dinner hours and dinner on Sundays was at two o'clock. Shortly before the time to ring the dinner chimes, Verily, the cook, opened the shutters of the dining room which had been closed all morning against the glare. The mid-summer heat and light beat at the windows and beyond there was the burnt lawn and the fever-bright border of flowers. Some elm trees at the end of the lawn were dark and breezeless in the lacquered brightness of the afternoon. Jester's dog responded first to the dinner summons – he walked slowly under the table, letting the long damask cloth linger against his spine. Then Jester appeared and stood waiting behind his grandfather's chair. When the old Judge entered, he seated him carefully and then took his own place at the table. The dinner began according to custom and as usual vegetable soup was the first course. With the soup two breads were served – beaten biscuits and cornsticks. The old Judge ate greedily, sipping buttermilk between swallows of bread. Jester could manage only a few spoonfuls of the hot soup and he drank iced tea and held the cold glass to his cheek and forehead from time to time. According to the habits of the house, there was no conversation during the soup course except for the Judge's customary Sunday remark: 'Verily, Verily, I say unto you; you shall dwell in the house of the Lord forever.' He added his little Sunday joke: 'If you cook this well.'

Verily said nothing – only pursed her purplish wrinkled lips.

'Malone has always been one of my most loyal constituents and best supporters,' the Judge said when the chicken was brought and Jester had stood up to carve. 'You keep the liver, Son, you ought to have liver at least once a week.'

'Yes, Grandfather.'

So far the meal was consonant with habits and the customs of the house. But later a strange dissonance appeared, a jolt in the usual harmony, a sense of cross purposes and communication deflected and estranged. Neither the old Judge nor his grandson realized what happened at the time, but at the end of the long, hot, customary meal they both felt that something had altered so that their relationship could never again be the same.

'The *Atlanta Constitution* today referred to me as a reactionary,' the Judge said.

Jester said softly: 'I'm sorry.'

'Sorry,' said the old Judge. 'It's nothing to be sorry about. I'm glad!'

Jester's brown eyes exchanged a long, asking stare.

'You must take the word "reactionary" literally these days. A reactionary is a citizen who *reacts* when the age-long standards of the South are threatened. When States' rights are trampled on by the Federal Government, then the Southern patriot is duty-bound to react. Otherwise the noble standards of the South will be betrayed.'

'What noble standards?' Jester asked.

'Why boy, use your head. The noble standards of our way of life, the traditional institutions of the South.'

Jester did not say anything but his eyes were sceptical and the old Judge, sensitive to all his grandson's reactions, noticed this.

'The Federal Government is trying to question the legality of the Democratic Primary so that the whole balance of Southern civilization will be jeopardized.'

Jester asked, 'How?'

'Why, boy, I'm referring to segregation itself.'

'Why are you always harping on segregation?'

'Why, Jester, you're joking.'

Jester was suddenly serious. 'No, I'm not.'

The Judge was baffled. 'The time may come in your generation – I hope I won't be here – when the educational system itself is mixed – with no colour line. How would you like that?'

Jester did not answer.

'How would you like to see a hulking Nigra boy sharing a desk with a delicate little white girl?'

The Judge could not believe in the possibility of this; he wanted to shock Jester to the gravity of the situation. His eyes challenged his grandson to react in the spirit of Southern gentlemen.

'How about a hulking white girl sharing a desk with a delicate little Negro boy?'

'What?'

Jester did not repeat his words, nor did the old Judge want to hear again the words that so alarmed him. It was as though his grandson had committed some act of incipient lunacy, and it is fearful to acknowledge the approach of madness in a beloved. It is so fearful that the old Judge preferred to distrust his own hearing, although the sound of Jester's voice still throbbed against his eardrums. He tried to twist the words to his own reason.

'You're right, Lambones, whenever I read such communist ideas I realize how unthinkable the notions are. Certain things are just too preposterous to consider.'

Jester said slowly: 'That's not what I meant.' From habit Jester glanced to see if Verily was out of the room. 'I can't see why coloured people and white people shouldn't mix as citizens.'

'Oh, Son!' It was a cry of pity, helplessness, and horror. Years ago when Jester was a child he had been occasionally subject to sudden vomiting fits at the table. Then, tenderness had overcome disgust, and afterwards the Judge had felt himself sickish in sympathy. Now the old Judge responded to this sudden situation in the same way. He held his good hand to his ear as if he had an earache and he stopped eating.

Jester noticed the old Judge's distress and he felt a tremor of sympathy. 'Grandfather, we all have our own convictions.'

'Some convictions are not tenable convictions. After all, what are convictions? They're just what you think. And you are too young, Son, to have learned the pattern of thought. You are just deviling your grandfather with foolish words.'

Jester's emotion of sympathy withered. He was staring at a picture over the mantelpiece. The picture was a Southern scene of a peach orchard and a Negro shack and a cloudy sky.

'Grandfather, what do you see in that picture?'

The Judge was so relieved that the tension had snapped that he chuckled a little. 'The Lord knows it ought to remind me of my folly. I lost a small fortune with those pretty peach trees. Your Great-aunt Sara painted it the year she died. And then right along afterwards the bottom dropped out of the peach market.'

'I mean, what do you actually see in the picture?'

'Why, there's an orchard and clouds and a Nigra shack.'

'Do you see there between the shack and the trees a pink mule?'

'A *pink mule*?' The Judge's blue eyes popped in alarm. 'Why naturally not.'

'It's a cloud,' Jester said. 'And it looks to me exactly like a pink mule with a grey bridle. Now that I see it that way, I can't see the picture any other way any more.'

'I don't see it.'

'Why you can't miss it, galloping upwards – a whole sky of pink mules.'

Verily came in with the dish of corn pudding: 'Why, mercy, what's the matter with you all. You ain't scarcely touch your dinner.'

'All my life I had seen the picture like Aunt Sara had intended it. And now this summer I can't see what I'm supposed to see in it. I try to look back as I used to see it – but it's no good. I still see the pink mule.'

'Do you feel dizzy, Lambones?'

'Why no. I'm just trying to explain to you that this picture is a sort of – symbol – I guess you might say. All my life I've seen things like you and the family wanted me to see them. And now this summer I don't see things as I used to – and I have different feelings, different thoughts.'

'That's only natural, Son.' The Judge's voice was reassuring, but his eyes were still anxious.

'A symbol,' Jester said. He repeated the word because it was the first time he had spoken it in conversation, although it was one of his favourite words in school compositions. 'A symbol of this summertime. I used to have ideas exactly like everybody else. And now I have my own ideas.'

'Such as?'

Jester did not answer for a moment. And when he spoke his voice broke with tension and adolescence. 'For one thing, I question the justice of white supremacy.'

The challenge was plain as a loaded pistol flung across the table. But the Judge could not accept it; his throat was dry and aching and he swallowed feebly.

'I know it's a shock to you, Grandfather. But I had to tell you, otherwise you would have taken it for granite I was like I used to be.'

'Take it for granted,' the Judge corrected. 'Not *granite*. What kind of wild-eyed radicals have you been consorting with?'

'Nobody. This summer I've been very –' Jester was going to say *I've been very lonely*, but he could not bring himself to admit this truth aloud.

'Well, all I say is, this talk about mixed races and pink mules in the picture are certainly – abnormal.'

The word struck Jester like a blow in the groin and he flushed violently. The pain made him strike back: 'All my life I have loved you – I even worshipped you, Grandfather. I thought you were the wisest, kindest man on earth. I listened to everything you said like gospel truth. I saved everything in print about you. My scrapbook on you was started as soon as I began to read. I always thought you ought to be – President.'

The Judge ignored the past tense and there was the warmth of self-pride in his veins. A mirrorlike projection reflected his own feelings for his grandson – the fair, unfolding child of his fair doomed son. Love and memory left his heart open and unaware.

'That time I heard about when that Negro from Cuba was making a talk in the House I was so proud of you. When the other congressmen stood up you sat back farther in your chair, propped your feet up and lighted a cigar. I thought it was wonderful. I was so proud of you. But now I see it differently. It was rude and bad manners. I am ashamed for you when I remember it. When I think back how I used to worship you –'

Jester could not finish, for the distress of the old Judge was obvious. His crippled arm tightened and his hand curled hard and spastic while the elbow joint crooked uncontrollably. The shock of Jester's words interacted with his disorder so that tears of emotional and physical hurt started. He blew his nose and said after some moments of silence: 'Far sharper than a serpent's tooth it is to have a thankless child.'

But Jester resented the fact that his grandfather was so vulnerable. 'But Grandfather, you've talked all you want to always. And I have listened and believed. But now that I have a few opinions of my own, you won't stand for it and start quoting the Bible. That isn't fair because it automatically puts a person in the wrong.'

'It's not the Bible – Shakespeare.'

'Anyway I'm not your child. I'm your grandson and my father's child.'

The fan turned in the breathless afternoon and the sun shone on the dining table with the platter of carved chicken and the butter melted in the butter dish. Jester held the cool tea glass to his cheek and fondled it before he spoke.

'Sometimes I wonder if I'm not beginning to suspect why my father – did what he did.'

The dead still lived in the ornate, Victorian house with the cumbersome furniture. The dressing room of the Judge's wife was still kept as it was in her lifetime with her silver appointments on the bureau and the closet with her clothes untouched except for occasional dusting. And Jester grew up with his father's photographs, and in the library there was the framed certificate of admittance to the bar. But though all through the house there were reminders of the lives of the dead, the actual circumstances of death were never mentioned, even by inference.

'What did you mean by that?' the old Judge asked with apprehension.

'Nothing,' Jester said. 'Except it is natural to wonder about my father's death under the circumstances.'

The Judge tinkled the dinner bell and the sound seemed to gather the tension in the room. 'Verily, bring a bottle of that elderberry wine Mr Malone brought me for my birthday.'

'Right now, today, sir?' she asked, as wine was usually

served only at Thanksgiving and Christmas dinners. She took the wineglasses from the sideboard and wiped off the dust with her apron. Noticing the platter of uneaten food, she wondered if a hair or a fly had been cooked in the candied yams or dressing. 'Is anything wrong with the dinner?'

'Oh, it's delicious. I just have a mite of indigestion, I suppose.'

It was true that when Jester talked of the mixing of races his stomach seemed to churn and all appetite had left him. He opened and poured the unaccustomed wine, then drank as soberly as if he had been drinking at a wake. For the break in understanding, in sympathy, is indeed a form of death. The Judge was hurt and grieving. And when hurt has been caused by a loved one, only the loved one can comfort.

Slowly he put his right hand palm upward on the table towards his grandson, and after a moment Jester placed his own palm on his grandfather's. But the Judge was not satisfied; since words had hurt him, his solace lay in words. He grasped Jester's hand in desperation.

'Don't you love your old grandfather any more?'

Jester took his hand away and drank some swallows of wine. 'Sure I do, Grandfather, but –'

And though the Judge waited, Jester did not finish the sentence and the emotion was left qualified in the strained room. The Judge's hand was left extended and the fingers fluttered a little.

'Son, has it ever occurred to you that I am not a wealthy man any longer? I have suffered many losses and our forebears suffered losses. Jester, I'm worried about your education and your future.'

'Don't worry. I can manage.'

'You've heard the old saw about the best things in life are free. It's both true and false like all generalizations. But this one thing is true: you can get the best education in this country absolutely and entirely free. West Point is free and I could get you an appointment.'

'But I don't want to be an army officer.'

'What do you want to be?'

Jester was perplexed, uncertain. 'I don't know exactly. I like music and I like flying.'

'Well go to West Point and enter the Air Corps. Anything you can get from the Federal Government you ought to take advantage of. God knows the Federal Government has done enough damage to the South.'

'I don't have to decide about the future until I graduate from high school next year.'

'What I was pointing out, Son, is my finances are not what they used to be. But if my plans materialize, then one day you will be a wealthy man.' The Judge had often made vague hints from time to time of future wealth. Jester had never paid much attention to these intimations, but now he asked:

'What plans, Grandfather?'

'Son, I wonder if you are old enough to understand the strategy.' The Judge cleared his throat. 'You're young and the dream is big.'

'What is it?'

'It's a plan to correct damages done and to restore the South.'

'How?'

'It's the dream of a statesman – not just a cheap political scheme. It's a plan to rectify an immense historical injustice.'

Ice cream had been served and Jester was eating, but the Judge let it melt in his saucer. 'I still don't get the drift, sir.'

'Think, Son. In any war between civilized nations what happens to the currency of the country who didn't win? Think of World War I and World War II. What happened to the German mark after the armistice? Did the Germans burn their money? And the Japanese yen? Did the Japanese make bonfires of their currency after their defeat? Did they, Son?'

'No,' Jester said, bewildered by the vehemence of the old man's voice.

'What happens in any civilized nation after the cannons are silenced and the battlefields are quiet? The victor allows the vanquished to rest and restore in the interests of the common economics. The currency of a conquered nation is always redeemed – devalued, but still redeemed. Redeemed: look what is happening now in Germany – in Japan. The Federal Government has redeemed the enemy money and helped the vanquished restore itself. From time immemorial the currency of a defeated nation has been left in circulation. And the lira in Italy – did the Federal Government confiscate the lira? The lira, the yen, the mark – all, all were redeemed.'

The Judge was leaning forward over the table and his tie brushed his saucer of melted ice cream, but he did not notice.

'But what happened after the War Between the States? Not only did the Federal Government of the United States free the slaves which were the *sine qua non* of our cotton economy, so that the very resources of the nation were gone with the wind. A truer story was never written than *Gone With the Wind*. Remember how we cried at that picture show?'

Jester said: 'I didn't cry.'

'You certainly did,' the Judge said. 'I wish I had written that book.'

Jester did not comment.

'But back to the issue. Not only was the economy of the nation deliberately wrecked, but the Federal Government completely invalidated all Confederate currency. Not one cent could be redeemed for the wealth of the entire Confederacy. I have heard of Confederate bills used as kindling for fires.'

'There used to be a whole trunk of Confederate bills in the attic. I wonder what happened to them.'

'They're in the library in my safety box.'

'Why? Aren't they worthless?'

The Judge did not answer; instead, he pulled from his vest pocket a Confederate thousand-dollar bill. Jester examined it with some of the wonder of his attic-playing childhood. The bill was so real, so green and believable. But the wonder illumined him only for a few instants, then was extinguished. Jester handed the bill back to his grandfather.

'It would be a lot of money if it was real.'

'One of these days it might be "real" as you say. It will be, if my strength and work and vision can make it so.'

Jester questioned his grandfather with his cold clear eyes. Then he said: 'The money is nearly a hundred years old.'

'And think of the hundreds of billions of dollars squandered by the Federal Government during those hundred years. Think of the wars financed and public spending. Think of the other currencies redeemed and put back into circulation. The mark, the lira, the yen – all foreign currencies. And the South was, after all, the same flesh and blood and should have been treated as brothers. The currency should have been redeemed and *not* devalued. Don't you see that, Lamb?'

'Well it wasn't and it's too late now.'

The conversation made Jester uneasy and he wanted to leave the table and go away. But his grandfather held him with a gesture.

'Wait a minute. It's never too late to redress a wrong. And I am going to be instrumental in allowing the Federal Government to redress this historic and monumental wrong,' the Judge stated pontifically. 'I am going to have a bill introduced in the House of Representatives if I win the next election that will redeem all Confederate monies, with the proper adjustment for the increase of cost-of-living nowadays. It will be for the South what F.D.R. intended to do in his New Deal. It will revolutionize the economy of the South. And you, Jester, will be a wealthy young man. There are ten million dollars in that safety box. What do you say to that?'

'How did that much Confederate money accumulate?'

'There are ancestors of vision in our family – remember that, Jester. My grandmother, your great-great-grandmother, was a great lady and a woman of vision. When the war was over she traded for Confederate money, swapping now and then a few eggs and produce – once I remember her telling me she even swapped a laying hen for three million dollars. Everybody was hungry in those days and everybody had lost faith. All except your great-great-grandmother. I will never forget her saying: "It will come back, it's bound to".'

'But it never has,' Jester said.

'Until now – but you wait and see. It will be a New Deal for the economy of the South and benefit the nation as a whole. Even the Federal Government will be benefited.'

'How?' Jester asked.

The Judge said calmly, 'What benefits one benefits the whole. It's simple to understand; if I had a few million, I would invest, employ a lot of people and stimulate local business. And I'm just one individual to be reimbursed.'

'Another thing,' Jester said. 'It's been about a hundred years. And how could the money be traced?'

The Judge's voice was triumphant. 'That's the least of our worries. When the Treasury announces that Confederate money is being redeemed, the money will be found all right. Confederate bills will be cropping up in attics and barns all over the South. Cropping up all over the nation and even in Canada.'

'What good would it do to have money cropping up in Canada?'

The Judge said with dignity: 'That's just a figure of speech – a rhetorical example.' The Judge looked hopefully at his grandson. 'But what do you think of the legislation as a whole?'

Jester avoided his grandfather's eyes and did not answer. And the Judge, desperate for his approval, persisted. 'What, Lamb? It's the vision of a great statesman,' he added more firmly. 'The *Journal* has many times referred to me as a "great statesman" and the *Courier* always speaks of me as the first citizen of Milan. Once it was written I was "one of the fixed stars in that glorious firmament of Southern statesmen". Don't you admit I am a great statesman?'

The question was not only a plea for reassurance, but a desperate command for emotional annealment. Jester could not answer. For the first time he wondered if his grandfather's reasoning power had been affected by the stroke. And his heart balanced between pity and the natural instinct for separation that divides the sound from the infirm.

The veins of age and excitement crawled in the Judge's temple and his face flushed. Only twice in his life had the Judge suffered from rejection: once when he was defeated in an election for Congress, and again when he sent a long story he had written to the *Saturday Evening Post* and it was returned to him with a form letter. The Judge could not believe this rejection. He read the story again and found it better than all the other stories in the *Post*. Then, suspecting that it had not been properly read, he glued certain pages of the manuscript together and when it was returned another time he never read a *Post* again, and never wrote another story. Now he could not believe that the separation between himself and his grandson was a reality.

'Do you remember how, when you were a little boy, you used to call me Grandy?'

Jester was not moved by the recollection and the tears in his grandfather's eyes irritated him. 'I remember everything.' He rose and stood behind the Judge's chair, but his grandfather would not get up and would not let him leave. He grasped Jester's hand and held it to his cheek. Jester stood stiff with embarrassment and his hand did not respond to the caress.

'I never thought I'd hear a grandson of mine speak as you have done. You said you didn't see why the races shouldn't mix. Think of the logical outcome. It would lead to intermarriage. How would you like that? Would you let your sister marry a Nigra buck if you had a sister?'

'I'm not thinking of that. I was thinking of racial justice.'

'But if your so-called "racial justice" leads to inter-marriage – as it will according to the laws of logic – would you marry a Nigra? Be truthful.'

Involuntarily, Jester was thinking of Verily and the other cooks and washerwomen who had worked at home, and of Aunt Jemima of the pancake ads. His face flushed bright and his freckles darkened. He could not answer immediately, so much did the image appal him.

'You see,' the Judge said. 'You were only making empty lip-service – for the Northerners, at that.'

Jester said: 'I still think that as a judge you judge one crime in two different ways – according to whether it is done by a Negro or a white man.'

'Naturally. They are two different things. White is white

and black is black – and never the two shall meet if I can prevent it.'

The Judge laughed and held Jester's hand when he tried to pull away again.

'All my life I have been concerned with questions of justice. And after your father's death I realized that justice itself is a chimera, a delusion. Justice is not a flat yardstick, applied in equal measure to an equal situation. After your father's death I realized there was a quality more important than justice.'

Jester's attention was always held by any reference to his father and his death. 'What is more important, Grandfather?'

'Passion,' the Judge said. 'Passion is more important than justice.'

Jester stiffened with embarrassment. 'Passion? Did my father have passion?'

The Judge evaded the question. 'Young people of your generation have no passion. They have cut themselves off from the ideals of their ancestors and are denying the heritage of their blood. Once when I was in New York, I saw a Nigra man sitting at a table with a white girl and something in my bloodstream sickened. My outrage had nothing particularly to do with justice – but when I saw those two laughing together and eating at the same table, my bloodstream – I left New York that same day and never went back to that Babel, nor will to my dying day.'

'I wouldn't have minded at all,' Jester said. 'Soon, as a matter of fact, I am going to New York.'

'That's what I meant. You have no passion.'

The words affected Jester violently; he trembled and blushed. 'I don't see –'

'One of these days you may have this passion. And when it comes to you, your half-baked notions of so-called justice will be forgotten. And you will be a man and my grandson – with whom I am well pleased.'

Jester held the chair while the Judge pushed himself up from the table with his stick and stood upright for a moment facing the picture above the mantelpiece. 'Wait a minute, Lamb.' He sought desperately some words that would abridge the chasm that had opened in the last two hours. And finally he said: 'You know, Jester, I can see the pink mule you were talking about – there in the sky over the orchard and the shack.'

The admission altered nothing and they both knew it. The Judge walked slowly and Jester stood near him ready to steady him if necessary. His pity mingled with remorse and he hated pity and remorse. When his grandfather was settled on the library sofa, he said: 'I'm glad you know how I stand. I'm glad I told you.' But the tears in his grandfather's eyes unnerved him so that he was forced to add: 'I love you anyway – I do love you – Grandy.' But when he was embraced, the smell of sweat and the sentimentality disgusted him, and when he had freed himself he felt a sense of defeat.

He ran out of the room and bounded up the staircase three steps at a time. At the head of the upstairs hall there was a window of stained glass which brightened Jester's auburn hair but cast a sallow light on his breathless face. He closed the door of his room and flung himself on the bed.

It was true he had no passion. The shame of his grandfather's words pulsed in his body and he felt that the old man knew that he was a virgin. His hard boy's hands unzipped his fly and touched his genitals for solace. Other boys he knew boasted of love affairs and even went to a house run by a woman called Reba. This place fascinated Jester; on the outside it was an ordinary frame house with a trellis on the porch and a potato vine. The very ordinariness of the house fascinated and appalled him. He would walk around the block and his heart felt challenged and defeated. Once, in the late afternoon, he saw a woman come out of the house and he watched her. She was an ordinary woman wearing a blue dress and with her lips gummed up with lipstick. He should have been passionate. But as she glanced at him casually, the shame of his secret defeat made him draw up one foot against the other leg and stand stricken until the woman turned away. Then he ran all the six blocks to his house and flung himself on the same bed where he lay now.

No, he had no passion, but he had had love. Sometimes,

for a day, a week, a month, once for a whole year. The one year's love was for Ted Hopkins who was the best all-around athlete in the school. Jester would seek Ted's eyes in the corridor and, although his pulses pounded, they only spoke to each other twice in that year.

One time was when they entered the vestibule together on a raining day and Ted said, 'It's foul weather.'

Jester responded in a faint voice, 'Foul.'

The other conversation was longer and less casual but completely humiliating. Because Jester loved Ted, he wanted more than anything to give him a gift and impress himself upon him. In the beginning of the football season, he saw in a jeweller's a little golden football. He bought this but it took him four days to give it to Ted. They had to be alone for him to give it and after days of following, they met in the locker room in Ted's section. Jester held out the football with a trembling hand and Ted asked, 'What's this?' Jester knew somehow, someway, he had made a mistake. Hurriedly, he explained, 'I found it.'

'Why do you want to give it to me?'

Jester was dizzy with shame. 'Just because I don't have any use for it and I thought I would give it to you.'

As Ted's blue eyes looked mockingly and suspiciously, Jester blushed the warm painful blush of the very fair and his freckles darkened.

'Well thanks,' Ted said, and put the gold football in his trousers pocket.

Ted was the son of an army officer who was stationed in a town fifteen miles from Milan, so this love was shadowed by the thought that his father would be transferred. And his feelings, furtive and secret as they were, were intensified by the menace of separation and the aura of distance and adventure.

Jester avoided Ted after the football episode and afterwards he could never think about football or the words 'foul weather' without a cringing shame.

He loved, too, Miss Pafford who taught English and wore bangs but put on no lipstick. Lipstick was repulsive to Jester, and he could not understand how anyone could kiss a woman who wore gummy smeary lipstick. But since nearly all girls and women wore lipstick, Jester's loves were severely limited.

Hot, blank and formless, the afternoon stretched ahead of him. And since Sunday afternoons are the longest afternoons of all, Jester went to the airport and did not come back until suppertime. After supper, he still felt blank, depressed. He went to his room and flung himself on his bed as he had done after dinner.

As he lay there sweating and still unsolaced, a sudden spasm lifted him. He was hearing from far away a tune played on the piano and a dark voice singing, although what the tune was or where it was coming from he did not know. Jester raised up on his elbow, listening and looking into the night. It was a blues tune, voluptuous and grieving. The music came from the lane behind the Judge's property where Negroes lived. As the boy listened the jazz sadness blossomed and was left unshattered.

Jester got up and went downstairs. His grandfather was in the library and he slipped into the night unnoticed. The music came from the third house in the lane, and when he knocked and knocked again the music stopped and the door was opened.

He had not prepared himself for what he would say, and he stood speechless in the doorway, knowing only that something overwhelming was about to happen to him. He faced for the first time the Negro with the blue eyes and, facing him, he trembled. The music still throbbed in his body and Jester quailed when he faced the blue eyes opposite him. They were cold and blazing in the dark and sullen face. They reminded him of something that made him quiver with sudden shame. He questioned wordlessly the overwhelming feeling. Was it fear? Was it love? Or was it – at last, was it – passion? The jazz sadness shattered.

Still not knowing, Jester went into the room and shut the door.

Three

The same midsummer evening while the scent of honey-
suckle lingered in the air, J.T. Malone made an unexpected
visit to the old Judge's house. The Judge went early to bed
and was an early riser; at nine in the evening he sloshed
mightily in his evening bath and the same procedure happened at four in the morning. Not that he liked it. He
would have liked to be safe in the arms of Morpheus until
six o'clock or even seven like other people. But the habit of
being an early riser had got into him and he couldn't break
it. The Judge held that a person as corpulent and free-
sweating as he was needed two baths a day, and those who
were around him would agree with this. So at those crepus-
cular hours the old Judge would be splashing, snorting and
singing – his favourite bathtub songs were 'On the Trail
of the Lonesome Pine' and 'I'm a Rambling Wreck from
Georgia Tech'. That evening he did not sing with the
usual gusto, as his talk with his grandson had troubled him,
nor did he put toilet water behind each ear as he might have
done. He had gone to Jester's room before his bath but the
boy was not there, nor did he answer from the yard. The
Judge was wearing a white dimity nightshirt and clutching
a dressing gown when the doorbell rang. Expecting his
grandson, he went downstairs and crossed the hall barefooted and with his robe slung negligently on his arm. Both
friends were surprised to see each other. Malone tried to
avoid looking at the too-small bare feet of the very fat
Judge, as the Judge struggled into his robe.

'What brings you here this time of the night?' the Judge
said in a tone as though midnight had long since passed.

Malone said, 'I was just out walking and thought I might
step in for a moment.' Malone looked frightened and desperate and the Judge was not deceived by his words.

'As you see I've just finished with my bath. Come up and

we can have a little nightcap. I'm always more comfortable in my own room after eight o'clock. I'll pile in my bed and you can lie in the long French chair . . . or vice versa. What's bothering you? You look like you've been chased by a banshee, J.T.'

'I feel like it,' Malone said. Unable to bear the truth alone, that evening he had told Martha about the leukemia. He had run from his own house in terror and alarm, fleeing for comfort or solace anywhere. He had dreaded in advance the intimacy that tragedy might have restored from the distant casualness of his married life, but the reality of that soft summer evening was worse than any dread. Martha had cried, insisted on bathing his face with cologne and talked of the children's future. In fact, his wife had not questioned the medical report and behaved as though she believed that her husband was incurably sick and was in fact a slowly dying man. This grief and credence exasperated and horrified Malone. As the hours passed the scene grew worse. Martha talked about their honeymoon at Blowing Rock, North Carolina, and the births of the children and the trips they had taken and the unexpected changes in life. She even mentioned, in connexion with the children's education, her Coca-Cola stock. Modest, Victorian lady – almost sexless it had seemed to Malone at times. This lack of interest in sex had often made him feel gross, indelicate, almost uncouth. The final horror of the evening was when Martha unexpectedly, so unexpectedly, referred to sex.

Martha was embracing the unnerved Malone when she cried, 'What can I do?' And she used the phrase that had not been said for years and years. It used to be the phrase for the act of love. It originated when Ellen was a baby who watched the older children do handsprings on the Malone summer lawn. The small Ellen would call out when her father came home from work, 'You want me to do a handspring for you, Daddy?' and that phrase of summer evenings, wet lawns, and childhood had been their word for the sexual act when they were young. Now the twenty-years-married Martha used the word, her bridges carefully placed in a glass of water. Malone was horrified knowing that, not only was he going to die, but some part of him had died also without his having realized. So quickly, wordlessly, he hurried out into the night.

The old Judge led the way, his bare feet very pink against the dark blue carpet, and Malone followed. They were both glad of the comfort of each other's presence. 'I told my wife,' Malone said, 'about that – leukemia.'

They passed into the Judge's bedroom where there was an immense four-poster bed with a canopy and feather pillows. The draperies were rich and musty and next to the window there was a chaise longue which he indicated to Malone before he turned his attention to the whisky and poured drinks. 'J.T., have you ever noticed that when someone has a failing, that fault is the first and foremost thing he attributes to another? Say a man is greedy – greed is the first thing he accuses in others, or stinginess – that is the first fault a stingy man can recognize.' Warming to his subject the Judge almost shouted his next words, 'And it takes a thief to catch a thief – a thief to catch a thief.'

'I know,' Malone replied, somewhat at a loss to find a hinge to the subject. 'I don't see –'

'I'm getting around to that,' the Judge said with authority. 'Some months ago you were telling me about Dr Hayden and those little peculiar things in the blood.'

'Yes,' Malone said, still puzzled.

'Well, this very morning while Jester and I were coming home from the drugstore, I chanced to see Dr Hayden and I was never so shocked.'

'Why?'

The Judge said: 'The man was a sick man. I never saw a man fall off so rapidly.'

Malone tried to digest the intimations involved. 'You mean –?'

The Judge's voice was calm and firm. 'I mean, if Dr Hayden has a peculiar blood disease, it is the most likely thing in the world to diagnose on to you instead of himself.' Malone pondered over this fantastic reasoning, wondering if there was a straw to grasp. 'After all, J.T., I have had a great fund of medical experience; I was in Johns Hopkins for close on to three months.'

Malone was remembering the doctor's hands and arms. 'It's true that Hayden has very thin and hairy arms.'

The Judge almost snorted: 'Don't be silly, J.T., hairiness has nothing to do with it.' Malone, abashed, was more willing to listen to the Judge's reasoning. 'The doctor didn't tell you that out of meanness or spite,' the Judge went on. 'It's just the logical, human way of contaging, bad things away from yourself. The minute I saw him today, I knew what had happened. I knew that look of a mortally sick man – looking sideways, his eyes averted as though ashamed. I have seen that look many a time at Johns Hopkins where I was a perfectly well, ambulatory patient who knew vvery soul at that hospital,' the Judge said truthfully. 'Whereas your eyes are straight as a die, although you're thin and ought to eat liver. Liver shots,' he said, almost shouting, 'aren't there things called liver shots for blood trouble?'

Malone looked at the Judge with eyes that flickered between bewilderment and hope. 'I didn't know you were in Johns Hopkins,' he said softly. 'I suppose you didn't bruit it around because of your political career.'

'Ten years ago I weighed three hundred and ten pounds.'

'You've always carried your weight well. I've never thought of you as a fat man.'

'Fat man: of course not. I was just stout and corpulent – the only thing, I would just have falling-out spells. It worried Miss Missy,' he said with a glance at his wife's portrait on the wall across from him. 'She even spoke about doctors – harped on the subject, in fact. I had never gone to a doctor in my adult life, feeling instinctively that doctors meant either cutting or, just as bad, diet. I was close friends with Doc Tatum who used to fish and hunt with me, but he was in a different category – otherwise I just let doctors alone and hoped they would leave me alone. Except for the falling-out spells I was in the pink of health. When Doc Tatum died I had a terrible toothache – I think it was psychosomatic, so I went to Doc's brother who was the best mule doctor in the county. I drank.'

'Mule doctor!' His faith in the Judge's reasoning echoed with a sick dismay. The old Judge did not seem to notice.

'Naturally, it was the week of Doc's funeral, and what

47

with the wake and cortege and all, my tooth hurt like an electric bell – so Poke, Doc's brother, just drew the tooth for me – with novocain and antibiotics which he uses for mules anyhow, as their teeth are strong and they are very stubborn about anybody fooling with their mouths and very sensitive.'

Malone nodded wonderingly, and as his disappointment still echoed, he changed the subject abruptly. 'That portrait is the living image of Miss Missy.'

'Sometimes I think so,' the Judge said complacently, as he was one of those persons who felt that anything he owned was greatly superior to the possessions of others – even if they were identical. He added reflectively:

'Sometimes when I am sad or pessimistic I think that Sara made a bad mistake with the left foot – at my worst moments it sometimes resembles a kind of odd tail.'

'I don't see that at all, sir,' Malone said comfortingly. 'Besides it's the face, the countenance that matters.'

'All the same,' the Judge said passionately, 'I wish my wife's portrait had been painted by Sir Joshua Reynolds or one of the great masters.'

'Well that's another story,' Malone said, looking at the badly drawn portrait done by the Judge's elder sister.

'I have learned not to settle for the cheapest, home-made product – especially when it comes to art. But at that time I never dreamed that Miss Missy was going to die and leave me.'

Tears brightened the dim, old eyes and he was silent, for the garrulous old Judge could never speak about his wife's death. Malone was also silent, remembering. The Judge's wife had died of cancer and it was Malone who had filled the doctor's prescriptions during her long illness, and he often visited her – sometimes bringing flowers from his garden or a bottle of cologne as though to soften the fact that he was delivering morphine. Often the Judge would be lumbering bleakly about the house, as he stayed with his wife as much as possible even, Malone thought, to the detriment of his political career. Miss Missy had developed cancer of the breast and it had been removed. The Judge's grief was boundless; he haunted the halls of the City Hospital, harrying even doctors who had nothing to do with the case, weeping, questioning. He organized prayers at the First Baptist Church and put a hundred dollars in her envelope every Sunday. When his wife returned home, apparently recovered, his joy and optimism were boundless; also, he bought a Rolls-Royce and hired a 'safe, coloured driver' for her daily airings. When his wife knew she was ill again she wanted to spare her husband the truth, and for a while he went on with his joyous extravagant ways. When it was apparent that his wife was failing, he didn't want to know and tried to deceive both her and himself. Avoiding doctors and questions, he accepted the fact that a trained nurse had become a member of the household. He taught his wife to play poker and they played frequently when she was well enough. When it was obvious that his wife was in pain, the Judge would tiptoe softly to the refrigerator, eat without tasting what he ate, thinking only that his wife had been very sick and was just recovering from a serious operation. So he steadied himself to his secret everyday grief, and would not let himself understand.

The day she died was a frosty day in December, with a cloudless blue sky and the sound of Christmas carols chiming in the icy air. The Judge, too dazed and worn to cry properly, had a terrible case of hiccups which let up, thank God, during the reading of the funeral service. Late that winter's day, when the ceremonies were finished and the guests were gone, he went alone in the Rolls-Royce to the cemetery (he sold the car the week afterwards). There, as the first frosty stars were appearing, he poked the newly laid cement of the grave with a walking stick, pondered over the workmanship of the job, and very slowly went back to the car driven by the 'safe, coloured driver', and there, exhausted, he went to sleep.

The Judge gave a final look at the portrait before he turned his brimming eyes away. A purer woman never lived.

After a proper time of mourning, Malone and the rest of the town expected that the Judge would marry again; and even he himself, lonesome and grieving as he rattled around the enormous house, felt a feeling of unknown expectancy. On Sunday he dressed very carefully and attended church, where he sat demurely on the second pew, his eyes glued to the choir. His wife had sung in the choir and he loved to watch the throats and bosoms of women when they sang. There were some lovely ladies in the First Baptist's choir, especially one soprano whom the Judge watched constantly. But there were other church choirs in the town. With a feeling of heresy, the Judge went to the Presbyterian church where there was a blond singer – his wife had been blond – whose singing throat and breasts fascinated him, although otherwise she was not quite to his taste. So, dressed to kill and sitting on one of the front rows, the Judge visited the various churches of the town and watched and judged the choirs, in spite of the fact that he had very little ear for music and was always singing off key and very loudly. No one questioned him about his changes of churches, yet he must have had some guilt for he often would declare in a loud voice, 'I like to be informed about what goes on in various religions and creeds. My wife and I have always been very broad-minded.'

The Judge never thought consciously of marrying again; indeed, he often spoke of his wife as though she were alive. Still there was this hollow yearning that he tried to fill with food or alcohol or watching choir ladies. And there had begun a veiled, subconscious search for his dead wife. Miss Missy was a pure woman, and automatically he considered only the pure. A choir singer, only choir singers attracted him. Those requirements were not too hard to fill. But Miss Missy had also been an excellent poker player, and unmarried pure choir singers who are also canny poker players are somewhat rare. One evening about two years after Miss Missy's death, the Judge invited Miss Kate Spinner for Saturday night supper. He also invited her elderly aunt as a chaperon and planned the supper with the forethought that was exactly like his wife's. The supper started with oysters. This was followed with a chicken dish and a curry of tomatoes, currants and almonds stewed together which was one of Miss Missy's favourite company dishes. Wine was served at each course and brandy followed the ice cream dessert. The Judge fidgeted over the preparations for days, making sure that the best plate and silver were used. The supper itself was a keen mistake. To begin with, Miss Kate had never eaten an oyster and was deadly afraid of having to eat one when the Judge tried to coax her. The unaccustomed wine made Miss Kate giggle in what seemed to the Judge a somewhat suggestive manner which obscuredly offended him. On the other hand, the old maiden aunt said she had never touched a drop of spirits in her life and was surprised that her niece would indulge. At the end of that dismal supper, the Judge, his hopes shaken but not yet gone, brought out a new deck of cards to have a game with the ladies. He had in mind his wife's slender fingers ringed with the diamonds he had given her. But it materialized that Miss Kate had never held a card in her life, and the old aunt added that, to her, cards were the entrance to the devil's playground. The party broke up early and the Judge finished the bottle of brandy before he went to bed. He blamed the fact that the Spinners were Lutherans and not quite expected to be in the same class as those who attended the First Baptist Church. So he consoled himself and soon his natural optimism returned.

However, he did not go so far afield in his broadmindedness about sects and creeds. Miss Missy had been born Episcopalian, changing over to First Baptist when they were married. Miss Hettie Peaver sang in the Episcopal choir and her throat was pulsing and vibrant as she sang. On Christmas the congregation stood up at the Hallelujah passage – year after year he was fooled by this passage, sitting there like a ninny until he realized that every soul had stood up and then trying to make amends by the loudest singing in the church ... but this Christmas the Hallelujah section came and went unnoticed as the Judge craned his neck at Miss Hettie Peaver. After church he scraped his feet and invited her and her aged mother to Saturday night supper the following week. Again he agonized over preparations. Miss Hettie was a short stout woman of good family; she was no spring chicken as the Judge well knew, but then neither was he, pushing seventy years old. And it was of course not a question of marriage as Miss Hettie was a widow. (The Judge had automatically in this unconscious search for love excluded widows and, of course, grass widows, as he had held it as a principle that second marriages were most unbecoming for a woman.)

That second supper was quite different from the Lutheran one. It turned out Miss Hettie adored oysters and was trying to get up nerve to swallow one whole. The old mother told a story about when she cooked an all-oyster dinner – raw oysters, scalloped oysters and so forth, which the old lady named in detail – for the business partner of Percy, 'my beloved spouse', and how it turned out that the partner couldn't eat oysters at all. As the old lady drank her wine, her stories grew longer and more tedious and the daughter would try to change the subject with little success. After dinner when the Judge brought cards, the old lady said she was too blind to make out the cards and she would be perfectly satisfied just finishing her port and looking at the fire. The Judge taught Miss Hettie blackjack and found her an able pupil. But he so much missed Miss Missy's slender hands and diamond rings. And another thing, Miss Hettie was a little buxom to his taste and he could not but compare his wife's slender bosom to her somewhat hefty form. His wife had had very delicate breasts, and indeed, he never forgot that one had been removed.

On Valentine's Day, sick with that hollow feeling, he bought a five-pound box of heart-shaped candy, much to the interest of J.T. Malone, who made the sale. On the way to Miss Hettie's house he reconsidered judiciously and walked slowly home. He ate the candy himself. It took two months. However, after some other little episodes like this that came to nothing, the Judge devoted himself solely to his grandson and his love for him.

The Judge spoiled his grandson beyond reason. It was the joke of the town that once at a church picnic the Judge had carefully picked the grains of pepper out of his small grandson's food, as the child did not like pepper. When the child was four years old he could recite the Lord's Prayer and the Twenty-Third Psalm, thanks to his grandfather's patient coaching, and it was the old man's delight when townspeople gathered to hear this prodigy perform.

Absorbed in his grandson, his hollowness of grief diminished, as well as his fascination for choir ladies. In spite of advancing age, which indeed the Judge did not admit, he went early every morning to his office in the court house – walking the morning way, being driven back at noon for a long midday dinner, and being driven back for the afternoon work hours. He argued vociferously in the court house square and in Malone's drugstore. On Saturday night he played poker in a game held in the back room of the New York Café.

All these years the Judge had as his motto: 'Mens sana in corpore sano.' His 'stroke' did not alter this as much as would have been supposed. After a cantankerous convalescence, he returned to his usual ways; although he went to the office only in the morning and did little but open his diminishing mail and read the *Milan Courier*, the *Flowering Branch Ledger* and, on Sundays, the *Atlanta Constitution*, which infuriated him. The Judge had fallen in the bathroom and had lain there for hours until Jester, sleeping his sound boy's sleep, finally heard his grandfather's cries. The 'little seizure' had happened instantaneously so that the Judge had at first hoped that his recovery would come about with the same instant speed. He would not admit it was a true stroke – spoke of 'a light case of polio', 'little seizure', etc. When he was up and around, he declared he used the walking stick because he liked it and that the 'little attack' had probably benefited him as his mind had grown keener because of contemplation and 'new studies'.

The old man waited restlessly for the sound of a door-latch. 'Jester is out so late,' he said, with a note of complaint. 'He's usually such a thoughtful boy about letting me know where he is when he goes out at night. Before my bath, when I heard some sound of music from not far away, I wondered if he had not stepped out in the yard to listen. But the music stopped and when I called there was only silence, and although it's past his bedtime, he has not come home.'

Malone put his long upper lip against his mouth, as he

53

did not like Jester, but he only said mildly: 'Well, boys will be boys.'

'Often I have worried about him, brought up in a house of sorrow. If ever there was one. Sometimes I think that's why he loves sad music, although his mother was a great one for music,' the Judge said, forgetting he had skipped a generation. 'I mean of course his grandmother,' he corrected. 'Jester's mother was with us only at that time of violence, sorrow and confusion – so much so that she passed through the family almost unnoticed, so that now I can hardly remember her face. Light hair, brownish eyes, a nice voice – although her father was a well-known rum runner. In spite of our feelings she was a blessing in disguise if ever there was one.

'The trouble was, she was just sandwiched in between Johnny's death, Jester's birth, and Miss Missy's second failing. It would take the strongest personality to not blur against all this and Mirabelle was not strong.' Indeed, the only memory that stood out was one Sunday dinner when the gentle stranger said: 'I love baked Alaskas' and the Judge took it upon himself to correct her. 'Mirabelle,' he said sternly, 'you love me. You love the memory of your husband. You love Miss Missy. But you don't love baked Alaskas, see?' He pointed out, with a most loving glance at the piece he was cutting, 'You like baked Alaskas. See the difference, child?' She saw, but her appetite had quite left her. 'Yes sir,' she said as she put down her fork. The Judge, feeling guilty, said angrily: 'Eat, child. You've got to eat in your condition.' But the idea of being in her condition only made her cry, and leave the table. Miss Missy, with a glance of reproach to her husband, followed soon after, leaving him to eat in solitary fury. As a punishment to them he deliberately deprived them of his presence most of the afternoon, playing solitaire in the library behind locked doors; it was a great satisfaction when the doorknob was rattled and he refused to budge or answer. He even went so far as to go to the cemetery alone instead of escorting his wife and daughter-in-law on the customary Sunday visit to Johnny's grave. The jaunt to the cemetery restored his usual good temper. After a stroll in the April twilight, he went to Pizzalatti's which was always open and bought sacks of candy, tangerines, and even a coconut, which the family enjoyed after supper.

'Mirabelle,' he said to Malone. 'If she had only been taken to Johns Hopkins for the confinement. But Clanes have always been born at home, and who could know how it would turn out. Besides, hindsight is always better than foresight,' he finished, dismissing his daughter-in-law who had died in childbirth.

'Such a sad thing about Mirabelle,' Malone said, just in order to say something. 'Women seldom die in childbirth in this generation, and when they do it's especially sad. She used to come to the drugstore every afternoon for an ice cream cone.'

'She craved sweets,' the Judge said with a peculiar satisfaction, as he had profited by this circumstance and would often say, 'Mirabelle is craving strawberry shortcake,' or some such delicacy, passing on his own desires to his pregnant daughter-in-law. Tactfully but firmly, his wife had kept the Judge within the three-hundred-pound weight range during her lifetime, although the words calorie or diet were never used. Secretly she read up on calorie lists and planned the meals accordingly, without the Judge's knowledge.

'Every baby doctor in town was consulted toward the end,' the Judge said almost defensively, as though he was being reproached for not caring for his kin. 'But it was some rare complication that had not been foreseen. To my dying day I will regret that we had not taken her to Johns Hopkins to begin with. They specialize in complications and rare complaints. If it hadn't been for Johns Hopkins, I would be under the sod today.'

Malone, who found solace in this talk of the sickness of others, asked delicately: 'Was your complaint complicated and rare?'

'Not so much complicated and rare, but curious,' the Judge said complacently. 'When my beloved wife died I was so miserable I began digging my grave with my teeth.'

Malone shuddered, having an instant, vivid image of his friend chewing gritty dirt in the graveyard, crying with misery. His own illness had left him defenceless against such sudden, random images, no matter how repellent. The subjectivity of illness was so acute that Malone responded violently to whole areas of the most placid and objective concepts. For instance, the mere mention of a commonplace thing such as Coca-Cola suggested shame and the disgrace of not being thought a good provider, just because his wife had some shares of Coca-Cola stock which she had bought with her own money and kept in a safety deposit box at the Milan Bank and Trust. These reactions, cavernous and involuntary, were hardly realized by Malone as they had the volatile vigour and backward grace of the unconscious.

'There came a time when I weighed at your drugstore and I weighed three hundred and ten pounds. But that didn't bother me particularly, and I was only troubled by those falling-out-spells. But something outlandish had to happen before I took much serious notice. And finally the outlandish thing happened.'

'What?' Malone asked.

'It was the time when Jester was seven.' The Judge broke off his story to complain of those years. 'Oh, the trouble for a man to raise a motherless child, and not only to raise but to rear him. Oh, the Clapps baby food, the sudden earaches in the night which I stopped with paregoric soaked in sugar and sweet oil dropped in his ear. Of course his nurse, Cleopatra, did most of the doing, but my grandson was my responsibility and no question about it.' He sighed before he continued his story. 'Anyway, when Jester was still a little nipper I decided to teach him to play golf, so one fair Saturday afternoon we set out to the Milan Country Club course. I was just playing away and showing Jester the various holds and positions. We came to that – that little pond near the woods – you know it, J.T.'

Malone, who had never played golf and was not a member of the Country Club, nodded with a certain pride.

'Anyway, I was just swinging away when I suddenly had one of those falling-out spells. And I fell right spang into the pond. There I was drowning with nothing but a seven-year-old boy and a little coloured caddy to save me. How they

hauled me out I don't know, being too drenched and confused to help myself much. It must have been a job, my
weighing over three hundred, but that coloured caddy was
both shrewd and smart and I was finally safe. However, that
falling-out spell made me think seriously enough to consider
going to a doctor. Since I didn't like or trust any doctor in
Milan it came to me in a divine flash – Johns Hopkins. I
knew they treated rare, uncommon diseases like mine. I
gave the caddy who had saved me a solid gold watch engraved in Latin.'

'Latin?'

'Mens sana in corpore sano,' the Judge said serenely, as
that was the only Latin he knew.

'Most appropriate,' said Malone, who did not know
Latin either.

'Unbeknownst to me, I had a peculiar and you might
say tragic connexion with the coloured boy,' the Judge said
slowly; and he closed his eyes as a kind of curtain for the
subject, leaving Malone's curiosity unsatisfied. 'Nonetheless,' he went on, 'I'm hiring him as a body servant.' The
old-fashioned term struck Malone.

'When I fell in the pond, I was sufficiently alarmed to
take myself to Johns Hopkins, knowing they studied rare
and curious diseases. I took little Jester with me to broaden
his education and as a reward for helping that caddy save
me.' The Judge did not admit that he could not face such a
horrendous experience as a hospital without his seven-year-
old grandson. 'So the day came I faced Dr Hume.'

Malone paled at the unconscious image of a doc-
tor's office with the smell of ether, the children's cries, Dr
Hayden's knife and a treatment table.

'When Dr Hume asked if I over-ate, I assured him I ate
just an ordinary amount. Then his questions chiselled finer.
He asked, for instance, how many biscuits I had at a meal
and I said, "Just the ordinary amount." Chiselling in closer
in the way that doctors do, he inquired what was the
"ordinary amount". When I told him, "Just a dozen or
two," I felt right then and there I had met my Waterloo.'

In a flash Malone saw soaked biscuits, disgrace, Napoleon.

'The doctor said I had two choices – either to go on

57

living as I had been, which would not be for long, or to go on a diet. I was shocked, I admit. And I told him it was much too serious a question to decide off hand. I told him to let me think it over for twelve hours before my final decision. "We won't find the diet too hard, Judge." Don't you loathe it when doctors use the word "we" when it applies only and solely to yourself? He could go home and gobble fifty biscuits and ten baked Alaskas – while me, I'm starving on a diet, so I meditated in a furious way.'

'I hate that "we" doctors use,' Malone agreed, feeling the sickening ricochet of his own emotions in Dr Hayden's office and the doomed words, 'We have here a case of leukemia.'

'Furthermore,' the Judge added, 'I hate it, God damn it, when doctors presume to tell me the so-called truth. I was so angry meditating about that diet problem I might have then and there had a stroke.' The Judge hastily corrected himself, 'A heart attack or a "little seizure".'

'No, it's not right,' Malone assented. He had asked for the truth, but in asking, he had asked only for reassurance. How could he dream that an ordinary case of spring fever would be a fatal disease? He had wanted sympathy and reassurance, and he got a death warrant. 'Doctors, by God; washing their hands, looking out windows, fiddling with dreadful things while you are stretched out on a table or half undressed on a chair.' He finished in a voice that wailed with weakness and fury: 'I'm glad I didn't finish medical school. I wouldn't have it on my soul nor conscience.'

'I meditated the full twelve hours as I said I would do. One portion of me said to go on the diet while another portion said, to hell, you live only once. I quoted Shakespeare to myself, "To be or not to be," and cogitated sadly. Then toward twilight a nurse came to the room with a tray. On the tray there was a steak twice as thick as my hand, turnip greens, lettuce and tomato salad. I looked at the nurse. She had dainty bosoms and a lovely neck . . . for a nurse, that is. I told her about my problem and asked her truthfully what that diet was. You could have struck me over with a feather when she said: "This, Judge, is the diet." When I was sure it was no trick, I sent word to Dr

Hume that I was on the diet and I fell to. I had forgotten to mention liquor or little toddies. I managed that.'

'How?' asked Malone, who knew the Judge's little weaknesses.

'The Lord works in strange ways. When I took Jester out of school to accompany me to the hospital, everybody thought it was mighty strange. Sometimes I thought so too, but secretly I was afraid I would die up North in that hospital. I didn't know the design beforehand, but a seven-year-old boy is just right to go to the nearest liquor store and get a bottle for his sick grandfather.

'The trick in life is to change a miserable experience into a happy one. Once my gut was shrunk, I got along fine in Johns Hopkins and I lost forty pounds in three months.'

The Judge, seeing Malone's long-eyed wistfulness, felt suddenly guilty because he had talked so much about his own health. 'You may think everything is roses and wine with me, J.T., but it's not and I'm going to tell you a secret I never breathed to a soul in this world, a serious, awful secret.'

'Why, what on earth –'

'I was pleased after the diet to lose all that corpulence, but that diet had got in my system and just a year later, on my annual visit to Johns Hopkins, I was told I had sugar in the blood and that means diabetes.' Malone, who had been selling him insulin for years, was not surprised but he did not comment. 'Not a fatal disease but a diet disease. I cussed out Dr Hume and threatened to bring suit but he reasoned with me and as a dyed-in-the-wool magistrate, I realized it wouldn't stand up in court. That brought certain problems. Do you know, J.T., while it's not a fatal disease, you have to have an injection every day. There is nothing catching about it but I felt there were too many health marks against me to make it known to the general public. I'm still in the zenith of my political career whether anybody recognizes it or not.'

Malone said, 'I won't tell anybody, although it is no disgrace.'

'Corpulence, that little seizure, and then on top of everything, diabetes – that's too much for a politician. Although there was a cripple in the White House for thirteen years.'

'I have every confidence in your political astuteness, Judge.' He said this, but that evening he had strangely lost faith in the old Judge – why he didn't know – medical faith anyhow.

'For years I put up with those public nurses for the injections and now chance has led me to another solution. I have found a boy who will look after me and give me those needles. He is the same boy you inquired about in the spring.'

Malone, suddenly remembering, said, 'Not the Nigra with the blue eyes.'

'Yes,' the Judge said.

'What do you know about him?' Malone asked.

The Judge was thinking about the tragedy of his life and how that boy had centred in it. But he only said to Malone, 'He was the coloured caddy who saved my life when I fell into that pond.'

Then came about between the two friends that laughter of disaster. It was focused consciously on the image of the three-hundred-pound old man being dragged out of a golf pond, but the hysterical laughter was reverberated in the gloom of the evening. The laughter of disaster does not stop easily, and so they laughed for a long time, each for his own disaster. The Judge stopped laughing first. 'Seriously, I wanted to find someone I could trust, and who else could I trust more than that little caddy who saved my life? Insulin is a very delicate, mysterious thing and has to be administered by someone who is mighty intelligent and conscientious, needles boiled and so forth.'

Malone thought the boy might be intelligent, but isn't there such a thing as a too intelligent coloured boy? He feared for the Judge, seeing those cold, blazing eyes and associating them with the pestle, rats and death. 'I wouldn't have hired that coloured boy, but maybe you know best, Judge.'

The Judge was back with his own worries. 'Jester doesn't dance, he doesn't drink liquor, he doesn't even go with girls, as far as I know. Where is that Jester? It's getting late. J.T., do you think I ought to call the police?'

60

The idea of calling the police and such commotion unnerved Malone. 'Why it's not late enough to worry about, but I think I'd better go home.'

'J.T., take a taxi at my expense and tomorrow we'll talk more about Johns Hopkins because, seriously, I think you ought to go there.'

Malone said, 'Thanks, sir, but I don't need a taxi – the fresh air will do me good. Don't worry about Jester. He'll be home soon.'

Although Malone said the walk would do him good, and although the night was warm, he was cold and weak as he walked home.

Noiselessly, he crept into the bed he shared with his wife. But when her warm buttocks touched his own, sick with the vibrance of their past livingness, he jerked away – for how can the living go on living when there is death?

Four

It was scarcely nine when Jester and Sherman first met that midsummer evening and only two hours had passed. But in first youth two hours can be a crucial period that can warp or enlighten a whole lifetime, and such an experience happened to Jester Clane that evening. When the emotion of the music and the first meeting steadied, Jester was aware of the room. The green plant growing in a corner. He steadied himself to realize the stranger had interrupted. The blue eyes challenged him to speak, but still Jester was silent. He blushed and his freckles darkened. 'Excuse me,' he said in a voice that trembled. 'Who are you and what was that song you were singing?'

The other youth, who was the same age as Jester, said in a voice meant to be creepy, 'If you want the sober ice-cold truth, I don't know who I am or any of my antecedents.'

'You mean you are an orphan,' Jester said. 'Why, so am I,' he added with enthusiasm. 'Don't you think that's sort of a sign?'

'No. You know who you are. Did your grandfather send you here?'

Jester shook his head.

When Jester first entered, Sherman had expected some message, then as the moments passed, some trick. 'Then why did you come busting in here?' Sherman said.

'I didn't come busting in. I knocked and said "Excuse me," and we got into a conversation.'

Sherman's suspicious mind was wondering what trick was being played on him, and he was very much on guard. 'We didn't get into any conversation.'

'You were saying how you didn't know about your parents. Mine died. Did yours?'

The dark boy with the blue eyes said, 'The sober ice-cold

truth is, I don't know anything about them. I was left in a church pew and therefore I was named Pew, in that somewhat Negroid and literal manner, according to the Nigerian race. My first name is Sherman.'

It would take a person far less sensitive than Jester to realize that the other youth was being deliberately rude to him. He knew he ought to go home, but it was as though he was hypnotized by the blue eyes set in the dark face. Then without a word, Sherman began to sing and play. It was the song Jester had heard in his own room and he felt that he had never been so moved. Sherman's strong fingers seemed very dark against the ivory keyboard and his strong neck was thrown back as he sang. After the first stanza of the song, he jerked his head and neck toward the sofa as an indication for Jester to sit down. Jester sat down, listening.

When the song was finished Sherman made a playful glissando before he went to the kitchenette in the next room and returned with two drinks already poured. He offered one to Jester who asked what it was as he took his glass.

'Lord Calvert's, bottled in bond, ninety-eight per cent proof.' Although Sherman did not say it, he had bought this whisky for the year he had been drinking because of the advertisement, 'The Man of Distinction'. He had tried to dress with the negligent care of the man in the ad. But on him it only looked sloppy, and he was one of the sharpest dressers in town. He had two Hathaway shirts and wore a black patch on his eye, but it only made him look pathetic instead of distinguished and he bumped into things. 'The best, the most distinguished,' Sherman said. 'I don't serve rotgut to my guests.' But he was careful to decant the drinks in the kitchen in case some juicehead would gobble it up; also he did not serve Lord Calvert's to known juiceheads. His guest tonight was no juicehead; in fact, he had never tasted whisky before. Sherman began to think that there was no dark plot on the Judge's behalf.

Jester held out a packet of cigarettes, which he proffered courteously. 'I smoke like a chimney,' he said, 'and drink wine practically every day.'

'I only drink Lord Calvert's,' Sherman said staunchly.

'Why were you so rude and ugly when I first came in here?' Jester asked.

'You have to be mighty careful about skitzes these days.'

'About what?' Jester asked, feeling somewhat at a loss.

'That means schizophrenics.'

'But isn't that a medical disease?'

'No, mental,' said Sherman with authority. 'A skitz is a crazy person. I actually knew one.'

'Who?'

'Nobody you would know. He was a Golden Nigerian.'

'A golden what?'

'That's a club I belonged to. It was started as a kind of protest club protesting against racial discrimination and with the very highest aims.'

'What highest aims?' Jester asked.

'First we registered for the vote in a body and if you don't think that takes nerve in this country you don't know nothing. Each member got a little cardboard coffin with his name in it and a printed sign, "A voting reminder". That actually happened,' Sherman said with emphasis.

Later Jester was to learn the significance of that little phrase, but not until he knew more about Sherman and the facts and phantasies of his life. 'I wish I had been there when you registered as a body,' Jester said wistfully. The phrase 'as a body' particularly appealed to him and heroic tears came suddenly to his eyes.

Sherman's voice was raw and cold, 'No you wouldn't. You would of been the first to chicken. Besides, you're not old enough to vote – the first to chicken.'

'I resent that,' Jester said. 'How do you know?'

'Little Bo-Peep told me so.'

Although Jester was hurt, he admired that answer, and thought he would use it himself very soon. 'Did many club members chicken?'

'Well,' Sherman said hesitantly, 'under the circumstances, with cardboard coffins slipped under doors – we continued our voting studies, learned the names and dates of all the Presidents, memorized the Constitution and so forth, but we had been aiming to vote, not aiming to be no Joan of Arc, so under the circumstances –' His voice trailed off. He did not tell Jester of the charges and countercharges exchanged as voting day neared, nor did he tell him that he was a minor and could not have voted anyhow. And that autumn day, Sherman exactly, with such lingering and exact detail, voted – in phantasy. He was also lynched in that phantasy to the tune of 'John Brown's Body', which always made him cry anyway and made him cry double that day, a martyr to his race. No Golden Nigerian voted and the subject of voting was never mentioned again.

'We had Parliamentary Procedure and were active in the Christmas Club which delegated in charge of donations for poor children. That's how we all knew Happy Henderson was a skitz.'

'Who's that?' Jester inquired.

'Happy was the chief active member in charge of the Christmas donations and he mugged an old lady on Christmas Eve. He was just skitz and didn't know what he was doing.'

'I've often wondered if crazy people know if they are crazy or not,' Jester said softly.

'Happy didn't know, or any of the Golden Nigerians either, otherwise we wouldn't have voted him into the club. Mugging an old lady in a fit of insanity.'

'I feel the sincerest sympathy for crazy people,' Jester said.

'The profoundest sympathy,' Sherman corrected. 'That's what we said on the flowers – I mean wreath, we sent his folks when he was electrocuted in Atlanta.'

'He was electrocuted?' Jester asked, appalled.

'Naturally, mugging an old white lady on Christmas Eve. Turned out Happy had been in institutions half of his life. There was no motive. In fact, he didn't snatch the old lady's purse after he mugged her. He just suddenly blew a fuse and went skitz – the lawyer made a case about the mental institutions and poverty and pressures – the lawyer the State hired to defend him, I mean – but anyway in spite of everything, Happy was fried.'

'Fried,' Jester exclaimed with horror.

'Electrocuted in Atlanta, June sixth, nineteen fifty-one.'

'I think it's simply terrible for you to refer to a friend and fellow member as being "fried".'

'Well he was,' Sherman said flatly. 'Let's converse about something more cheerful. Would you like me to show you Zippo Mullins' apartment?'

With pride he pointed out each piece of the crowded, fancy, dreary room. 'This rug is pure Wilton and the hide-a-bed sofa cost one hundred and eight dollars secondhand. It can sleep four if necessary.' Jester eyed the three-quarter-size sofa, wondering how four people could sleep in it. Sherman was stroking an iron alligator with an electric light bulb in its gaping jaws. 'A house-warming present from Zippo's aunt, not too modern or attractive, but it's the thought that counts.'

'Absolutely,' Jester agreed, cheered by any spark of humanness in his new-found friend.

'The end tables are genuine antique as you can see. The plant was a birthday gift for Zippo.' Sherman did not point out the red lamp with ragged fringes, two obviously broken chairs and other pieces of sad-looking furniture. 'I wouldn't have anything to happen to this apt' (he said the abbreviation). 'You haven't seen the rest of the apt – just gorgeous.' Sherman's voice was proud. 'When I'm alone here at night I don't hardly open the door.'

'Why?'

'Afraid I might be mugged and the muggers would haul off Zippo's furniture.' He added, in a voice that almost broke with self-pride, 'You see, I'm Zippo's house guest.' Until six months ago he had said he boarded with Zippo, then he heard the phrase 'house guest' which enchanted him and he used it frequently. 'Let's proceed to the rest of the apt,' Sherman said with the air of a host. 'Look at the kitchenette,' he said ecstatically, 'see the most modern conveniences.' Reverently he opened the door of the refrigerator for Jester. 'The bottom compartment is for crispies – crisp celery, carrots, lettuce, etc.' Sherman opened the door to the compartment, but there was only a head of wilted lettuce there. 'We keep caviar in this section,' he said emptily. Sherman gestured to the other parts of the magical box. Jester saw only a dish of cold black-eyed peas jellied in their own grease, but Sherman said, 'Last Christmas we had champagne iced in this compartment.' Jester, who seldom opened his own well-stocked refrigerator, was mystified.

'You must eat caviar and drink loads of champagne at your grandpapa's house,' Sherman said.

'No, I never tasted caviar, nor champagne either.'

'Never drank Lord Calvert's bottled in bond, nor had champagne, nor eaten caviar – personally, I just guzzle it,' Sherman said, having tasted caviar once, and having wondered silently why it was supposed to be so high-class. 'And look,' he said with enthusiasm, 'a genuine electric beater – plugs in here.' Sherman plugged in the beater and it began to beat furiously. 'A Christmas gift for Zippo Mullins from yours truly. I bought it on credit. I have the best credit record in town and can buy anything.'

Jester was bored standing in the cramped dingy kitchenette, and Sherman soon sensed it, but his pride was undaunted; so they went into the bedroom. Sherman indicated a trunk against the wall. 'This is the trunk,' he said superfluously, 'where we keep our valuables.' Then he added, 'I shouldn't have told you that.'

Jester was naturally offended by that last remark, but he said nothing.

In the room there were twin beds, each with a rose-coloured spread. Sherman stroked the spread appreciatively and said, 'Pure rayon silk.' There were portraits over each of the beds, one of an elderly coloured woman, the other of a dark young girl. 'Zippo's mother and sister.' Sherman was still stroking the bedspread and the Negro-coloured hand against the rose gave Jester an inexplicable creepy thrill. But he dared not touch silk, and he felt that if his own hand would touch the outspread one he would feel a shock like an electric eel, so carefully he placed both his own hands against the headboard of the bed.

'Zippo's sister is a nice-looking girl,' Jester remarked, as he felt that Sherman was expecting some comment about his friend's relatives.

'Jester Clane,' Sherman said, and though his voice was hard, Jester felt again the creepy thrill from the simple

67

calling of his name, 'if you ever, ever,' Sherman continued in a voice that lashed at Jester, 'if you ever, ever have the teeniest least lewd lascivious thought about Cinderella Mullins I'll string you up by your heels, tie your hands, light fire to your face and stand there and watch you roast.'

The sudden fury of the attack made Jester hold on tight to the headboard. 'I only said –'

'Shuddup, shuddup,' Sherman shouted. He added in a low hard voice, 'When you looked at the picture I didn't like the look on your puss.'

'What look?' asked Jester, baffled. 'You showed me the picture and I looked at it. What else could I have done? Cry?'

'Any further wisecracks and I will string you up and make the slowest barbecue that anybody ever made, smothering up the flames so it will last and keep on lasting.'

'I don't see why you talk so ugly, especially to somebody you just met.'

'When it's a question of Cinderella Mullins's virtue, I talk how I please.'

'Are you in love with Cinderella Mullins, passionately, I mean?'

'Any further personal questions and I'll have you fried in Atlanta.'

'How silly,' Jester said. 'How could you? It's a matter of legality.'

Both boys were impressed by that last phrase, but Sherman only muttered, 'I'll turn the juice personally and set it for very slow.'

'I think all this talk about electrocution and roasting people is childish.' Jester paused to deliver a stinging blow. 'In fact, I suspect it's because you have a limited vocabulary.'

Sherman was properly stung. 'Limited vocabulary,' he shouted with a little quiver of rage. Then he paused for a long time before he asked, belligerently, 'What does the word "stygian" mean?'

After Jester thought for a while he had to admit, 'I don't know.'

'– and epizootical and pathologinical,' Sherman went on, making up phony words like crazy.

'Isn't pathologinical something about being sick –'

'No,' Sherman said, 'I just made it up.'

'Made it up,' Jester said, shocked. 'It's utterly unfair to make up words when you are testing another person's vocabulary.'

'Anyway,' Sherman concluded, 'you have a very limited and putrid vocabulary.'

Jester was left in the situation of trying to prove his vocabulary; he tried in vain to make up long fancy words but nothing that made sense occurred to him.

'Forchrissake,' Sherman said, 'less change the subject. You wish me to sweeten your Calvert's?'

'Sweeten it?'

'Yes, goofy.'

Jester sipped his whisky and choked on it. 'It's kind of bitter and hot –'

'When I said sweeten it, did your dim mind suppose I was going to put sugar in this Calvert's whisky? I wonder more and more if you come from Mars.'

That was another remark Jester thought he would use later.

'What a nocturnal evening,' Jester said to prove his vocabulary. 'You are certainly fortunate,' he added.

'You mean about Zippo's apt?'

'No, I was just thinking – ruminating you might say – about how fortunate it is when you know what it is you're going to do in life. If I had a voice like yours I would never have to worry about that particular headache any more. Whether you know it or not, you have a golden voice, where I don't have any talent – can't sing or dance and the only thing I can draw is a Christmas tree.'

'There are other things,' Sherman said in a superior voice, as Jester's praise had been sweet to hear.

'– not too good at maths, so nuclear physics are out.'

'I suppose you could do construction work.'

'I suppose so,' Jester said dolefully. Then he added in a suddenly cheerful voice: 'Anyway, this summer I'm taking flying lessons. But that's just an advocation. I think every person ought to learn to fly.'

'I utterly disagree with you,' said Sherman, who was afraid of heights.

'Suppose your baby was dying, like say one of those blue babies you read about in the paper, and you have to fly to see him before the end, or suppose your crippled mother was sick and wanted to see you before she died; besides, flying's fun and I look on it as a kind of moral obligation that everyone ought to learn to fly.'

'I utterly disagree with you,' said Sherman, who was sick of talking about something he couldn't do.

'Anyway,' Jester went on, 'what was that song you were singing this evening?'

'This evening I was singing just plain jazz, but earlier this afternoon I was practising genuine Simon-pure German lieder.'

'What's that?'

'I knew you would ask me that.' Sherman's ego was glad to get on the subject. 'Lieder, goofy, means song in German and German means German, like in English.' Softly he began to play and sing and the new strange music throbbed in Jester's body and he trembled.

'In German,' Sherman boasted. 'They tell me I don't have a trace of accent in German,' he lied.

'What does it mean in English?'

'It's a kind of love song. This youth is singing to his maiden – goes something like this: "The two blue eyes of my beloved, I've never seen anything like them."'

'Your eyes are blue. It sounds like a love song to yourself; in fact, when I know the words of the song it makes me feel creepy.'

'German lieder is creepy music. That's why I specialize in it.'

'What other music do you like? Personally, I adore music, passionately, I mean. Last winter I learned the "Winter Wind" étude.'

'I bet you didn't,' Sherman said, unwilling to share his musical laurels with another.

'Do you think I would sit here and tell you a lie about the "Winter Wind" étude?' said Jester who never lied under any circumstances.

'How would I know?' answered Sherman who was one of the world's worst liars.

'I'm out of practice.'

As Jester went to the piano Sherman watched intently, hoping Jester couldn't play.

Loudly and furiously the 'Winter Wind' étude thundered into the room. When, after the first few bars, Jester's furiously playing fingers faltered, he stopped. 'Once you get off the track of the "Winter Wind" it's hard to get back on.'

Sherman, who had been listening jealously, was relieved when the music stopped. Furiously Jester attacked the étude at the beginning.

'Stop it,' Sherman shouted, but Jester played on, the music punctured frantically with Sherman's shouted protests.

'Well that's pretty fair,' Sherman said at the frantic, rickety end. 'However, you don't have tone.'

'Didn't I tell you I could play it?'

'There are all kinds of ways of playing music. Personally, I don't like yours.'

'I know it's just an advocation, but I enjoy it.'

'That's your privilege.'

'I like the way you play jazz better than the way you play German lieder,' Jester said.

'When I was a youth,' Sherman said, 'for a while I played in this band. We had hot sessions. The leader was Bix Beiderbecke and he tooted a golden horn.'

'Bix Beiderbecke, why, that's impossible.'

Sherman lamely tried to correct his lie. 'No, his name was Rix Hiederhorn. Anyway, I really wanted to sing Tristan at the Metropolitan Opera House but the role is not adaptable to me. In fact, most of the roles of the Metropolitan are severely limited for people of my race; in fact, the only role I can think of off-hand is the role of Othello who was a Negro Moor. I like the music all right, but on the other hand, I don't dig his feeling. How anybody can be that jealous over a white dame is beyond me. I would think about Desdemona – me – Desdemona – me –? No, I can't dig it.' He began to sing 'O! now, for ever farewell the tranquil mind.'

'It must give you a funny feeling, not to know who your mother was.'

'No it don't,' said Sherman, who had spent all his childhood trying to find his mother. He would pick out one woman after another who had a gentle touch and a soft voice. Is this my mother? he would think in wordless expectancy that ended always in sorrow. 'Once you get accustomed to it, it don't bother you at all.' He said this because he had never gotten accustomed to it. 'I loved very much Mrs Stevens, but she told me outright I wasn't her son.'

'Who is Mrs Stevens?'

'A lady I was boarded out with five years. It was Mr Stevens who boogered me.'

'What does that mean?'

'Sexually assaulted, goofy. I was sexually assaulted when I was eleven years old.'

Jester was speechless until he finally said, 'I didn't know anybody ever sexually assaulted a boy.'

'Well they do, and I was.'

Jester, who always had been subject to propulsive vomiting, suddenly began to vomit.

Sherman cried, 'Oh, Zippo's Wilton rug,' and took off his shirt to scrub the rug. 'Get towels in the kitchen,' he said to Jester who was still vomiting, 'or get out of this house.'

Jester, still vomiting, stumbled out. Jester sat on the porch until he stopped vomiting, then he came back to help Sherman clean up the mess, although the smell of his own vomit made him feel sickish again. 'I was just wondering,' he said, 'since you don't know who your mother is, and since you have a voice like yours, if your mother wouldn't be Marian Anderson?'

For the first time Sherman, who soaked up compliments like a sponge because he had had so few, was truly impressed. In all of his search for his mother he had never thought about Marian Anderson.

'Toscanini said she had a voice like once in a century.'

Sherman, who felt it was almost too good to be true, wanted to think about it alone, and, as a matter of fact, hug the idea to himself. Sherman changed the subject abruptly. 'When I was boogered by Mr Stevens' – Jester turned white and swallowed – 'I couldn't tell nobody. Mrs Stevens asked why I was always hitting Mr Stevens. I couldn't tell her. It's the kind of thing you can't tell a lady, so at that period I began to stammer.'

Jester said, 'I don't see how you can even bear to talk about it.'

'Well, it happened, and I was just eleven years old.'

'What a queer thing to do,' Jester said, who was still wiping the iron alligator.

'I'll borrow a vacuum tomorrow and vacuum this rug,' Sherman said, who was still concerned about the furniture. He flung a towel at Jester: 'If you feel anything like that is coming on again, kindly use this . . . Since I was stammering and always hitting Mr Stevens, Reverend Wilson talked to me one day. At first he would not believe me, as Mr Stevens was a deacon in the church and as I had made up so many things.'

'What other things?'

'Lies I would tell people about my mother.' The thought of Marian Anderson returned to him and he wanted Jester to go home so he could brood about it. 'When are you going home?' he asked.

Jester, who was still feeling sorry for Sherman, did not want to take the hint. 'Have you ever heard Marian Anderson sing "Were You There When They Crucified My Lord"?' he asked.

'Spirituals, that's another item that makes me blow a fuse.'

'It occurs to me your fuses blow awfully easy.'

'What's that to you?'

'I was just commenting how I love "Were You There When They Crucified My Lord" sung by Marian Anderson. I practically cry every time I hear it.'

'Well, cry ahead. That's your privilege.'

'–in fact, most spirituals make me cry.'

'Me, I wouldn't waste my time and trouble. However, Marian Anderson sings a creepy species of German lieder.'

'I cry when she sings spirituals.'

'Cry ahead.'

'I don't understand your point of view.'

Spirituals had always offended Sherman. First, they made him cry and make a fool of himself which was mortally hateful to him; second, he had always lashed out that it was nigger music, but how could he say that if Marian Anderson was his true mother?

'What made you think up Marian Anderson?' Since that worry-wart Jester wouldn't take the hint and go home to let him daydream in peace, he wanted to talk about her.

'On account of your voices. Two golden, once-in-a-century voices are quite a coincidence.'

'Well, why did she abandon me? I read somewhere where she loves her own old mother,' he added cynically, unable to give up his marvellous dream.

'She might have fallen in love, passionately, I mean, with this white prince,' Jester said, carried away with the story.

'Jester Clane,' Sherman's voice was mild but firm, 'never say "white" just out like that.'

'Why?'

'Say Caucasian, otherwise you would refer to my race as coloured or even Negro, while the proper name is Nigerian or Abyssinian.'

Jester only nodded and swallowed.

'– otherwise you might hurt people's feelings, and you're such a tenderhearted sissy, I know you wouldn't like that.'

'I resent you calling me a tenderhearted sissy,' Jester protested.

'Well, you are one.'

'How do you know?'

'Little Bo-Peep told me so.' Jester's admiration for this remark was not lessened because he had heard it before.

'Even if she had fallen for this Caucasian, I wonder why she left me in a church pew at the Holy Ascension Church in Milan, Georgia, of all places.'

Jester, who had no way of sensing the anxious, fallow search which had lasted all Sherman's childhood, was worried that a random suggestion on his part could have been blown up to such certainty. Jester said conscientiously, 'Maybe she wasn't exactly Marian Anderson; if it was, she must have considered herself wedded to her career. Still it

74

would be a kind of crummy thing to do and I never thought of Marian Anderson as the least bit crummy. In fact, I adore her. Passionately, I mean.'

'Why are you always using the word "passionately"?'

Jester, who had been drunk all evening and for the first time with passion, could not answer. For the passion of first youth is lightly sown but strong. It can spring into instant being by a song heard in the night, a voice, the sight of a stranger. Passion makes you daydream, destroys concentration on arithmetic, and at the time you most yearn to be witty, makes you feel like a fool. In early youth, love at first sight, that epitome of passion, turns you into a zombie so that you don't realize if you're sitting up or lying down and you can't remember what you have just eaten to save your life. Jester, who was just learning about passion, was very much afraid. He had never been intoxicated and never wanted to be. A boy who made A grades in high school, except for a sprinkling of B's in geometry and chemistry, he daydreamed only when he was in bed and would not let himself daydream in the morning after the alarm clock went off, although sometimes he would have dearly liked to. Such a person is naturally afraid of love at first sight. Jester felt that if he touched Sherman it would lead to a mortal sin, but what the sin was, he didn't know. He was just careful not to touch him and watched him with the zombie eyes of passion.

Suddenly Sherman began to pound on middle C, over and over.

'What's that?' asked Jester, 'just middle C?'

'How many vibrations are there in the treble?'

'What kind of vibrations are you talking about?'

'The teeny infinitesimal sounds that vibrate when you strike middle C or any other note.'

'I didn't know that.'

'Well, I'm telling you.'

Again Sherman pounded middle C, first with the right forefinger, then with the left. 'How many vibrations do you hear in the bass?'

'Nothing,' Jester said.

'There are sixty-four vibrations in the treble and another

sixty-four in the bass,' Sherman said, magnificently unaware of his own ignorance.

'What of it?'

'I'm just telling you I hear every teeniest vibration in the
whole diatonic scale from here,' Sherman struck the lowest
bass note, 'to here', the highest treble note was sounded.

'Why are you telling me all this? Are you a piano tuner?'

'As a matter of fact, I used to be, smarty. But I'm not
talking about pianos.'

'Well, what the hell are you talking about?'

'About my race and how I register every single vibration
that happens to those of my race. I call it my black book.'

'Black book? – I see, you are talking of the piano as a sort
of symbol,' Jester said, delighted to use the brainy word.

'Symbol,' repeated Sherman, who had read the word but
never used it, 'yeah, man, that's right – when I was fourteen years old a crowd of us got in a rage against the Aunt
Jemima signs, so we suddenly decided to tear them off. We
scraped and chiselled away to get the sign off. Upshot –
cops caught us in the middle and all four of the gang was
sent to jail, sentenced to two years on the road for destroy-
ing public property. I wasn't caught because I was just a
lookout, but what happened is in my black book. One guy
died from overwork, another came back a living zombie.
Have you heard of the Nigerians and that quarry in
Atlanta, who broke their legs with hammers so they
wouldn't be worked to death? One of them was one that
was caught on the Aunt Jemima signs.'

'I read that in the paper and it made me sick, but is that
the solemn truth, was he one of those Golden Nigerian
friends of yours?'

'I didn't say he was a Golden Nigerian, I just said he was
somebody I knew, and that's what I mean by vibrations. I
vibrate with every injustice that is done to my race. Vibrate
– vibrate – and vibrate, see?'

'I would too, if I were of your race.'

'No you wouldn't . . . tenderhearted, chicken, sissy.'

'I resent that.'

'Well resent – resent – resent. When are you going home?'

'You don't want me?'

'No. For the last time, no – no – NO.' He added lowly in a venomous voice, 'You fatuous, fair, redheaded boy. Fatuous,' Sherman said, using a word that had been hurled at him by a brainy vocabulary-wise boy.

Jester automatically ran his hand down his rib cage. 'I'm not a bit fat.'

'I didn't say fat – I said fatuous. Since you have such a putrid and limited vocabulary, that means fool – fool – fool.'

Jester held up his hands as though warding off a blow as he backed out of the door. 'Oh, sticks and stones,' he screamed as he ran away.

He ran all the way to Reba's house and when he reached the door he rapped with the firm rap of anger.

The inside of the house was not like he had expected. It was an ordinary house, and a whore-lady asked him, 'How old are you boy?' and Jester, who never lied, said desperately 'Twenty-one.'

'What would you like to drink?'

'Thanks a million, but nothing, nothing at all, I'm on the wagon tonight.' It was so easy he did not tremble when the whore-lady showed him upstairs, nor did he tremble when he lay in bed with a woman with orange hair and gold in her teeth. He closed his eyes, and having in mind a dark face and blue flickering eyes, he was able to become a man.

Meanwhile, Sherman Pew was writing a letter in ice-cold sober black ink; the letter started, 'Dear Madame Anderson'.

Five

Although the Judge was up the night before until far past his bedtime and had spent a restless night, he awakened at four in the morning as usual. After sloshing in the bathtub so mightily that he waked his grandson, who was also having a restless night, he dried himself, dressed slowly, using mainly the right hand because of his infirmity . . . he could not manage the shoestrings so he left them flopping . . . and bathed, dressed and in command of himself, he tiptoed down to the kitchen. It promised to be a fair day; the grey of the dawn sky was changing to the rose and yellow of sunrise. Although the kitchen was still grey, the Judge did not turn on the light, as he liked to look at the sky at this hour. Humming a little song without a tune, he put on the coffee and began preparing his breakfast. He selected the two brownest eggs in the icebox as he had convinced himself that brown eggs were more nourishing than the white ones. After months of practice, with many a gooey slip, he had learned to crack an egg and slip it carefully into the poacher. While the eggs were poaching he buttered his bread lightly and put it in the oven as he disliked toaster toast. Finally, he put a yellow cloth on the breakfast table and blue salt and pepper shakers. Although it was a solitary meal, the Judge did not want it to be a dismal one. The breakfast finished, he carried it item by item to the table, using only the good hand. Meanwhile the coffee was perking merrily. As a final touch he brought mayonnaise from the refrigerator and put a careful dollop on each poached egg. The mayonnaise was made of mineral oil and had, thank God, few calories. The Judge had found a wonderful book, *Diet Without Despair*, which he read constantly. The only trouble was that mineral oil was laxative and it behoved you to be careful not to eat too much for fear of sudden bathroom accidents, bathroom accidents which he knew were unbecoming to a magistrate – especially if it occurred in the courthouse office as it had two times. Being sensitive to his own dignity, the Judge was careful to ration the helpings of the delicious, low-calorie mayonnaise.

The small yellow tablecloth and others of the same size which he used and cherished, having them carefully hand laundered, were the ones that had been used on his wife's breakfast trays that he had brought up to her every morning. The robin's-egg blue salt and pepper set had been hers too, as well as the silver coffeepot the Judge now used for his own breakfast. In the old days when he became, little by little, an early riser, he would make his own breakfast, then lovingly prepare his wife's tray, often stopping to go out into the garden and pick some posies to decorate the tray. Then he would walk up carefully, bearing her breakfast, and if his wife was sleeping he would awaken her with kisses, as he was loath to start the day without her gentle voice and encouraging smile before he left for the office. (Except when she became ill he did not waken her; but he could not start out on his day until he saw her, which meant that sometimes toward the end he did not get to the office until afternoon.)

But surrounded by his wife's possessions, his grief subdued by the years, the Judge seldom thought consciously of Miss Missy, especially at breakfast time. He just used her things and sometimes would stare at the blue salt and pepper set with the stun of grief in his eyes.

Anxiety always put a keen edge on the Judge's appetite, and he was especially hungry this morning. When his grandson had come in at nearly one the night before, he had gone straight to bed, and when the Judge had followed, the boy had said in a cold, angry voice, almost shouting: 'Don't bother me, for Christ sake, don't bother me. Why can't I ever be left in peace?' The explosion was so loud and sudden that quietly, almost humbly, the Judge went away in his bare, pink feet and his dimity nightshirt. Even when he heard Jester sobbing in the night he was too timid to go in to him.

So for these due and good reasons the Judge was ravenous

this morning. He ate the whites of his eggs first – the least delicious part of his breakfast – then he carefully mashed up the peppered and mayonnaised yolks and spread them delicately on his toast. He ate with careful relish, his maimed hand curved lovingly around the rationed food as though to defend it from some possible aggressor. His eggs and toast finished, he turned now to the coffee which he had carefully decanted into his wife's silver pot. He loaded the coffee with saccharine, blew on it to cool it somewhat, and sipped it slowly, very slowly. After the first cup, he prepared his first morning cigar. It was now going on seven and the sky was a pale tender blue that precedes a fair bright day. Lovingly, the Judge alternated his attention between his coffee and his first cigar. When he had that little seizure and Doc Tatum took him off cigars and whisky, the Judge had been worried to death at first. He slipped around smoking in the bathroom, drinking in the pantry. He argued with Doc, and then came the irony of Doc's death – a confirmed teetotaler who never smoked and only enjoyed a chew on rare occasions. Although the Judge was overwhelmed by grief and an inconsolable mourner at the wake, when the shock of death was over, the Judge felt a secret, such a secret relief that he was almost unaware of what had happened and never acknowledged it. But within a month after Doc's death he was smoking cigars in public and drinking openly as before, but prudently he cut down to seven cigars a day and a pint of bourbon.

Breakfast over, the old Judge was still hungry. He picked up *Diet Without Despair* which was on the kitchen shelf and commenced to read studiously, hungrily. It almost comforted him to know that anchovies, large-sized, were only twenty calories and a stalk of asparagus only five, and that a medium-sized apple was a hundred. But though this knowledge almost comforted him, he was not quite soothed, for what he wanted was more toast, dripping with butter and spread with the home-made blackberry jam that Verily had made. He could see in his mind's eye the delicately browned toast and feel in his mouth the sweet, grainy blackberries. Although he had no intention of digging his grave with his teeth, the anxiety that had sharpened his appetite had at the same time weakened his will; stealthily he was limping to the breadbox when a low growl in his stomach made him stop, his hand outstretched toward the breadbox, and start toward the bathroom which had been put in for him after the 'little seizure'. He veered on his way to pick up *Diet Without Despair* in case there should be any waiting.

After slipping down his trousers hastily, he balanced himself with his good hand and sat gingerly on the stool; then when he was sure of himself, his great buttocks relaxed and he settled. There was not long to wait; he had only time to read the recipe for lemon crustless pie (only ninety-six calories when made with sucaryl) thinking with satisfaction that he would have Verily make the dish for lunch that noon. He was also satisfied when he felt his bowels open noiselessly, and thinking of 'mens sana in corpore sano', he smiled a little. When the odour in the bathroom rose, he was not annoyed by this; on the contrary, since he was pleased by anything that belonged to him, and his faeces were no exception, the smell rather soothed him. So he sat there, relaxed and meditative, pleased with himself. When he heard a noise in the kitchen, he wiped himself hastily and put himself right before leaving the bathroom.

His heart, suddenly light and volatile as a boy's, had expected Jester. But when, still struggling with his belt, he reached the kitchen, no one was there. He could just hear Verily doing her Monday morning cleaning in the front part of the house. A little cheated (he could have stayed longer in the bathroom) he looked at the sky which now had the blaze of full morning, the blue unbroken by a cloud, and he smelled from the open window the fresh, faint smell of summer flowers. The old Judge regretted the fact that the routine of breakfast and bowels was over because there was nothing to do now but wait for the *Milan Courier*.

Since waiting is as tedious in old age as it is in childhood, he found his kitchen spectacles (he had spectacles in the library, the bedroom, aside from his pair at the courthouse) and began to read the *Ladies' Home Journal*. Not to read, really, but to look at the pictures. There, for instance, was a marvellous picture of a chocolate cake, and on the following page a mouth-watering picture of a coconut pie made with condensed milk. Picture after picture the Judge scrutinized wistfully. Then, as though ashamed for his greed, he reminded himself of the truth that, quite aside from the pictures, the *Ladies' Home Journal* was a very superior magazine. (Far, far superior to that dreadful *Saturday Evening Post* whose good-for-nothing editors had never read the story he had once sent them.) There were serious articles about pregnancy and childbirth which he enjoyed, also sound essays on child rearing which the Judge knew were sound because of his own experience. Also articles on marriage and divorce which might well have benefited him as a magistrate if his mind had not been occupied by the plans of a great statesman. Finally, in the *Ladies' Home Journal* there were little extra lines, blocked and inserted in the stories – sayings of Emerson, of Lin Yu-tang, and the great sages of the world. Several months ago he had read in these bylines the words: 'How can the dead be truly dead when they are still walking in my heart?' It was from an old Indian legend and the Judge could not forget it. He had seen in his mind's eye a barefooted, bronzed Indian walking silently in the forest and heard the silent sound of a canoe. He never cried about his wife's death, never even cried about the diet any more. When his nervous system and tear ducts made him cry, he thought of his brother Beau, and Beau was like a lightning rod that could ground and safely conduct his tears. Beau was two years older than he was and had died when he was eighteen years old. As a young boy, Fox Clane had worshipped his brother, yea, worshipped the ground he walked on. Beau acted, could recite, was the president of the Milan Players Club. Beau could have been anything. Then one night he had come in with a sore throat. The next morning he was delirious. It was an infected throat, and Beau was muttering, 'I am dying, Egypt, dying, ebbs the crimson lifetide fast.' Then he began to sing, 'I feel, I feel, I feel like the morning star; I feel, I feel, I feel like the morning star. Shoo, fly, don't bother me; shoo, fly, don't bother me.' At the end Beau had begun to laugh although it wasn't laughter. The young Fox had shuddered so violently that his mother had sent him to the back room. It was a bare bleak room that was a sickroom playroom where the children had their measles, mumps, and childhood diseases, and where they were free to rough-house when they were well. The Judge remembered an old forgotten rocking horse, and a sixteen-year-old boy had put his arms around the wooden horse and cried – and even as an eighty-five-year-old man he could cry whenever he wanted to, just thinking about that early sorrow. The Indian walking silently in the forest and the silent sound of the canoe. 'How can the dead be truly dead when they are still walking in my heart?'

Jester came clattering down the stairs. He opened the ice-box and poured himself some orange juice. At the same time Verily came into the kitchen and began to prepare Jester's breakfast.

'I want three eggs this morning,' Jester said. 'Hey, Grandfather.'

'Are you all right today, Son?'

'Natch.'

The Judge did not mention the crying in the night and neither did Jester. The Judge even restrained himself from asking where Jester had been the night before. But when Jester's breakfast was served, his will broke and he took a golden brown piece of toast, added more butter and spread it with blackberry jam. The forbidden extra toast broke his will even further so that he asked, 'Where were you last night?' well knowing as he spoke he shouldn't have asked the question.

'Whether you realize it or not, I'm a grown man now,' Jester said in a voice that squeaked a little, 'and there's such a thing called sex.' The Judge, who was prudish about such topics, was relieved when Verily poured him a cup of coffee. He drank silently, not knowing what to say.

'Grandfather, have you ever read the *Kinsey Report*?'

The old Judge had read the book with salacious pleasure, first substituting for the jacket the dust cover of *The Decline and Fall of the Roman Empire*. 'It's just tomfoolery and filth.'

'It's a scientific survey.'

'Science, my foot. I have been an observer of human sin and nature for close on to ninety years, and I never saw anything like that.'

'Maybe you ought to put on your glasses.'

'How dare you sass me, John Jester Clane.'

'Close to ninety years old,' the Judge repeated, for now he was a little coquettish about his advancing age, 'I've observed human sin as a magistrate and human nature as a man with natural curiosity.'

'A bold invaluable scientific survey,' said Jester, quoting from a review.

'Pornographic filth.'

'A scientific survey of the sexual activities in the human male.'

'The book of an impotent, dirty old man,' said the old Judge who had relished the book as he marvelled behind the covers of *The Decline and Fall of the Roman Empire* which he had never read but kept in his law office library for show.

'It proves that boys my age have sexual affairs, boys even younger, but at my age it's a necessity – if they're passionate I mean.' Jester had read the book in the lending library and it had shocked him. He had read the report a second time and worried terribly. He was afraid, so terribly afraid, that he was not normal and the fear corkscrewed within him. No matter how many times he circled Reba's house, he had never felt the normal sexual urge and his heart quaked with fear for himself, as more than anything else he yearned to be exactly like everyone else. He had read the words 'jewel-eyed harlot' which had a beautiful sound that tingled his senses; but the eyes of the woman he had seen leaving Reba's place that spring afternoon were not 'jewel-eyed' but only dull and baggy, and yearning to lust and be normal he could only see the gooey lipstick and the vacant smile. And the orange-haired lady he had slept with last night was not a bit 'jewel-eyed'. Secretly Jester thought sex was a fake, but this morning, now that he had become a man, he felt cocksure and free.

'That's all very well,' the Judge said, 'but in my youth we went to church and attended B.Y.P.U. meetings and had a raring good time. We went courting and dancing. Believe it or not, Son, in those days I was one of the best dancers in Flowering Branch, limber as a willow and the very soul of grace. The waltz was fashionable those days.

84

We danced to "Tales of the Vienna Woods", "The Merry Widow", "Tales of Hoffmann" –' The old, fat Judge broke off to wave his hands in waltz time and sang in a monotone he imagined was the tune

'Lovely night, oh, lo-o-vely night.'

'You're not a bit introverted,' Jester said when his grandfather had put down his waving hands and stopped that croaking singing.

The Judge, who had felt this as a criticism, said, 'Son, everybody has a right to sing, Every mortal has the right to sing.

Lovely night, oh, lo-o-vely night.'

That was all the beautiful tune he could remember. 'I danced like a willow and sang like an angel.'

'Possibly.'

'No possibly about it. In my youth I was as light and radiant as you and your father until the layers of corpulence began to hold me down, but I danced and sang and had a raring good time. I never moped around reading dirty books on the sly.'

'That's what I say. You're not a born introvert.' Jester added, 'Anyway I didn't read the *Kinsey Report* on the sly.'

'I had it banned at the public library.'

'Why?'

'Because I am not only the leading citizen in Milan but the most responsible one. I am responsible that innocent eyes are not offended nor the calm heart troubled by such a book.'

'The more I listen to you the more I wonder if you came from Mars.'

'Mars?' The old Judge was bewildered and Jester let it go.

'If you were more introverted you could understand me better.'

'Why are you so hipped on that word?'

Jester, who had read the word and never spoken it, deeply regretted he had not used it the night before.

'Lovely night, oh, lov-ely night.'

Not being introverted, his grandfather had never wondered if he himself was normal or not. It had never entered
his singing and dancing mind if he was normal or queer.

If it turned out he was homosexual like men in the *Kinsey
Report*, Jester had vowed that he would kill himself. No, his
grandfather was utterly not an introvert, and Jester dearly
wished he had used the word the night before. Extrovert,
that was the opposite word – while he was an introvert.
And Sherman? Anyhow, he would use both words.

'I could have written that book myself.'

'You?'

'Why certainly. The truth is, Jester, I could have been a
great, great writer if I had put my mind to it.'

'You?'

'Don't sit there saying, "You? You?" like an imbecile,
Son. All you have to have to be a great writer is appli-
cation, imagination, and a gift for language.'

'You have imagination all right, Grandfather.'

The Judge was thinking of *Gone With the Wind* which he
could have written easily. He wouldn't have let Bonnie die
and he would have changed Rhett Butler; he would have
written a better book. He could have written *Forever Amber*
with his left foot – a much better book, more refined.
Vanity Fair he could have written too; why, he saw through
that Becky as slick as a whistle. He could have written
Tolstoy, for although he had not actually read the books,
he had seen them in the picture shows. And Shakespeare?
He had read Shakespeare at law school and even seen *Hamlet*
in Atlanta. An English cast, speaking with English accents,
naturally. It was the first year of their marriage and Miss
Missy had worn her pearls and her first wedding rings.
After three performances of the Atlanta Shakespeare
Festival, Miss Missy had enjoyed it so much and was so
impressed that she picked up an English accent which
lasted a month after they had come home to Milan. But
could he have made up 'To be or not to be'? Sometimes
when he considered the question he thought so, and sometimes he thought not; for after all, even a genius can't do
everything and Shakespeare had never been a congressman.

'There have been learned arguments about the authorship of Shakespeare. It was argued that an illiterate strolling player could never have written poetry like that. Some say it was Ben Jonson who wrote the plays. I know durn well I could have written "Drink to me only with thine eyes, and I will drink with mine." I'm sure I could have done that.'

'Oh, you can do wonders and eat rotten cucumbers,' Jester muttered.

'What's that?'

'Nothing.'

'–and if Ben Jonson wrote "Drink to me only with thine eyes" and wrote Shakespeare too, then –' After a great leap of the imagination, the Judge pondered.

'You mean you are comparing yourself to Shakespeare?'

'Well, maybe not the Bard himself, but after all Ben Jonson was a mortal too.' Immortality, that was what the Judge was concerned with. It was inconceivable to him that he would actually die. He would live to a hundred years if he kept to his diet and controlled himself – deeply he regretted the extra toast. He didn't want to limit his time for just a hundred years, wasn't there a South American Indian in the newspaper who lived to be a hundred and fifty – and would a hundred and fifty years be enough? No. It was immortality he wanted. Immortality like Shakespeare, and if 'push came to shovel', even like Ben Jonson. In any case he wanted no ashes and dust for Fox Clane.

'I always knew you were the biggest egotist in the round world, but in my wildest dreams it never occurred to me you could compare yourself to Shakespeare or Ben Jonson.'

'I was not comparing myself to the Bard himself; in fact, I have the proper humility. Anyway, I never set out to be a writer and you can't be everything.'

Jester, who had been cruelly hurt the night before, was cruel to his grandfather, deliberately ignoring the fact that he was old. 'Yes, the more I hear you, the more I wonder if you come from Mars.' Jester got up from the table, his breakfast almost untouched.

The Judge followed his grandson. 'Mars,' he repeated, 'you mean you think I'm off on another planet?' His voice was suddenly high, almost shrill. 'Well, let me tell you this, John Jester Clane, I'm not off on another planet, I'm right here on this earth where I belong and want to be. I'm rooted in the very centre of the earth. I may not be immortal yet, but you wait and see, my name will be synonymous with George Washington or Abraham Lincoln – more beloved than Lincoln's, for I am the one who will redress the wrongs in my country.'

'Oh, the Confederate money – I'm off now.'

'Wait, Son, this coloured boy is coming today and I thought you would screen him with me.'

'I know about that,' Jester said. He did not want to be there when Sherman arrived.

'He's a responsible boy, I know all about him, and he will help me with my diet, give me my injections, open my mail, and be my general amanuensis. He will be a comfort to me.'

'If that Sherman Pew is a comfort to you, just let me know.'

'He will read to me – an educated boy – immortal poetry.' His voice was suddenly shrill. 'Not dirty trash like that book I banned at the public library. I had to ban it because as a responsible man I'm determined that things in this town and state are going to be in order, and this country too, and the world if I can accomplish it.'

Jester slammed out of the house.

Although he had not set the alarm clock and could very well have daydreamed for a long time before getting out of bed, the spring of energy and life stirred violently that morning. The golden summer was with him and he was still free. When he slammed out of the house, Jester did not race but took his mortal time, for after all it was summer vacation and he was not going to any fire. He could stop to look at the world, he could imagine, he could look with summer vacation freedom at the border of verbena that lined the drive. He even stooped down and examined a vivid flower and joy was with him. Jester was dressed in his best clothes that morning, wearing a white duck suit and even a coat. He just wished his beard would get a hump on and grow so he could shave. But suppose he never grew a beard, what would people think of him? For a moment the vacation joy darkened until he thought of something else.

He had dressed fit to kill because he knew that Sherman was coming, and he had slammed out of the house because he did not want to meet Sherman that way. Last evening he had not been the least bit witty or sparkling; in fact, he had just goofed off, and he did not want to meet Sherman until he could be witty and sparkling. How Jester was going to accomplish that this morning he didn't know, but he would talk about introverts and extroverts . . . where that would lead him, he wondered. In spite of the fact that Sherman utterly disagreed with him about his theories of flight and was unimpressed about Jester's flying, he walked automatically to J.T. Malone's pharmacy and stood at the corner waiting for the bus that went to the airport. Happy, confident, free, he lifted his arms and flapped them for a moment.

J.T. Malone, who saw that gesture through the window of the pharmacy, wondered if, after all, the boy was dotty.

Jester was trying to be witty and sparkling and he thought that being alone in the airplane would help him in this. It was the sixth time that he had soloed. A great part of his mind was taken up with the instruments. In the blue, wind-rushing air his spirits lifted, but witty and sparkling in his conversation . . . he didn't know. Of course it would depend a great deal on what Sherman said himself, so he would have to hinge the conversation and he just dearly hoped that he would be witty and sparkling.

It was an open Moth Jester was flying and the wind pulled his red hair backward from his scalp. He deliberately had not worn a helmet because he liked the sensation of wind and sun. He would put on the helmet when he went to the house and met Sherman there. Careless he would be, and busy, a helmeted aviator. After a half an hour of wind-rushing cobalt and sun, he began to think of landing. Zooming carefully, circling to get just the proper distance, he had no room in his thoughts for Sherman even, because he was responsible for his own life and for the training Moth. The landing was bumpy, but when he put on his helmet and jumped out with careful grace he wished somebody could have seen him.

The bus ride back from the airport always made him feel

squashed, and the old bus itself was plodding and terribly restricted compared to the air; and the more he flew the more he was convinced that every adult had the moral obligation to fly, no matter what Sherman Pew's convictions were about this matter.

He left the bus at the corner of J.T. Malone's drugstore which was in the centre of town. He looked at the town. On the next block was the Wedwell Spinning Mill. From the open basement window the heat from the dye vats made wavy lines in the sweltering air. Just to stretch his legs, he strolled around the business section of town. Pedestrians stayed close to the awnings and it was the time of late morning when their shadows cast on the glittering sidewalk were blunt and dwarfed. His unaccustomed coat made him very hot as he walked through town, waving to people he knew and blushing with surprise and pride when Hamilton Breedlove of the First National Bank tipped his hat at him – very likely because of the coat. Jester circled back to Malone's drugstore thinking of a cherry coke with cool crushed ice. On the corner, near where he had waited for the bus, a town character called Wagon sat in the shade of the awning with his cap on the sidewalk next to him. Wagon, a light-coloured Negro who had lost both legs in a sawmill accident, was toted every day by Grown Boy and transported in the wagon where he would beg before awninged stores. Then when the stores closed, Grown Boy would wheel him back home in the wagon. When Jester dropped a nickel in the cap, he noticed that quite a few coins were there, and even a fifty-cent piece. The fifty-cent piece was a decoy coin Wagon always used in hope of further generosity.

'How you do today, Uncle?'

'Just tollable.'

Grown Boy, who often showed up at dinnertime, was standing there just watching. Wagon today had fried chicken instead of his usual side-meat sandwich. He ate the chicken with the lingering delicate grace with which coloured people eat chicken.

Grown Boy asked, 'Why don you gimme a piece of chicken?' although he had already eaten dinner.

'Go on, nigger.'

'Or some biscuits and molasses?'

'I ain payin no min to you.'

'Or a nickel for a cone?'

'Go on, nigger. You come before me like a gnat.'

So it would go on, Jester knew. The hulking, dimwitted coloured boy begging from the beggar. Tipped panama hats, the separate fountains for white and coloured people in the courthouse square, the trough and hitching post for mules, muslin and white linen and raggedy overalls. Milan. Milan. Milan.

As Jester turned into the dim, fan-smelling drugstore, he faced Mr Malone who stood behind the fountain in his shirt-sleeves.

'May I have a coke, sir?'

Fancy and overpolite the boy was, and Malone remembered the dotty way he flapped his arms when he was waiting for the airport bus.

While Mr Malone made up the Coca-Cola, Jester moseyed over to the scales and stood on them.

'Those scales don't work,' Mr Malone said.

'Excuse me,' Jester said.

Malone watched Jester and wondered. Why did he say that, and wasn't it a dotty thing to say, apologizing because the pharmacy scales didn't work. Dotty for sure.

Milan. Some people were content to live and die in Milan with only brief visits to relatives and so forth in Flowering Branch, Goat Rock, or other smaller towns near by. Some people were content to live their mortal lives and die and be buried in Milan. Jester Clane was not one of those. Maybe a minority of one, but a definitely *not* one. Jester pranced with irritation as he waited and Malone watched him.

The coke was frostly-beaded on the counter and Malone said, 'Here you are.'

'Thank you, sir.' When Malone went to the compounding room, Jester sipped his icy coke, still brooding about Milan. It was the broiling season when everybody wore shirtsleeves except dyed-in-the-wool sticklers who put on their coats when they went to lunch in the Cricket Tea Room or the New York Café. His Coca-Cola still in hand, Jester moved idly to the open doorway.

The next few moments would be forever branded in his brain. They were kaleidoscopic, nightmare moments, too swift and violent to be fully understood at the time. Later Jester knew he was responsible for the murder and the knowledge of that fact brought further responsibility. Those were the moments when impulse and innocence were tarnished, the moments which end the end, and which, many months later, were to save him from another murder – in truth, to save his very soul.

Meanwhile Jester, Coca-Cola in hand, was watching the flame-blue sky and the burning noonday sun. The noon whistle blew from the Wedwell Mill. The millworkers straggled out for lunch. 'The emotional scum of the earth,' his grandfather had called them, although he had a great hunk of Wedwell Spinning Mill stock which had gone up very satisfactorily. Wages had increased, so that instead of bringing lunch pails the hands could afford to eat at luncheonettes. As a child, Jester had feared and abhorred 'factory tags', appalled by the squalor and misery he saw in Mill Town. Even now he didn't like those blue-denimed, tobacco-chewing mill hands.

Meanwhile, Wagon had only two pieces of fried chicken left – the neck and the back. With loving delicacy he started on the neck which has as many stringy bones as a banjo and is just as sweet.

'Just a teeny bit,' Grown Boy begged. He was looking yearningly at the back and his rusty black hand reached toward it a little. Wagon swallowed quickly and spat on the back to insure it for himself. The phlegmy spit on the crusty brown chicken angered Grown. As Jester watched him, he saw the dark, covetous eyes fix on the change in the begging cap. A sudden warning made him cry, 'Don't, don't,' but his stifled warning was lost by the clanging of the town clock striking twelve. There were the scrambled sensations of glare and brassy gongs and the resonance of the static midday; then it happened so instantly, so violently, that Jester could not take it in. Grown Boy dived for the coins in the begging cap and ran.

'Git him. Git him,' Wagon screamed, hoisting himself on his sawed-off legs with the leather 'shoes' to protect them, and jumping from leg to leg in helpless fury. Meantime Jester was chasing Grown. And the hands from the mill, seeing a white-coated white man running after a nigger, joined in the chase. The cop on Twelfth and Broad saw the commotion and hastened to the scene. When Jester caught Grown Boy by the collar and was struggling to seize the money from Grown's fist, more than half a dozen people had joined in the fray, although none of them knew what it was about.

'Git the nigger. Git the nigger bastard.'

The cop parted the mêlée with the use of his billy stick and finally cracked Grown Boy on the head as he struggled in terror. Few heard the blow, but Grown Boy limpened instantly and fell. The crowd made way and watched. There was only a thin trickle of blood on the black scalp, but Grown Boy was dead. The greedy, lively, wanting boy who had never had his share of sense lay on the Milan sidewalk – forever stilled.

Jester threw himself on the black boy. 'Grown?' he pleaded.

'He's dead,' somebody in the crowd said.

'Dead?'

'Yes,' said the cop after some minutes. 'Break it up you all.' And doing his duty, he went to the telephone booth at the pharmacy and called an ambulance, although he had seen that look of death. When he came back to the scene, the crowd had drifted back closer to the awning and only Jester remained near the body.

'Is he really dead?' Jester asked, and he touched the face that was still warm.

'Don't touch him,' the cop said.

The cop questioned Jester about what had happened and took out his notebook and paper. Jester began a dazed account. His head felt light like a gas balloon.

The ambulance shrilled in the static afternoon. An intern in a white coat leaped out and put his stethoscope on Grown Boy's chest.

'Dead?' the cop asked.

'As a doornail,' the intern said.

'Are you sure?' Jester asked.

The intern looked at Jester and noticed his panama hat that had been knocked off. 'Is this your hat?' Jester took the hat, which was grimy now.

The white-coated interns carried the body to the ambulance. It was so callous and swift and dreamlike that Jester turned slowly toward the drugstore, his hand on his head. The cop followed him.

Wagon, who was still eating his spat-on back, said, 'What happened?'

'Dunno,' said the cop.

Jester felt lightheaded. Could it be possible he was going to faint? 'I feel funny.'

The cop, glad to be doing something, steered him to a chair in the pharmacy and said, 'Sit down here and hold your head between your legs.' Jester did so and when the blood rushed back to his head he sat up, although he was very pale.

'It was all my fault. If I hadn't been chasing him and those people piling in on top of us,' he turned to the cop, 'and why did you hit him so hard?'

'When you are breaking up a crowd with a billy stick you don't know how hard you are hitting. I don't like violence any more than you do. Maybe I shouldn't even have joined the force.'

Meantime Malone had called the old Judge to come and get his grandson and Jester was crying with shock.

When Sherman Pew drove up to bring him home, Jester, who was not thinking about impressing Sherman any more, was led to the car while the cop tried to explain what had happened. After listening, Sherman only commented, 'Well, Grown Boy has always been just a feeb, and in my case, if I was just a feeb, I'd be glad if it happened to me. I put myself in other people's places.'

'I do wish you would shut up,' Jester said.

At the Judge's household there were tears and disorder when they arrived. Verily was sobbing for her nephew and the Judge patted her with awkward little pats. She was sent home to her own people to mourn over that sudden noonday death.

Before the news came, the Judge had had a happy fruitful

morning. He had been working joyfully; there had been none of the idle tedium that day, that endlessness of time that is as hard to bear in old age as it is in early childhood. Sherman Pew was panning out to his utmost expectations. Not only was he an intelligent coloured boy who understood about insulin and the needles as soon as he was told and sworn to secrecy, he also had imagination, talked of diet and substitutions for calories, and so forth. When the Judge had impressed on him that diabetes was not catching, Sherman had said: 'I know all about diabetes. My brother had it. We had to weigh his food on a teensy little balancing scale. Every morsel of food.'

The Judge, who suddenly recalled that Sherman was a foundling, wondered a second about this information but said nothing.

'I know all about calories too, sir, on account of I am a house guest of Zippo Mullins and his sister went on a diet. I whipped the fluffy mashed potatoes with skimmed milk for her and made sucaryl jello. Yessireebob, I know all about diets.'

'Do you think you would make me a good amanuensis?'

'A good what, Judge?'

'An amanuensis is a kind of secretary.'

'Oh, a super-dooper secretary,' Sherman said, his voice soft with enchantment. 'I would adore that.'

'Harrumph,' said the Judge, to hide his pleasure. 'I have quite a voluminous correspondence, serious, profound correspondence and little niggling letters.'

'I adore writing letters and write a lovely hand.'

'Penmanship is most indicative.' The Judge added, 'Calligraphy.'

'Where are the letters, sir?'

'In my steel file in my office at the courthouse.'

'You want me to get them?'

'No,' the Judge said hastily, as he had answered every letter; indeed, that was his chief occupation when he went in the morning to his office – that and the persual of the *Flowering Branch Ledger* and the *Milan Courier*. Last week there had come a day when not a letter of moment had been received – only an advertisement for Kare Free

Kamping Equipment which was probably meant for Jester anyway. Cheated that there were no letters of moment, the Judge had answered the ad, posing trenchant questions about sleeping bags and the quality of frying pans. The static tedium of old age had troubled him so often. But not today; this morning with Sherman he was on a high horse, his head literally teeming with plans.

'Last night I wrote a letter that lasted to the wee hours,' Sherman said.

'A love letter?'

'No.' Sherman thought over the letter which he had posted on the way to work. At first the address had puzzled him, then he addressed it to: 'Madame Marian Anderson, The steps of the Lincoln Memorial.' If she wasn't right there, they would forward it. Mother ... Mother ... he was thinking, you are too famous to miss.

'My beloved wife always said I wrote the most precious love letters in the world.'

'I don't waste time writing love letters. This long letter I wrote last night was a finding letter.'

'Letter writing is an art in itself.'

'What kind of letter do you wish me to write today?' Sherman added, timidly, 'Not a love letter, I presume.'

'Of course not, silly. It's a letter concerning my grandson. A letter of petition, you might say.'

'Petition?'

'I am asking an old friend and fellow congressman to put my boy up for West Point.'

'I see.'

'I have to draft it carefully in my mind beforehand. They are the most delicate letters of all ... petition letters.' The Judge closed his eyes and placed his thumb and forefinger over his eyelids, thinking profoundly. It was a gesture almost of pain, but that morning the Judge had no pain at all; on the contrary, after the years of boredom and endless blank time, the utter joy of having important letters to compose and a genuine amanuensis at his disposal made the Judge as buoyant as a boy again. He sat furrowed and immobile so long that Sherman was concerned.

'Head hurt?'

The Judge jerked and straightened himself. 'Mercy no, I was just composing the structure of the letter. Thinking to whom I'm writing and the various circumstances of his present and past life. I'm just thinking of the individual I'm writing to.'

'Who is he?'

'Senator Thomas of Georgia. Address him: Washington, D.C.'

Sherman dipped the pen in the inkwell three times and straightened the paper very carefully, thrilled at the thought of writing to a senator.

'My Dear Friend and Colleague, Tip Thomas.'

Again Sherman dipped the pen in ink and began to write with a flourish. 'Yes, sir?'

'Be quiet, I'm thinking – Proceed now.'

Sherman was writing that when the Judge stopped him. 'You don't write that. Start again. When I say "proceed" and things like that, don't actually write them.'

'I was just taking dictation.'

'But, by God, use common sense.'

'I am using common sense, but when you dictate words I naturally write them.'

'Let's start at the very beginning. The salutation reads: My Dear Friend and Colleague, Tip Thomas. Get that?'

'I shouldn't write the get that, should I?'

'Of course not.'

The Judge was wondering if his amanuensis was as brilliant as he first supposed, and Sherman was wondering privately if the old man was nuts. So both regarded each other with mutual suspicions of mental inadequacy. The work went badly at first.

'Don't write this in the letter. I just want to level with you personally.'

'Well, level personally.'

'The art of a true amanuensis is to write down everything in the letter or document, but not to record personal reflections or, in other words, things that go on in my mind that are more or less extraneous to the said letter. The trouble with me, boy, is my mind works too quick and so many random thoughts come into it that are not pertinent to any particular train of thought.'

'I understand, sir,' said Sherman, who was thinking that the job was not what he had imagined.

'Not many people understand me,' the Judge said simply.

'You mean you want me to read your mind about what to write in the letter and what to not.'

'Not read my mind,' the Judge said indignantly, 'but to gather from my intonations which is personal rumination and which is not.'

'I'm a wonderful mind reader.'

'You mean you are intuitive? Why so am I.'

Sherman did not know what the word meant, but he was thinking that if he stayed on with the old Judge he would pick up a grand vocabulary.

'Back to the letter,' the Judge said sternly. 'Write after the salutation, "It has recently come to my attention that –"' The Judge broke off and continued in a lower voice which Sherman, who was reading the Judge's mind, did not write down. 'How recently is recently, boy? One – two – three years? I guess it happened ten years ago.'

'I wouldn't say recently in that case.'

'You are quite correct,' the Judge decided in a firm voice. 'Start the letter on a completely different tack.'

The gilt clock in the library sounded twelve strikes. 'It's noon.'

'Yea,' said Sherman, pen in hand and waiting.

'At noon I interrupt my endeavours to have the first toddy of the day. The privilege of an old man.'

'Do you wish me to prepare it for you?'

'That would be most kindly, boy. Would you like a little bourbon and branch water?'

'Bourbon and branch water?'

'I'm not a solitary drinker. I don't like to drink alone.' Indeed, in the old days he used to call in the yardman, Verily, or anyone else to drink with him. Since Verily did not drink and the yardman was dead, the Judge was many times forced to drink alone, but he didn't like it. 'A little toddy to keep me company.'

This was the delightful part of the job that Sherman

hadn't thought about. He said, 'I'd be very pleased, sir. What measure drink do you like?'

'Half and half, and don't drown it.'

Sherman bustled to the kitchen to make the drinks. He was already worrying about dinner. If they had the drink together and became friends, he would hate to be sent to the kitchen to have dinner with the cook. He knew it would happen, but he would hate it. He rehearsed carefully what he would say. 'I never eat dinner,' or 'I ate such a hearty breakfast I'm not hungry.' He poured the half and halfs, both of them, and returned to the library.

After the Judge had sipped his drink once and smacked his lips, he said, 'This is ex-cathedral.'

'What?' Sherman said.

'That's what the Pope says when he's speaking frankly. I mean that nothing that I say to you now while we're drinking is in the letter. My friend Tip Thomas took to himself a helpmeet – or is it helpmate? I mean by this, he took to himself a second wife. As a rule I don't approve of second marriages, but when I think about it I just think, "Live and let live." You understand, boy?'

'No, sir. Not exactly, sir.'

'I wonder if I should overlook the second marriage and talk about his first wife. Talk in praise about his first wife and not mention the second.'

'Why mention either one of them?'

The Judge leaned his head back. 'The art of letter writing is like this; you first make gracious personal remarks about health and wives and so forth, and then when that's covered, you come plumb to the subject of what the letter is really about.'

The Judge drank blissfully. As he drank a little miracle was happening.

When the telephone rang, the Judge could not understand all at once. J.T. Malone was talking to him, but what he was saying seemed to make no sense. 'Grown Boy killed in a street fight – and Jester in the fight?' he repeated. 'I'll send somebody to get Jester at the drugstore.' He turned to Sherman. 'Sherman, will you go drive to Mr Malone's drugstore and pick up my grandson?' Sherman, who had never driven a car in his life, agreed with pleasure. He had watched people drive and thought he knew how it went. The Judge put down his drink and went to the kitchen. 'Verily,' he started, 'I have some serious news for you.'

After one look at the old Judge's face, Verily said, 'Somebody daid?' When the Judge did not answer she said, 'Sister Bula?'

When the Judge told her it was Grown Boy, she flung her apron over her head and sobbed loudly. 'And in all these years he never had his share of sense.' She told this as though it was the most poignant and explicable truth about the unreasonable fact that was shattering her.

The Judge tried to comfort her with little bearlike pats. He went to the library, finished his drink and the drink that Sherman had left unfinished and then went to the front porch to wait for Jester.

Then he realized the little miracle that had happened. Every morning for fifteen years he had waited so tediously for the delivery of the *Milan Courier*, waiting in the kitchen or in the library, his heart leaping up when he heard that little plop. But today, after all these years, his time was so occupied he had not even thought about the paper. Joyfully, the old Judge limped down the steps to pick up the *Milan Courier*.

Six

Since livingness is made up of countless daily miracles, most of which are unnoticed, Malone, in that season of sadness, noticed a little miracle and was astonished. Each morning that summer he had waked up with an amorphous dread. What was the awful thing that was going to happen to him? What was it? When? Where? When consciousness finally formed, it was so merciless that he could lie still no longer; he had to get up and roam the hall and kitchen, roaming without purpose, just roaming, waiting. Waiting for what? After his conversation with the Judge, he had filled the freezing compartment of the refrigerator with calf liver and beef liver. So morning after morning, while the electric light fought with the dawn, he fried a slice of the terrible liver. He had always loathed liver, even the Sunday chicken liver that the children squabbled over. After it was cooked, smelling up the whole house like a stink bomb, Malone ate it, every loathsome bite. Just the fact that it was so loathsome comforted him a little. He swallowed even the gristly pieces that other people removed from their mouths and put on the sides of their plates. Castor oil also had a nasty taste, and it was effective. The trouble with Dr Hayden, he had never suggested any cures, nasty or otherwise, for that – leukemia. Name a man a fatal disease and not recommend the faintest cure – Malone's whole being was outraged. A pharmacist for close on to twenty years, he had listened to and prescribed for trillions of complaints: constipation, kidney trouble, smuts in the eye, and so forth. If he honestly felt the case was beyond him he would tell the customer to consult a doctor, but that was not often – Malone felt he was as good as any bona fide M.D. in Milan, and he prescribed for trillions of complaints. A good patient himself, dosing himself with nasty Sal Hepatica, using Sloan's

Liniment when needed, Malone would eat every living bite of the loathsome liver. Then he would wait in the brightly lighted kitchen. Waiting for what? And when?

One morning toward the end of summer, Malone was wakening and fought against wakening. He struggled for the soft, sweet limbo of sleep, but he could not recapture it. The shrill birds were already up and at him, slicing to shreds his soft, sweet sleep. That morning he was exhausted. The terror of consciousness washed over his tired body and limpened spirit. He was going to force himself to sleep. Think of counting sheep – black sheep, white sheep, red sheep all hippity-hoppity and with plumping tails. Think of nothingness, oh, soft sweet sleep. He would not get up and turn on lights and roam the hall and kitchen, and roam and wait and dread. He would never fry that loathsome liver at dawn, smelling up the whole house like a stink bomb. Never no longer. Never no more. Malone switched on the bedside lamp and opened the drawer. There were the Tuinal capsules he had prescribed for himself. There were forty of them, he knew. His trembling fingers slid amongst the red and green capsules. Forty of them, he knew. He would no longer have to get up at dawn and roam the house in terror. No longer go to the pharmacy just because he had always gone to the pharmacy as it was his living and the support of his wife and family. If J.T. Malone was not the sole support, because of those shares of Coca-Cola stock his wife had bought with her own money and because of the three houses she had inherited from her mother – dear old Mrs Greenlove who had died fifteen years ago – if because of his wife's various resources he was not the utter and sole provider, the pharmacy was the mainstay of the family and he was a good provider, no matter what people might think. The pharmacy was the first store open in Milan and the last to close. Standing faithfully, listening to complaints, prescribing medicine, making cokes and sundaes, compounding prescriptions . . . no more, no more! Why had he done it so long? Like a plodding old mule going round and round a sorghum mill. And going home every night. And sleeping in bed with his wife whom he had long since ceased to love. Why? Because there was no fitting place to be except the pharmacy? Because there was no other fitting place to sleep except in bed beside his wife? Working at the pharmacy, sleeping with his wife, no more! His drab livingness spread out before him as he fingered the jewel-bright Tuinal.

Malone put one capsule in his mouth and drank half a glass of water. How much water would he have to drink to swallow the forty capsules?

After the first capsule he swallowed another, then a third. Then he stopped and refilled the water glass. When he came back to bed again he wanted a cigarette. As he smoked it he grew drowsy. While he was smoking his second cigarette it fell from between his lifeless fingers for J.T. Malone at last had gone to sleep again.

He slept until seven that morning and the household was awake when he went into the busy kitchen. For one of the few times in his life he failed to bathe and shave, for fear of being late at the pharmacy.

That morning he saw with his eyes the little miracle, but he was too swivetty and occupied to take it in. He took the short cut through the back yard and back gate, the miracle was there but his eyes were blind as he loped toward the gate. Yet when he reached the pharmacy he wondered why he had been hurrying so; no one was there. But already he had begun his day. He let down the awnings with a slam and turned on the electric fan. When the first customer entered his day had begun, although the first customer was only Herman Klein, the jeweller next door. Herman Klein was always in and out of the drugstore all day long, drinking Coca-Colas. He also kept a bottle of liquor in the compounding room of the pharmacy, as his wife hated liquor and did not allow it in the home. So Herman Klein spent the whole day at his shop doing his watchwork and visiting the drugstore frequently. Herman Klein did not go home for noonday dinner as did most Milan businessmen; he had a little snifter, then ate one of the neatly wrapped chicken sandwiches that Mrs Malone supplied. After Herman Klein had been attended to, a flurry of customers came in all at once. A mother came in with a bed-wetting child, and Malone sold her a Eurotone, a device that rings a bell when the bed is being wet. He had sold Eurotones to many parents, but privately he wondered why the ring of the bell would really be effective. Privately he wondered if it might not scare the be-Jesus out of a sleeping child, and what good would it do if the whole house was alarmed just because little Johnny made some quiet little pee-pee in his sleep? He thought privately it would be better to let Johnny just pee in peace. Malone advised the mothers sagely: 'I've sold a lot of these devices but the main thing I've always felt about toilet training is the co-operation of the child.' Malone scrutinized the child, a squarish little girl who did not look at all co-operative. He fitted a woman who had varicose veins with a surgical stocking. He listened to complaints of headaches, backaches and bowel trouble. He studied each customer carefully, made his diagnosis and sold the medicines. Nobody had leukemia, nobody went away empty handed.

By one o'clock when that wife-ridden, hag-ridden, little Herman Klein came in for his sandwich, Malone was tired. He was also meditating. He wondered who else in the world was worse off than he was. He looked at that little Herman Klein munching his sandwich at the counter. Malone loathed him. Loathed him for being so spineless, for working so hard, for not going to the Cricket Tea Room or the New York Café like other decent businessmen who did not go home for dinner. He did not feel sorry for Herman Klein. He just despised him.

He put on his coat to go home to dinner. It was a sweltering day, with a sky like white lightning. He walked slowly this time, feeling the weight of his white linen coat or a weight somehow on his shoulders. He always took his time and had a home-cooked dinner. Not like that mousy little Herman Klein. He went through the back-yard gate and then, though he was tired, he recognized the miracle. The vegetable garden, which he had sown so carelessly and forgotten in that long season of fear, had grown up. There were the purple cabbages, little frills of carrots, the green, green turnip greens and tomatoes. He stood looking at the garden. Meanwhile, a crowd of children had entered the open gate. They were the Lank brood. It was a curious thing about the Lanks. They had one multiple birth after the other. Twins, Triplets. They rented one of his wife's houses that she had inherited – a crummy, beatup house, as you would expect with all those hoards of children. Sammy Lank was a foreman at the Wedwell Spinning Mill. When at times he was laid off, Malone did not press him for the rent. Malone's house, which Martha had also inherited from old Mrs Greenlove, God bless her, was the corner house facing a very respectable street. The other three houses which adjoined each other were around the corner, and the neighbourhood there was running down. The Lank family house was the last house, that is, the last house in the row of three that Mrs Malone had inherited. So Malone saw the Lank brood frequently. Grimy, sniffly-nosed, they just hung around since there was nothing at home to do. One especially cold winter when Mrs Lank was confined with twins, Malone had sent some coal to their house because he was fond of children and knew they were cold. The children were called Nip and Tuck, Cyrily and Simon, and Rosemary, Rosamond, and Rosa. The children now were growing up. The eldest triplets, who were already married and having babies on their own, were born the night the Dionne quins were born and the *Milan Courier* had had a little article about 'Our Milan Trio' which the Lanks framed and put in their sitting room.

Malone looked again at the garden. 'Sugar,' he called.

'Yes, Hon,' Mrs Malone answered.

'Have you seen the vegetable garden?' Malone went into the house.

'What vegetable garden?' Mrs Malone asked.

'Why, our vegetable garden.'

'Of course I've seen it, Hon. We've been eating out of it all summer. What's the matter with you?'

Malone, who had no appetite these days and never remembered what he ate, said nothing, but it was indeed a miracle that that garden, planted so carelessly and never tended, had flourished. The collards were growing like crazy as collards will do. Plant a collard in the garden and they just grow like crazy, pushing out the other plants. The same as morning-glories – a collard or a morning-glory.

There was little conversation at the noonday dinner. They had meat loaf and double-trouble potatoes, but although the meal was well cooked, Malone did not taste it. 'I've been telling you all summer that the vegetables were home grown,' Mrs Malone said. Malone heard the remark but paid no attention, let alone replied; for years his wife's voice had been like a sawmill to him, a sound you hear but pay no attention to.

Young Ellen and Tommy bolted their dinner and were about to run.

'You ought to chew, darlings. Otherwise nobody knows what intestinal trouble lies in wait for you. When I was a girl they had what they called the Fletcher cure, you were supposed to chew seven times before you actually swallowed. If you continue to eat like firehorses . . .' But already the Malone children had said 'Excuse me,' and had run from the house.

From then on the dinner was a silent one, and neither voiced their thoughts. Mrs Malone was thinking about her 'Mrs Malone Sandwiches' – plump kosher chickens (it did not matter if the fowls were Jewish), the A & P hens she prodded carefully, midget turkeys, twenty-pound turkeys. She labelled the turkey sandwiches 'Mrs Malone's Turkey Salad Sandwich', although it was an amazing thing how many people could not taste the difference between turkey salad and chicken salad. Meanwhile, Malone was occupied with his own professional considerations; should he have sold the Eurotone this morning? It had slipped his mind that a few months ago a woman had complained about the Eurotone. It seemed that her little Eustis had slept through all the bells of the Eurotone, but the family had waked up and stood around watching the quietly peeing and sound asleep little Eustis, while the Eurotone bells were ringing like mad. Finally, it seemed, the daddy had yanked the child out of the wet bed and warmed his behind in front of the whole family. Was that fair? Malone pondered the subject and decided it was definitely not fair. He had never laid a hand on his children, whether they deserved it or not. Mrs Malone disciplined the children, as Malone felt it was the wife's duty, and she always cried when it was her clear duty to spank one of the children. The only time Malone felt impelled to act in such a manner was the time four-year-old Ellen built a secret fire under her grandmother's bed. How old Mrs Greenlove had cried, both for her own terror and for the fact that her favourite grandchild was being chastised. But playing with fire was the only mis-behaviour that Malone dealt with, as it was too serious a thing to trust to a tenderhearted mother who invariably cried as she chastised. Yes, forbidden matches and fires were the only things he had to handle. And the Eurotone? Although it was a recommended product, he regretted having sold it that morning. With a painful, final swallow that made his Adam's apple struggle in his frail throat, Malone excused himself and rose from the table.

'I'm going to call Mr Harris to take over the pharmacy for the balance of the day.'

Anxiety flickered across Mrs Malone's placid face. 'Aren't you feeling well, Hon?'

Rage made Malone fist his hands until the knuckles whitened. A man with leukemia not feeling well? What the hell did the woman think he had . . . chicken pox or spring fever? But although his fisted knuckles were white with rage, he only said, 'I feel no better nor no worse than I deserve.'

'You work too hard, Hon. Altogether too hard. You're a regular workhorse.'

'A mule,' Malone corrected. 'A mule going round and round a cane mill.'

'J.T., don't you want me to put you in a tub of nice, tepid water?'

'I certainly do not want it.'

'Don't be mulish, Hon. I'm just trying to comfort you.'

'I can be mulish as I please in my own house,' Malone said stubbornly.

'I was just trying to comfort you, but I see it's no use.'

'No use at all,' he answered bitterly.

Malone took a steaming shower, washed his hair, shaved, and darkened the bedroom. But he was too angry to rest. From the kitchen he could hear Mrs Malone beating batter for a wedding cake or something, and this made him still angrier. He went out into the glaring afternoon.

He had lost the summer that year; the vegetables had grown and been eaten unnoticed. The hard blaze of summer shrivelled his spirit. The Judge had insisted that nothing ailed him that a spell of Milan summer would not cure. Thinking of the old Judge, he went to the back porch and found a paper sack. Although he was free for the afternoon, there was no sense of freedom in him. Wearily he began to pick a mess of greens for the Judge, both turnip greens and collards. Then he added the largest tomato and stood for a moment weighing it in his hand.

'Hon,' Mrs Malone called from the kitchen window, 'what are you doing?'

'What? What?'

'What are you doing just standing there in the heat of the afternoon?'

Things had come to a pretty pass when a man has to account for himself for just standing alone in his own back yard. But though his thoughts were brutal he only answered, 'Picking greens.'

'You ought to have a hat on if you are going to linger long in this broiling sun. Might save you a sunstroke, Hon.'

Malone's face paled as he shouted, 'Why is it your goddamn business?'

'Don't swear, J.T., for mercy's sake.'

So Malone stayed longer in the broiling heat, just because his wife had questioned and interfered. Then, hatless, and carrying the sack of vegetables, he trudged over to the Judge's house. The Judge was in the darkened library and the nigger with the blue eyes was with him.

'High-ho, J.T., high-ho, my hearty. You're just the man I was looking for.'

'What for?' For Malone was both pleased and taken aback by this hearty reception.

'This is the hour for immortal poetry. My amanuensis reads to me.'

'Your what?' Malone asked sharply, as the word suggested to him Eurotone and bed-wetting.

'My secretary here. Sherman Pew. He is an excellent reader, and the reading hour is one of the pleasantest portions of the day. Today we're reading Longfellow. Read on, MacDuff,' the Judge said jovially.

'What?'

'I was just paraphrasing Shakespeare, so to say.'

'Shakespeare?' Sherman felt out of his element, left out and cloddish. He hated Mr Malone for coming in at the poetry hour. Why wasn't that old sourpuss at the drugstore where he belonged?

'Go back to:

> By the shore of Gitche Gumee,
> By the shining Big-Sea-Water,
> At the doorway of his wigwam . . .'

The Judge's eyes were closed and his head gently wagged with the rhythm. 'Proceed, Sherman.'

'I don't want to,' said Sherman sullenly. Why should he make a monkey of himself in front of that fuss-body Mr Malone? He'd be damned if he would.

The Judge felt something amiable was going amiss. 'Well, just recite, "I shot an arrow into the air."'

'I don't feel like it, sir.'

Malone watched and listened to the scene, his sack of greens still on his lap.

The Judge, feeling that something *very* amiable was going amiss, and craving to finish the lovely poem, continued himself:

> 'Daughter of the moon, Nakomis
> Dark behind it rose the forest
> Rose the black and gloomy pine-trees
> Bright before it beat the water
> Beat the clear and sunny water
> Beat the shining big sea water . . .

My eyes are tired in this darkened room. Can't you take over, Sherman?'

'No, sir.'

> 'Ewa yea, my little owlet
> Who is this that lights the wigwam
> With his great eyes lights the wigwam . . .

Oh the tenderness, the rhythm and tenderness of this. Why can't you feel it, Sherman? You always read immortal poetry so beautifully.'

Sherman scrooched up his behind and did not comment.

Malone, still with the sack of greens in his lap, felt the tension in the room. It was apparent that this sort of thing went on every day. He wondered who was crazy. The old Judge? The nigger with the blue eyes? Himself? Longfellow? He said with careful tact, 'I brought you a mess of turnip greens from my garden, and a mess of collards.'

With arrogant rudeness Sherman said, 'He can't eat them.'

The Judge's voice was dismayed. 'Why, Sherman,' he said pleadingly, 'I adore turnip greens and collards.'

'It's not on the diet,' Sherman insisted. 'They belong to be cooked with side meat, streak of lean and streak of fat. And that's not on the diet.'

'Hows about just a slither of the lean portion of streak of lean, streak of fat?'

Sherman was still mad that Mr Malone had come in at the reading hour which he loved, and the sourpuss old drugstore man had looked at the two of them like they were loony and spoiled the immortal poetry hour. However, he had not read Hiawatha aloud. He had not made himself a monkey; he had left that to the old Judge who did not seem to care if people thought he had just escaped from Milledgeville or not.

Malone said soothingly, 'Yankees eat greens with butter or vinegar.'

'While I'm certainly no Yankee, I'll try the greens with vinegar. On our honeymoon in New Orleans I ate snails. One snail,' the old Judge added.

From the parlour, there was the sound of the piano. Jester was playing the 'Lindenbaum'. Sherman was furious because he played it so well.

'I eat snails all the time. Picked up the habit when I was in France.'

'I didn't know you were ever in France,' Malone said.

'Why certainly. I had a brief stint in the service.' Zippo Mullins had been in the service, and that was the actual truth, and had told Sherman many stories, most of which Sherman took with a grain of salt.

'J.T., I'm sure you need some refreshment after your broiling walk. How about some gin and quinine water?'

'That would be most acceptable, sir.'

'Sherman, will you make Mr Malone and me some gin and quinine water?'

'Quinine, Judge?' His voice was incredulous, for even if that old Mr Malone was a drugstore man, he surely wouldn't like bitter quinine on his day off.

The Judge said in a bossy voice, as if to a servant, 'It's in the refrigerator. On the bottle it says "tonic".'

Sherman wondered why he had not said so at first. Tonic water was not the same as quinine. He knew because he had tasted little drinks ever since he had been with the Judge.

'Put plenty of ice in it,' the Judge said.

Sherman was fit to be tied, not only because the reading hour was spoiled but because he had been ordered around like a servant. He hurried in to take it out on Jester. 'Is that "Rockabye Baby" you're playing?'

'No, it is "Lindenbaum"; I borrowed it from you.'

'Well, it is the utter end in German lieder.'

Jester, who had been playing with tears of emotion in his eyes, stopped playing, to Sherman's content because he had been playing much too well, especially for a sight-reading job.

Sherman went to the kitchen and fixed the drinks with very little ice. Who was he to be ordered around? And how was it that that puny-faced Jester could play genuine German lieder so well, especially on a sight-reading job?

He had done everything for the old Judge. The afternoon when Grown Boy died, he had cooked supper himself, waiting on the table; however, he would not eat the supper he had cooked. He would not eat the supper, even at the library table. He had found a cook for them. He had found Cinderella Mullins to pinch-hit for them while that Verily was away.

Meanwhile, the Judge was telling his friend Malone, 'That boy is a veritable treasure, a jewel. Writes letters for me, reads for me, let alone giving me the injections and making me toe the line on my diet.'

Malone's scepticism showed on his face. 'How did you happen to run across this paragon?'

'I didn't run across him. He has affected my very life since before he was born.'

Malone was hesitant even to conjecture about this mysterious remark. Could it be that the snooty blue-eyed nigger was the Judge's natural son? Improbable as it seemed, it could be possible. 'But wasn't he found in a pew at one of the coloured churches?'

'He was.'

'But how does this affect your very life?'

'Not only my very life but my life's blood – my own son.'

Malone tried to think of Johnny having a sexual relation with a coloured girl. The fair-haired, decent Johnny Clane with whom he had many times gone hunting at Sereno. It was highly improbable but again not impossible.

The Judge seemed to read his puzzled mind. With his good hand he gripped his stick until the hand turned purple. 'If you think for one single moment that my Johnny ever slept with nigger wenches or such immoral doings . . .' The Judge could not finish for rage.

'I never supposed any such thing,' Malone said soothingly. 'You just put it so mysteriously.'

'It is a mystery, if ever there was one. But it's such a bad business that even a garrulous old man like myself can hardly discuss it.'

Yet Malone knew he wanted to discuss it further, but at that moment Sherman Pew banged two glasses on the library table. When Sherman bolted out of the room, the Judge continued: 'However, now that boy is a golden skein in my old age. Writes my letters with the calligraphy of an angel, gives me my injections and makes me toe the line on the diet. Reads to me in the afternoons.'

Malone did not point out that the boy had refused to read that afternoon, so that the old Judge himself had had to finish Longfellow.

'Sherman reads Dickens with such pathos. Sometimes I cry and cry.'

'Does that boy ever cry?'

'No, but often he smiles at the humorous places.'

Malone, puzzled, waited for the Judge to say something more pertinent about the mystery he had intimated, but he only said, 'Well it only goes to show again that "out of this nettle, danger, we pluck this flower, safety".'

'Why, what's the matter, sir? Were you in danger?'

'Not exactly in danger – that's just the expression of the Bard. But since my dear wife's death I've been so much alone.'

Malone was not only puzzled about the Judge, but suddenly worried. 'Alone, sir? You have your grandson, and you're the most revered citizen in all Milan.'

'You can be the most revered citizen in town, or in all the state, and still feel alone. And *be* alone, by God!'

'But your grandson who is the apple of your eye?'

'It's the nature of young boys to be selfish. I know boys through and through. The only thing that's the matter with Jester is – adolescence. I have a profound knowledge of all boys and it all comes down to – selfish, selfish, selfish.'

Malone was pleased to hear Jester criticized, but very properly he said nothing. He only asked, 'How long have you had the coloured boy?'

'About two months.'

'That's a short time for him to be so well established in the household . . . so cozily settled, one might say.'

'Sherman is cozy, thank God. Although he's an adolescent like my grandson, we have a quite different relationship.'

Malone was thankful to hear this, but again very properly said nothing. Knowing the capriciousness of the Judge, his fits of instant delight and instant disappointment, he wondered how long this situation would last.

'A veritable jewel,' the Judge was saying enthusiastically. 'A treasure.'

Meanwhile, 'the veritable jewel' was reading a movie magazine and drinking gin and tonic with loads of ice. He was alone in the kitchen as that old Verily was cleaning upstairs. Although he was replete with the comforts of taste and imagination – it was a very good article about one of his favourite movie stars – he was very, very mad. Not only had his special hour of the day been spoiled by the fusspot Mr Malone, he had lived for three months in suspense, suspense that little by little grew into anxiety. Why hadn't Madame Anderson replied to his letter? If it had been wrongly addressed, it could have been forwarded, for his mother was too famous to miss. When Jester's dog, Tige, walked into the room, Sherman kicked him.

Verily came down from upstairs and looked at Sherman reading the magazine, drinking the gin and tonic. She was going to comment about him but the look of the fierce eyes in the dark face silenced her. She only said, 'In my day I never sat around reading books and drinking liquor.'

Sherman said, 'You were probably born a slave, old woman.'

'Slave I was not, my grandfather was.'

'They probably put you on the block in this very town.'

Verily began to wash the dishes, turning on the water spigot very loud. Then she said, 'If I knew who your mother was I would tell her to switch you to a frazzle.'

Sherman went back into the parlour to rile Jester for a while, having nothing else to do. Jester was playing again, and he wished he knew what the name of the music was. Suppose he said something bad about the composer and it was the wrong composer. Was it Chopin, Beethoven, Schubert? Because he did not know he could not trust himself to be insulting and that made him more furious. Suppose he said, 'That's terrible Beethoven you're playing,' and Jester said, 'It's not Beethoven, it's Chopin.' Sherman, out of pocket, did not know what to do. Then he heard the front door open and close and knew that that busybody, Mr Malone, had gone. Having embarrassed himself, he went in, meek as Moses, to the Judge. On his own accord he resumed Longfellow, starting with:

'I shot an arrow into the air.'

Malone had never felt the heat so much as he had this summer. As he walked he felt the blazing sky, the sun, weigh down his shoulders. An ordinary, practical man who seldom daydreamed, he was daydreaming now that in the autumn he was going to a northern country, to Vermont or Maine where again he would see snow. He was going alone without Mrs Malone. He would ask Mr Harris to take over the pharmacy and he would stay there for two weeks, or who knows, two months, alone and at peace. He saw in his mind's eye the polar enchantment of snow and felt the cool of it. He would stay in a hotel by himself, which he had never done before, or would it be a ski resort? As he thought of snow he felt a freedom, and a guilt gnawed him as he walked, shoulders bent, under the terrible heat of the day. Once, and only once, he had had the guilt of freedom. Twelve years ago he had sent his wife and the small Ellen to Tallulah Falls for a cool summer vacation, and while they were gone Malone chanced to meet Malone's sin. At first he did not think it was a sin at all. It was just a young lady he met at the drugstore. She had come in with a cinder in her eye and very carefully he had removed the cinder with his clean linen handkerchief. He remembered her trembling body and the tears in her black eyes as he held her head to remove the cinder. She left and that night he thought of her, but that seemed to be the end. But it happened they met the next day when he was paying the dry goods bill. She was a clerk in the office. She had said, 'You were so sweet to me yesterday. I wonder what I could do for you now?' He said, 'Why, why don't you go to lunch with me tomorrow?' and she had accepted, a little slip of a young thing, working in the dry goods store. They had lunch in the Cricket Tea Room, the most respectable place in town. He talked to her about his family and he never dreamed it would come to anything else. But it did, and at the end of two weeks he had sinned and the awful thing was, he was glad. Singing as he shaved and putting on his finest garments every day. They went to the picture show in town, and he even took her to Atlanta on the bus and took her to the cyclorama. They went to the Henry Grady Hotel for dinner and she ordered caviar. He was strangely happy in this transgression, although he knew it was soon to end. It ended in September when his wife and child came back to town, and Lola was very understanding. Maybe a thing like that had happened to her once before.

After fifteen years he still dreamed of her although he had changed dry goods stores and never saw her. When he learned that she had married he was sad, but in another portion of his soul, relieved.

Thinking of freedom was like thinking of snow. Surely, in the autumn of that year, he would have Mr Harris take over the pharmacy and he would take a vacation. He would know again the secret stealth of snow and feel the blessed cold. So Malone walked wearily to his own home.

'When you have a vacation like this, hon, I don't think it's a real vacation just to trudge around town, not in this heat.'

'I wasn't thinking of the heat, although this town in summer is hot as the hinges of hell.'

'Well, Ellen's been trying herself.'

'What do you mean?' Malone said, alarmed.

'Just trying herself, and crying, crying all afternoon in her bedroom.'

Quickly Malone went up to Ellen's bedroom and Mrs Malone followed. Ellen was in the bed in her pretty little blue and pink girl's room, sobbing. Malone could not bear to see Ellen cry, for she was his heart. A little tremor came over his tired body. 'Baby, baby, what is it?'

Ellen turned her face to him, 'Oh, Daddy, I'm so much in love.'

'Well, why does that make my heart-child cry?'

'Because he doesn't even know I'm on the earth. We pass on the street and everywhere and he just waves in a casual way and goes on.'

Mrs Malone said, 'That's all right, darling, one of these days when you are older you will meet Mr Right and all will end well.'

Ellen sobbed more vehemently and Malone hated his wife for it was the silliest thing a mother could say. 'Baby, baby, who is it? '

'Jester. I'm so much in love with Jester.'

'Jester Clane!' Malone thundered.

'Yes, Jester. He is so handsome.'

'Darling, love,' Malone said, 'Jester Clane is not worth one inch of your little finger.' As Ellen still sobbed, he regretted that he had toted the turnip greens to the old Judge, although the old Judge was innocent of all this. Trying so much to make amends, he said, 'And after all, heart-child, this is only puppy love, thank goodness.' But as he said these words he knew they were just as silly and comfortless as Mrs Malone's were. 'Darling, in the cool of the afternoon, why don't we go to the pharmacy and pick up a quart of that ripple-fudge ice cream for supper.' Ellen cried for a while, but later in the afternoon, which was not cool, they went in the family car to the pharmacy and picked up some ripple-fudge ice cream.

Seven

J.T. Malone was not the only one who was worried about the Judge those months; Jester had begun to be concerned about his grandfather. Selfish, selfish, selfish as he was, with a hundred problems of his own, he still worried about his grandfather. The Judge's wild enthusiasm for his 'amanuensis' just carried him away. It was Sherman this, Sherman that, all day long. His grandfather dictated letters in the morning, then at noon they had a drink together. Then when he and his grandfather had their dinner in the dining room, Sherman made himself a 'slight sandwich' and ate it in the library. He had told the Judge that he wanted to think over the morning's correspondence, that he didn't want to be distracted by conversations with Verily in the kitchen, and that a heavy noon dinner was bad for his work and concentration.

The Judge had agreed with this arrangement, pleased that his correspondence was pondered so seriously, pleased as pie about everything these days. He had always spoiled servants, giving them costly, but often very peculiar, gifts for Christmas and birthdays. (A fancy dress nowhere near the right size or a hat nobody would be caught dead in or brand new shoes that did not fit.) Although most of the servants had been female churchgoers who never drank, a few had been in a different category. Yet whether they were teetotallers or the drinking kind, the Judge never checked his liquor shelf in the sideboard. Indeed, Paul, the old gardener (a wizard with roses and border flowers), had died of cirrhosis of the liver after gardening and drinking twenty years at the Judge's.

Although Verily knew the Judge was a born spoiler, she was amazed at Sherman Pew and the liberties he took in the Judge's household.

'Won't eat in the kitchen because he says he wants to think about letters,' she grumbled. 'It's because he's too uppity to eat with me in the kitchen as he belongs. Fixing himself party sandwiches and eating in the liberry, if you please! He's going to ruin the liberry table.'

'How?' the Judge asked.

'Eating them party sandwiches on them trays,' Verily said stubbornly.

Although the Judge was very sensitive to his own dignity, he was not so sensitive to the dignity of others. Sherman stifled his sudden rages in the Judge's presence and took them out on Gus, the new yardman, Verily, and most of all on Jester. But although the actual rage fits were smothered, the anger remained and, indeed, increased. For one thing he hated reading Dickens, there were so many orphans in Dickens, and Sherman loathed books about orphans, feeling in them a reflection on himself. So when the Judge sobbed aloud over orphans, chimney sweeps, stepfathers, and all such horrors, Sherman read in a cold, inflexible voice, and glanced with cool superiority when the old fool acted up. The Judge, obtuse to the feelings of others, noticed none of this and was as pleased as pie. Laughing, drinking, sobbing at Dickens, writing whole mailsacks of letters, and never an instant bored. Sherman continued to be a jewel, a treasure, and no world could be said against him in the house. Meanwhile, in Sherman's dour but quailing heart things went steadily from bad to worse so that by the middle of autumn his feelings for the Judge were those of veiled but ever present hate.

But in spite of the soft, clean, bossy job; in spite of the fun of riling that soppy, chicken-outing Jester Clane, that autumn was the most miserable one in Sherman's entire life. Day after day he waited, his livingness suspended in the blank vacuum of suspense. Day after day he waited for the letter, and day after day, week after week, there was no answer. Then by chance one day he met a musician friend of Zippo Mullins who actually knew Marian Anderson, owned a signed photograph of her and everything, and from this hideous stranger he learned the truth: Madame Anderson was not his mother. Not only was she wedded to her career and too busy studying to have had the time for love affairs with princes, let alone borning him and leaving him so peculiarly in a church pew, she had never once been to Milan and could not possibly have touched his life in any way. So the hope that had lifted and made so luminous his searching heart was shattered. Forevermore? He thought so at that time. That evening he took down his records of German lieder sung by Marian Anderson and stomped on them, stomping with such despair and fury that not a groove of the records remained unshattered. Then, as the hope and the music could not be altogether silenced, he threw himself with his muddy shoes on the fine rayon bedspread and scraped his body on it as he wailed aloud.

Next morning he could not go to work as his fit had left him exhausted and hoarse. But at noon when the Judge sent him a covered tray of fresh vegetable soup with piping hot cornsticks and a lemony dessert, he was sufficiently recovered to eat the food slowly, languidly – glad with the feeling-sick feeling and eating the cornsticks with his little finger delicately crooked. He stayed home a week and somebody else's cooking and the rest restored him. But his smooth, round face hardened and, although he did not think consciously about that cheating creep of a Madame Anderson after a while he yearned to rob as he had been robbed.

The first of that fall was the happiest time Jester had ever known. At first lifted by the wings of song, his passion now had quieted to friendship. Sherman was in his home every day, and the security of constant presence alters passion which is fed by jeopardy and the dread of change, of loss. Sherman was at his house every day and there was no reason to believe it would not go on forever. True, Sherman went out of his way to insult him, which wounded Jester. But as the weeks passed he had learned not to let the wounding remarks be felt too deeply or too long; indeed, he was learning to defend himself. Hard as it was for Jester to make up jazzy hurtful remarks, he was learning to do it. Furthermore he was learning to understand Sherman, and understanding which conflicts with the ruthless violence of passion leads to both pity and love. Nevertheless, when Sherman was away that week, Jester was a little bit relieved;

he did not have to be on his P's and Q's every instant and could relax without the fear of having to defend his pride at any moment. Another element of their relationship was Jester's dim awareness that he was the chosen one; that he was the one that Sherman used to lash out against when he wanted to lash out against the world. For Jester knew dimly that fury is unleashed more freely against those you are most close to – so close that there is the trust that anger and ugliness will be forgiven. Jester, himself, would be angry only with his grandfather as a child – his fits of head-banging temper were directed only toward his grand-father – not Verily, Paul, or anybody else – for he knew that his grandfather would forgive and love. So while Sherman's wounding remarks were certainly no blessing, he sensed in them a kind of trust for which he was grateful. He had bought the score of *Tristan,* and when Sherman was away it was a relief to practise it without fear of belittling wisecracks. However, when his grandfather roamed the house like a lost soul and almost couldn't eat, Jester was concerned. 'I just don't see what you see in Sherman Pew.'

'That boy's a jewel, a veritable treasure,' the Judge said placidly. His voice changed when he added, 'Besides, it's not a short time I've known the boy and I feel responsible for him.'

'Responsible how?'

'It's because of me that the boy is an orphan.'

'I don't dig it,' Jester protested. 'Don't talk in riddles.'

'It's too sorry a business to be discussed, especially between you and me.'

Jester answered, 'Anything I despise is for somebody to tell just half a story, work up a person's interest and then don't go on.'

'Well, forget it,' his grandfather said. He added with a glib addendum that Jester knew was only a sort of camou-flage to the truth, 'After all, he was the coloured caddy who saved my life when I was flailing and drowning in the golf pond.'

'That's just a detail and not the real truth.'

'Ask me no questions and I'll tell you no lies,' the Judge said in a maddening voice.

Deprived of the joys and the busyness of Sherman, the Judge wanted to rope in Jester, who was too busy with his own life and school to be roped in. Jester would not read immortal poetry, or play poker, and even the correspondence did not interest Jester a hoot. So the sadness and tedium returned to the Judge. After the manifold interests and activities of those months, solitaire bored him and he had read every speck of all the issues of the *Ladies' Home Journal* and *McCall's*.

'Tell me,' Jester said suddenly, 'since you imply you know so much about Sherman Pew, did you ever know his mother?'

'Unfortunately, I did.'

'Why don't you tell Sherman who she is. Naturally he wants to know.'

'That is a pure case where ignorance is bliss.'

'One time you say knowledge is power and another time you say ignorance is bliss. Which side are you on? Anyway I don't believe a particle in any of those old saws.'

Absentmindedly Jester was tearing up the spongy rubber ball the Judge used to exercise his left hand. 'Some people think it's the act of a weakling ... to commit suicide ... and other people think, it takes a lot of guts to do it. I still wonder why my father did it. And an all-around athlete, graduated with all honours from the University of Georgia, why did he do it?'

'It was just a fleeting depression,' the Judge said, copying J.T. Malone's words of consolation.

'It doesn't seem an all-around athlete thing to do.'

While his grandfather carefully laid out the cards for a game of solitaire, Jester wandered to the piano. He began to play *Tristan*, his eyes half closed and his body swaying. He had already inscribed the score:

> For my dear friend Sherman Pew
> Ever faithfully,
> John Jester Clane

The music gave Jester goose pimples, it was so violent yet shimmering.

Nothing pleased Jester more than giving a fine present to Sherman, whom he loved. On the third day of Sherman's absence Jester picked some mums and autumn leaves from his garden and bore them proudly to the lane. He put the flowers in an iced-tea pitcher. He hovered over Sherman as though he was dying, which annoyed Sherman.

Sherman lay languidly on the bed and when Jester was arranging the flowers he said in a sassy, languid voice: 'Have you ever stopped to consider how much your face resembles a baby's behind?'

Jester was too shocked to take it in, let alone reply.

'Innocent, dopey, the very living image of a baby's behind.'

'I'm not innocent,' Jester protested.

'You certainly are. It shows in your dopey face.'

Jester, like all young things, was a great one for gilding the lily. Hidden in his bouquet of flowers was a jar of caviar which he had bought from the A & P that morning; now with the violence and insolence of this new attack he did not know what to do with the hidden caviar which Sherman claimed to eat by the ton-fulls. Since his flowers had been set so peculiarly at nought – not a word of thanks or even an appreciative look – Jester did wonder what to do with the hidden caviar, for he could not stand to be humiliated further. He hid the caviar in his hip pocket. So he had to sit gingerly in a sideways position. Sherman, with pretty flowers in the room which he appreciated but didn't bother to thank Jester for or mention, well fed with somebody else's cooking, and rested, felt well enough to tease Jester. (Little did he know that he had already teased himself out of a jar of genuine caviar which he would have displayed in the most conspicuous shelf in the frigidaire for many months before serving it to his most distinguished guests.)

'You look like you have tertiary syphilis,' Sherman said as a starter.

'Like what?'

'When you sit wonkensided like that it's a sure sign of syphilis.'

'I'm just sitting on a jar.'

Sherman did not ask why he was sitting on a jar and

naturally Jester did not volunteer. Sherman only wise-cracked: 'Sitting on a jar – a slop jar?'

'Don't be so crude.'

'People in France sit like that a lot of times on account of they have syphilis.'

'How do you know?'

'Because in my brief stint in the service I was in France.'

Jester suspected this was one of Sherman's lies but said nothing.

'When I was in France I fell in love with this French girl. No syphilis or anything like that. Just this beautiful, lily-white French virgin.'

Jester changed his position because it's hard to sit long on a jar of caviar. He was always shocked by dirty stories and even the word 'virgin' gave him a little thrill; but shocked or no he was fascinated so he let Sherman go on and he listened.

'We were engaged, this lily-white French girl and I. And I knocked her up. Then, like a woman, she wanted to marry me and the wedding was going to take place in this ancient old church called Notre Dame.'

'A cathedral,' Jester corrected.

'Well, church ... cathedral ... or however you call it, that's where we were going to be married. There were loads of invited guests. French people have families like carloads. I stood outside the church and watched them coming in. I didn't let anybody see me. I just wanted to see the show. This beautiful old cathedral and those French people dressed to kill. Everybody was chick.'

'You pronounce the word "sheik",' Jester said.

'Well, they were sheik and chick too. These carloads of relatives all waiting for me to come in.'

'Why didn't you go in?' Jester asked.

'Oh, you innocent dope. Don't you know I had no intention of marrying that lily-white French virgin? I just stayed there the whole afternoon watching these dressed up French people who were waiting for me to marry the lily-white French virgin. She was my "feancee" you understand, and come night they realized I was not going to be there. My "feancee" fainted. The old mother had a heart attack. The old father committed suicide right there in the church.'

'Sherman Pew, you're the biggest liar who ever walked in shoe leather,' Jester said.

Sherman, who had been carried away with his story, said nothing.

'Why do you lie?' Jester asked.

'It's not exactly lying, but sometimes I think up situations that could very well be true and tell 'em to baby-ass dopes like you. A lot of my life I've had to make up stories because the real, actual was either too dull or too hard to take.'

'Well, if you pretend to be my friend, why try to make me be a sucker?'

'You're what the original Barnum described. Barnum and Bailey Circus, in case you don't remember. "A sucker is born every minute on this earth".' He could not bear to think of Marian Anderson. And he wanted Jester to stay but he did not know how to ask him. Sherman had on his best blue rayon pyjamas with white piping, so he was glad to get out of bed to show them off. 'Would you like a little Lord Calvert's bottled in bond?'

But whisky and best pyjamas were far away from Jester. He was shocked by the dirty story, but he was touched by Sherman's explanation of why he lied. 'Don't you know that I'm one friend you don't have to lie to?'

But gloom and rage had settled in Sherman. 'What makes you think you're a friend?'

Jester had to ignore this and he only said, 'I'm going home.'

'Don't you want to see the fine food Zippo's Aunt Carrie sent to me?' Sherman walked to the kitchen and opened the icebox door. The frigidaire had a faintly sour smell. Sherman admired Aunt Carrie's fancy food. 'It's a tomato aspic moulded ring with cottage cheese in the middle.'

Jester looked dubiously at the food and said, 'Do you lie to Aunt Carrie, Cinderella Mullins, and Zippo Mullins?'

'No,' Sherman said simply. 'They got my number.'

'I've got your number too, and I do wish you wouldn't lie to me.'

'Why?'

'I hate stating obvious facts and the fact why I don't like you to lie to me is too obvious for me to state.'

Jester squatted by the side of the bed and Sherman lay in his best pyjamas, propped with pillows and pretending to be at ease.

'Have you ever heard the saying that truth is stranger than fiction?'

'Of course I've heard it.'

'When Mr Stevens did that thing to me it was a few days before Halloween and it was my eleventh birthday. Mrs Stevens had given me this wonderful birthday party. Many invited guests attended, some wearing party clothes and other people Halloween outfits. It was my first birthday party and was I thrilled. There were guests in witches' costumes and in pirates' outfits as well as party best clothes they wore to Sunday School. I started the party wearing my first brand-new pair of navy-blue long trousers and a new white shirt. The state paid my board, but that didn't include birthday parties nor brand-new birthday clothes. When the invited guests brought presents, I minded what Mr Stevens said, didn't snatch at the presents but said "Thank you" and opened them very slowly. Mrs Stevens always said I had beautiful manners and I truly had beautiful manners on that birthday party. We played all kinds of games.' Sherman's voice trailed off and finally he said, 'It's a funny thing.'

'What's funny?'

'From the time the party began until in the evening after it was over I don't remember hardly a single thing. For it was the evening of the fine party that Mr Stevens boogered me.'

In a swift unconscious gesture Jester half raised his right hand as though warding off a blow.

'Even after it was done and over the real Halloween had already gone, I remember only snitches and snatches of my b-bi-birthday p-party.'

'I wish you wouldn't talk about it.'

Sherman waited until his stammer was under control, then went on fluently: 'We played all kinds of games, then refreshments were served. Ice cream and white iced cake with eleven pink candles. I blew out the candles and cut the birthday cake as Mrs Stevens said for me to do. But I didn't eat a bite on account of I wished so much to have beautiful manners. Then after the refreshments we played running and hollering games. I had put on a sheet like a ghost and a pirate hat. When Mr Stevens called out behind the coal house I ran to him quickly, my ghost sheet flying. When he caught me I thought he was just playing and I was laughing fit to kill. I was still laughing fit to kill when I realized he wasn't playing. Then I was too surprised to know what to do but I quit laughing.'

Sherman lay on the pillow as if he were suddenly tired. 'However, I have a charmed life,' he continued with a tone of zest that Jester found hard to believe at first. 'From then on I never had it so good. Nobody ever had it so good. Mrs Mullins adopted me – not a real adoption, the state still paid for me, but she took me to her bosom. I knew she wasn't my mother, but she loved me. She would beat Zippo and spank Cinderella with a hairbrush, but she never laid a hand on me. So you see I almost had a mother. And a family too. Aunt Carrie, Mrs Mullins's sister, taught me singing.'

'Where is Zippo's mother?' Jester asked.

'Died,' Sherman said bitterly. 'Passed on to glory. That's what broke up the home. When Zippo's father remarried, neither Zippo or I liked her a bit so we moved out and I've been Zippo's house guest ever since. But I did have a mother for a little while,' Sherman said, 'I did have a mother even though that cheating creep of a Marian Anderson is not my mother.'

'Why do you call her a cheating creep?'

'Because I prefer to. I've ripped all thought away from her. And stomped on all her records.' Sherman's voice broke.

Jester, who was still squatting by the bed, steadied himself and suddenly kissed Sherman on the cheek.

Sherman rared back in the bed, put his feet down for balance and slapped Jester, using his whole arm.

Jester was not surprised although he had never been

slapped before. 'I only did that,' he said, 'because I felt sorry for you.'

'Save your peanuts for the zoo.'

'I don't see why we can't be serious and sincere,' Jester said.

Sherman, who was half out of the bed, slapped him again on the other cheek so hard that Jester sat down on the floor. Sherman's voice was strangled with rage. 'I thought you were a friend and you turn out like Mr Stevens.'

The slap and his own emotions stunned Jester, but quickly he got up, his hands clenched, and biffed Sherman straight in the jaw, which surprised Sherman so that he fell on the bed. Sherman muttered, 'Sock a fellow when he's down.'

'You weren't down, you were sitting on the bed so's you could slap me hardest. I take a lot of things from you, Sherman Pew, but I wouldn't take that. Besides you slapped me when I was squatting.'

So they went on arguing about sitting up and squatting and which was a more sportsmanlike position to slap or to punch somebody. The argument went on so long that they quite forgot the words that had preceded the blows.

But when Jester went home he was still thinking: I don't see why we can't be serious and sincere.

He opened the caviar, but it smelled like fish which he didn't like. Neither did his grandfather like fish, and Verily just said 'Ugh' when she smelled it. The part-time yard-man, Gus, who would eat anything, took it home.

Eight

In November Malone had a remission and was admitted for a second time to the City Hospital. He was glad to be there. Although he had changed doctors, the diagnosis had not changed. He had changed from Dr Hayden to Dr Calloway and changed again to Dr Milton. But though the last two doctors were Christians (members of the First Baptist and Episcopal churches) their medical verdict was the same. Having asked Dr Hayden how long he would live, and having received the unexpected and terrifying answer, he was careful not to ask again. Indeed, when he changed to Dr Milton, he had insisted he was a well man and just wanted a routine checkup and that one doctor had said that there was just a slight suspicion of leukemia. Dr Milton confirmed the diagnosis and Malone asked no questions. Dr Milton suggested that he check in at the City Hospital for a few days. So Malone again watched the bright blood dripping drop by drop, and he was glad because something was being done and the transfusions strengthened him.

On Mondays and Thursdays an aide wheeled in some shelves of books and the first book Malone selected was a murder mystery. But the mystery bored him and he could not keep track of the plot. The next time the aide came around with the books, Malone returned the mystery and glanced at the other titles; his eyes were drawn to a book called *Sickness unto Death*. His hand had reached for the book when the aide said, 'Are you sure you want this one? It doesn't sound very cheerful.' Her tone reminded him of his wife so that he immediately became determined and angry. 'This is the book I want and I'm not cheerful and don't want to be cheerful.' Malone, after reading for a half hour, wondered why he had made such a fuss about the book and dozed for a while. When he awoke he opened the

129

book at random and began to read just to be reading. From the wilderness of print some lines struck his mind so that he was instantly awake. He read the lines again and then again: *The greatest danger, that of losing one's own self, may pass off quietly as if it were nothing; every other loss, that of an arm, a leg, five dollars, a wife, etc., is sure to be noticed.* If Malone had not had an incurable disease those words would have been only words and he wouldn't have reached for the book in the first place. But now the thought chilled him and he began to read the book from the first page. But again the book bored him so that he closed his eyes and thought only of the passage he had memorized.

Unable to think of the reality of his own death, he was thrown back into the tedious labyrinth of his life. He had lost himself – he realized that surely. But how? When? His father had been a wholesale druggist from Macon. He had been ambitious for J.T., his eldest son. Those years of boyhood were good for the forty-year-old Malone to dwell on. He had not been lost then. But his father was ambitious for him, too ambitious it seemed later to Malone. He had decided that his son would be a doctor as that had been his own youthful ambition. So the eighteen-year-old Malone matriculated at Columbia, and in November he saw snow. At that time he bought a pair of ice skates and he actually tried to skate in Central Park. He had had a fine time at Columbia, eating the chow mein he had never tasted before, learning to ice skate, and marvelling at the city. He had not realized he had started to fail in his studies until he was already failing. He tried to bone up – studying until two o'clock on examination nights – but there were so many Jew grinds in the class who ran up the average Malone finished the first year by the skin of his teeth and rested at home, a bona fide premedical student. When the fall came round again the snow, the ice, the city was not a shock to him. When he failed at the end of his second year at Columbia, he felt himself to be a no-good. His young man's pride would not let him stay in Macon, so he moved to Milan and got a job as a clerk with Mr Greenlove, in the Greenlove drugstore. Was it this first humiliation that made him fumble in the beginning of life?

Martha was the daughter of Mr Greenlove and it was only natural, or seemed natural, when he asked her to a dance. He was dressed up in his best blue suit and she had on a chiffon dress. It was an Elk's Club dance. He had just become an Elk. What had he felt as he touched her body and why had he asked her to the dance? After the dance he had dated her a number of times because he knew few girls in Milan and her father was his boss. But still he never thought of love, let alone marriage, with Martha Greenlove. Then suddenly old Mr Greenlove (he was not old, he was only forty-five but the young Malone thought of him as old) died of a heart attack. The drugstore was put up for sale. Malone borrowed fifteen hundred dollars from his mother and bought it on a fifteen year mortgage. So he was saddled with a mortgage, and before he even realized it his own self, with a wife. Martha did not actually ask him to marry her, but she seemed to assume so much that Malone would have felt an irresponsible man if he had not spoken. So he spoke to her brother who was now the head of the family, and they shook hands and had a drink of Blind Mule together. And it all happened so naturally that it seemed supernatural; yet he was fascinated by Martha who wore afternoon dainty dresses and a chiffon dress for dances and who, above all, restored the pride he had lost when he failed at Columbia. But when they were married in the Greenloves' living room in the presence of his mother, her mother, the Greenlove brothers, and an aunt or two, her mother had cried, and Malone felt like crying also. He didn't cry, but listened to the ceremony, bewildered. After the rice had been thrown they had gone on the train to their honeymoon in Blowing Rock, North Carolina. And ever afterward there was no particular time when he regretted marrying Martha, but regret, or disappointment was certainly there. There was no particular time when he asked, 'Is this all there is of life?' but as he grew older he asked it wordlessly. No, he had not lost an arm, or a leg, or any particular five dollars, but little by little he had lost his own self.

If Malone had not had a fatal disease he would not have brooded about this. But dying had quickened his livingness as he lay in the hospital bed, seeing the bright blood drop, drop by drop. He said to himself he didn't care about the hospital expenses, but even while he was there he was worried about the twenty-dollars-a-day bill.

'Hon,' Martha said on one of her daily visits to the hospital, 'why don't we take a nice relaxing trip?'

Malone stiffened on his sweaty bed.

'Even resting here at the hospital you always seem tense and worried up. We could go to Blowing Rock and breathe the nice mountain air.'

'I don't feel like it,' Malone said.

'. . . or the ocean. I've seen the ocean only once in my life and that was when I was visiting my cousin, Sarah Greenlove, in Savannah. It's a nice climate at Sea Island Beach, I hear. Not too hot, not too cold. And the little change might perk you up.'

'I've always felt that travelling is exhausting.' He did not tell his wife about the trip he was planning later on to Vermont or Maine where he could see snow. Malone had carefully hidden *Sickness unto Death* beneath the pillow for he did not want to share anything that was intimate with his wife. He did say fretfully, 'I'm sick of this hospital.'

'One thing I'm sure you ought to do,' Mrs Malone said, 'you ought to make a habit of turning the pharmacy over to Mr Harris in the afternoons. All work and no play makes Jack a dull boy.'

Home from the hospital with every afternoon off, Malone blundered through his days. He thought of the mountains, the North, snow, the ocean – thought of all the life he had spent unlived. He wondered how he could die since he had not yet lived.

He took hot baths after his morning work and even darkened the bedroom to try to take a nap, but it had never been his habit to sleep in the middle of the day and he could not sleep. Instead of waking at four or five o'clock in the morning to roam the house in fear, the flashes of terror had flickered for a season, leaving boredom and a dread that he could not formulate. He hated the blank afternoons when Mr Harris took over the pharmacy. He was always fearing that something might go wrong, but what could go wrong?

The lose of another Kotex sale? A bad judgement on a physical complaint? He actually had no reason to advise in the first place, having never finished medical school. Other dilemmas plagued him. He was now so thin that his suits hung in baggy folds. Should he go to a tailor? Though the suits would long outlast him, he did go to a tailor instead of going to Hart, Schaffner & Marx, where he had always gone, and ordered an Oxford grey suit and a blue flannel suit. The fittings were tiresome. Another thing, he had paid so much on orthodontist's bills for Ellen that he had neglected his own teeth, so that suddenly so many teeth had to be pulled that the dentist gave him a choice of pulling twelve teeth and having false teeth or making expensive bridges. Malone decided on the bridges, even knowing he couldn't get the good of them. So dying, Malone took more care of himself than he had done in life.

A new chain drugstore opened in Milan which did not have the quality and trustworthiness of Malone's pharmacy, but it was a competitor which undercut fair prices and this annoyed Malone immoderately. Sometimes he even wondered if he shouldn't sell the pharmacy while he could supervise the sale. But the thought was more shocking and bewildering than the thought of his own death. So he did not dwell on it. Besides, Martha could be trusted to dispose of the property, including stock, good will and reputation, when the occasion arose. Malone spent whole days with a pencil and paper, writing down his assets. Twenty-five thousand (it comforted Malone that his figures were conservative) for the pharmacy, twenty thousand life insurance, ten thousand for the home, fifteen thousand for the three run-down houses Martha had inherited ... while the combined assets were not a fortune, they were considerable when added up; Malone totalled the figures several times with a fine-sharpened pencil and twice with a fountain pen. Deliberately he had not included his wife's Coca-Cola stock. The mortgage on the pharmacy had been burned two years ago and the insurance policy converted from retirement insurance to plain life insurance, as it had been to begin with. There were no outstanding debts or mortgages. Malone knew that his financial affairs were in better order than they had ever been before, but this comforted him little. Better, perhaps, if he had been harried by mortgages and unpaid bills than to feel this flat solvency. For Malone still felt he had unfinished business which the ledgers and his figuring did not show. Although he had not talked more about his will with the Judge, he felt that a man, a bread-winner, should not die intestate. Should he set five thousand legally aside for the children's education, the residue going to his wife? Or should he leave it all to Martha, who was a good mother if she was anything? He had heard of widows buying Cadillac cars when their husbands had died and left them in full charge of the estate. Or widows being rooked into phony oil well deals. But he knew that Martha would neither breeze around in Cadillac cars nor buy any stock more chancy than Coca-Cola or A.T.&T. The will would probably read: To my beloved wife, Martha Greenlove Malone, I bequeath all monies and properties that comprise my entire estate. Although he had long since ceased loving his wife, he respected her judgement, and it was the ordinary will to make.

Until that season, few of Malone's friends or relatives had died. But his fortieth year seemed a time for death. His brother from Macon died of cancer. His brother had been only thirty-eight years old and he was the head of the Malone Wholesale Drug Company. Also, Tom Malone had married a beautiful wife and J.T. had often envied him. But blood being thicker than jealousy, Malone began packing his suitcase when Tom's wife telephoned he was failing. Martha objected to the trip because of his own ill-health, and a long argument followed which made him miss the Macon train. So he was unable to see Tom again in life, and in death the body was too much rouged and terribly shrunken.

Martha came the next day when she had arranged for someone to care for the children. Malone, as the elder brother, was the chief spokesman in financial matters. The affairs of the Malone Wholesale Drug Company were in worse shape than anyone had imagined. Tom had been a drinking man, Lucille extravagant, and the Malone Wholesale Drug Company was faced with bankruptcy.

Malone went over the books and figures for days. There were two boys of high school age and Lucille, when faced with the necessity of earning a living, said vaguely that she would get a job in an antique shop. But there were no vacancies in an antique shop in Macon, and besides, Lucille didn't know scat about antiques. No longer a beautiful woman, she cried less for her husband's death than that he had managed the Malone Wholesale Drug Company so badly, leaving her a widow with two growing children and no ideas about work or jobs. J.T. and Martha stayed for four days. After the funeral when they left, Malone gave Lucille a cheque for four hundred dollars to tide the family over. A month later Lucille got a job in a department store.

Cab Bickerstaff died, and Malone had seen and talked with him that very same morning before he just fell over dead at his desk in the Milan Electric and Power Company. Malone tried to remember every act and word of Cab Bickerstaff that morning. But they were so ordinary that they would have been unnoticed if he had not slumped at his desk at eleven o'clock, dying instantly of a stroke. He had seemed perfectly well and absolutely ordinary when Malone had served him the coke and some peanut butter crackers. Malone remembered that he had ordered an aspirin along with the coke, but there was nothing unusual about that. And he had said on entering the pharmacy, 'Hot enough for you, J.T.?' Again perfectly ordinary. But Cab Bickerstaff had died an hour later and the coke, the aspirin, the peanut butter crackers, the hackneyed phrase were fixed in an inlay of mystery that haunted Malone. Herman Klein's wife died and his shop was closed for two full days. Herman Klein no longer had to hide his bottle in the compounding room at the pharmacy, but could drink at his own home. Mr Beard, a deacon at the First Baptist Church, died also that summer. None of these people had been close to Malone, and in life he had not been interested in them. But in death they were all fixed in the same curious inlay of mystery that compelled an attention that they had not exerted in life. So Malone's last summer had passed in this way.

Afraid to talk to the doctors, unable to speak of anything

intimate with his own wife, Malone just blundered silently. Every Sunday he went to church, but Dr Watson was a folksy preacher who spoke to the living and not to a man who was going to die. He compared the Holy Sacraments with a car. Saying that people had to be tanked up once in a while in order to proceed with their spiritual life. This service offended Malone, although he did not know why. The First Baptist Church was the largest church in town with a property worth, offhand, two million dollars. The deacons were men of substance. Pillars of the church, millionaires, rich doctors, owners of utility companies. But though Malone went every Sunday to church, and though they were holy men, in his judgement, he felt strangely apart from them. Though he shook hands with Dr Watson at the end of every church service, he felt no communication with him, or any of the other worshippers. Yet he had been born and reared in the First Baptist Church, and there was no other spiritual solace he could think of, for he was ashamed and timid to speak of death. So one November afternoon, shortly after his second stay at the hospital, he dressed up in his new tailored Oxford grey suit and went to the parsonage.

Dr Watson greeted him with some surprise. 'How well you are looking, Mr Malone.' Malone's body seemed to shrink in the new suit. 'I'm glad you've come. I always like to see my parishioners. What can I do for you today? Would you like a coke?'

'No thanks, Dr Watson. I would like to talk.'

'Talk about what?'

Malone's reply was muted and almost indistinct. 'About death.'

'Ramona,' Dr Watson bawled to the servant who quickly answered him, 'serve Mr Malone and me some cokes with lemon.'

As the cokes were served, Malone crossed and uncrossed his withered legs in their fine flannel pants. A flush of shame reddened his pale face. 'I mean,' he said, 'you are supposed to know about things like that.'

'Things like what?' Dr Watson asked.

Malone was brave, determined. 'About the soul, and what happens in the afterlife.'

In church, and after twenty years of experience, Dr Watson could make glib sermons about the soul; but in his own home, with only one man asking, his glibness turned to embarrassment and he only said, 'I don't know what you mean, Mr Malone.'

'My brother died, Cab Bickerstaff died in this town, and Mr Beard died all in the course of seven months. What happened to them after death?'

'We all have to die,' said the plump, pale Dr Watson.

'Other people never know when they are going to die.'

'All Christians should prepare for death.' Dr Watson thought the subject was getting morbid.

'But how do you prepare for death?'

'By righteous living.'

'What is righteous living?' Malone had never stolen, had seldom lied, and the one episode in his life that he knew was a mortal sin had happened years ago and lasted only one summer. 'Tell me, Dr Watson,' he asked, 'what is eternal life?'

'To me,' Dr Watson said, 'it is the extension of earthly life, but more intensified. Does that answer your question?'

Malone thought of the drabness of his life and wondered how it could be more intensified. Was afterlife continual tedium and was that why he struggled so in order to hold on to life? He shivered although the parsonage was hot. 'Do you believe in heaven and hell?' Malone asked.

'I'm not a strict fundamentalist, but I believe that what a man does on earth predicates his eternal life.'

'But if a man does just the ordinary things, nothing good, nothing bad?'

'It's not up to man's judgement to decide what is good and what is bad. God sees the truth, and is our Saviour.'

These days Malone had often prayed, but what he was praying to he did not know. There seemed no sense in continuing the conversation, for he was getting no answer. Malone put the Coca-Cola glass carefully on the doily beside him and stood up. 'Well, thanks very much, Dr Watson,' he said bleakly.

'I'm glad you dropped in to talk with me. My home is

always open to my parishioners who want to speak of spiritual things.'

In a daze of weariness and vacuity, Malone walked through the November twilight. A bright woodpecker pecked hollowly at a telephone pole. The afternoon was silent except for the woodpecker.

It was strange that Malone, who loved singsong poetry, would think of those memorized lines: *The greatest danger, that of losing one's own self, may pass off quietly as if it were nothing; every other loss, that of an arm, a leg, five dollars, a wife, etc., is sure to be noticed.* The incongruity of these ideas, fateful and ordinary as his own life, sounded like the brassy clamour of the city clock, uncadenced and flat.

Nine

That winter the Judge made a grave mistake about Sherman and Sherman made a still graver mistake about the Judge. Since both mistakes were phantasies which flowered as richly in the senile brain of the old man as they did in the heart of the thwarted boy, their human relationship was going very much amiss, choked as it were with the rank luxuriance of their separate dreams. So that the relationship which had begun with such joy and lucidity was, by the end of November, already tarnished.

It was the old Judge who spoke first of his dream. One day with an air of secrecy and zest he opened his safety deposit box and handed Sherman a sheaf of papers. 'Read carefully, boy, for this may be my final contribution as a statesman to the South.'

Sherman read and was puzzled, less by the ornate and badly spelled manuscript than by the contents of what he read. 'Don't bother about the calligraphy or spelling,' the Judge said airily. 'It's the trenchancy of ideas that matters.' Sherman was reading about the Confederate money while the Judge looked on, glowing with pride and anticipated compliments.

Sherman's delicately fluted nostrils widened and his lips fluttered but he said nothing.

Passionately the old Judge began to speak. He described the history of devaluations of foreign monies and the rights of conquered nations to the redemption of their own currencies. 'In every civilized nation the currencies of defeated nations have been redeemed – devaluated, to be sure, but redeemed. Look at the franc, the mark, the lira and look at, by God, even the yen.' This last redemption particularly infuriated the old man.

Sherman's slate-blue eyes stared at the deeper blue eyes of

the old Judge. At first bewildered by the talk of all the foreign money, he wondered if the Judge was drunk. But it was not yet twelve o'clock and the Judge never started his toddies until noon. But the old Judge was speaking passionately, drunk with his dream, and Sherman responded. Knowing nothing about what the Judge was discussing, Sherman responded to rhetoric, repetition and rhythm, to the language of passionate demagoguery, senseless and high flown, of which the old Judge was a past master. So Sherman's delicately fluted nostrils widened and he said nothing. The Judge, who had been hurt by his grandson's casual indifference to his dream, knew a spellbound listener when he had one and pressed on triumphantly. And Sherman, who seldom believed a word that Jester said, listened to the Judge's tirade, heedful and wondering.

It happened that some time ago the Judge received a letter from Senator Tip Thomas in reply to the first petition letter that Sherman had written concerning Jester's admittance to West Point. The senator had replied with cumbersome courtesy that he would be glad to put his old friend and fellow statesman's grandson up at his first opportunity. Again the old Judge and Sherman had struggled with a letter to Senator Tip Thomas. This time with the same cumbersome courtesy the old Judge wrote of the dead Mrs Thomas, as well as the living Mrs Thomas. It always seemed a miracle to Sherman that the old Judge had actually been a congressman in the House of Representatives in Washington, D.C. The glory was reflected in Sherman, the genuine amanuensis who had his trays on the library table. When Senator Thomas replied, referring to past favours the Judge had shown him and promising that Jester would get an appointment at West Point – playing footsie with the old Judge – it seemed magical to Sherman. So magical that he even fought down his rebellious jealousy that his own letter to Washington had not been answered.

The Judge, in spite of his oratory, was a great one for putting his own foot in his mouth, and soon, sure enough, his foot was in the middle of his mouth. He began to talk about reparation for burnt houses, burnt cotton, and to Sherman's shame and horror, of reparation for slaves.

'Slaves,' Sherman said in a voice almost inaudible with shock.

'Why certainly,' the old Judge continued serenely. 'The institution of slavery was the very cornerstone and pillar of the cotton economy.'

'Well Abe Lincoln freed the slaves and another Sherman burnt the cotton.'

The Judge, fixed in his dream, had forgotten that his amanuensis was coloured. 'And a sad time that was, to be sure.'

The Judge wondered helplessly why he had lost his spell-bound listener, for Sherman, far from being spellbound, was now trembling with insult and fury. Deliberately, he picked up one of the pens and broke it in two. The Judge did not even notice. 'It will take a lot of statistical work, a pile of arithmetic, in fact a lot of doing. But my motto for my election campaign is "rectify" and justice is on my side. I only have to get the ball rolling, so to say. And I'm a born politician, know how to work with people and handle delicate situations.'

The Judge's dream had flattened for Sherman, so he could see it in all its detail. The first flush of enthusiasm with which he had responded to the Judge's dream had faded utterly. 'It would take a lot of doing,' he said in a dead voice.

'What strikes me is the simplicity of the whole idea.'

'Simplicity,' Sherman echoed in the same dead voice.

'Yes, the simplicity of genius. Maybe I couldn't have thought up "To be or not to be," but my ideas of the restoration of the South are sheer genius.' The old voice quivered for confirmation. 'Don't you think so, Sherman?'

Sherman, who was looking round for a fast escape in case the Judge did anything suddenly wild, said simply: 'No. I don't think it's genius or even common sense.'

'Genius and common sense operate at two different polarities of thought.'

Sherman wrote down the word 'polarities' thinking he would look it up later; he was benefiting from the Judge's vocabulary if nothing else. 'All I would say is that your plan would turn back the clock for a hundred years.'

'I would like nothing better,' said the mad old foolhardy Judge. 'And furthermore I think I can do it. I have in high place friends who are deadly sick of this so-called liberalism and who are only waiting for a rallying cry. I am after all one of the Senior Statesmen in the South and my voice shall be attended; maybe some weak sisters will hesitate because of the details of statistics and bookkeeping involved. But, by God, if the Federal Government can screw every nickel out of me for income tax, my plan will be child's play to carry out.'

The Judge lowered his voice. 'I never filed State income tax yet and never will. I wouldn't bruit this around, Sherman, as I tell you in strictest confidence. And I pay the Federal Income Tax under the utmost duress and mighty unwillingly. As I say, many a Southerner in high power is in my same boots and they will harken to the rallying call.'

'But what does your income tax have to do with this?'

'A lot,' the old man said. 'A mighty lot.'

'I don't dig it.'

'Of course the N.A.A.C.P. will be dead set against me. But the brave long for battle if the battle is just. For years I've yearned to tangle with the N.A.A.C.P., force them to a showdown, put them out of business.'

Sherman just looked at the blue and passionate eyes of the old Judge.

'All Southern patriots feel the same about the scurrilous pressure group that aims to destroy the very axioms of the South.'

Sherman's lips and nostrils fluttered with emotion when he said: 'You talk like you believe in slavery.'

'Why of course I believe in slavery. Civilization is founded on slavery.'

The old Judge, who still thought of Sherman as a jewel, a treasure, had forgotten, in his passionate prejudice, that Sherman was coloured. And when he saw his jewel so agitated he tried to make amends.

'If not actual slavery at least a state of happy peonage.'

'Happy for who?'

'For everybody. Do you believe for a single instant that the slaves wanted to be freed? No, Sherman, many a slave

142

remained faithful to his old master, would not be freed till the day he died.'

'Bullshit.'

'Beg your pardon,' said the old Judge, who was conveniently deafer at times. 'Now I've been told that the conditions of the Negro in the North are appalling – mixed marriages, nowhere to live and lay his head, and just downright appalling misery.'

'Still a nigger would rather be a lamppost in Harlem than the Governor of Georgia.'

The Judge inclined his good ear. 'Didn't quite catch,' he said softly.

All Sherman's life he had thought that all white men were crazy, and the more prominent their positions the more lunatic were their words and behaviour. In this matter, Sherman considered he had the sober ice-cold truth on his side. The politicians, from governors to congressmen, down to sheriffs and wardens, were alike in their bigotry and violence. Sherman brooded over every lynching, bombing, or indignity that his race had suffered. In this Sherman had the vulnerability and sensitivity of an adolescent. Drawn to broodings on atrocities, he felt that every evil was reserved for him personally. So he lived in a stasis of dread and suspense. This attitude was supported by facts. No Negro in Peach County had ever voted. A schoolteacher had registered and been turned down at the polls. Two college graduates had been turned down likewise. The Fifteenth Amendment of the American Constitution had guaranteed the right to vote to the Negro race, yet no Negro Sherman had known or heard tell of had ever voted. Yes, the American Constitution itself was a fraud. And if his story he had told Jester was not true, about the voting of the Golden Nigerians and the cardboard coffins, he had heard the actual story about a club in another county; and if it had not actually happened to the Golden Nigerians of Milan, he knew it had happened to others somewhere else. Since his imagination enveloped all disasters, he felt that any evil he read or heard about could just as well have happened to himself.

This state of anxiety made Sherman take the old Judge

more seriously than he would have under calmer conditions. Slavery! Was the old Judge planning to make slaves of his race? It did not make sense. But what the fuckin' hell made sense in the relation between the races? The Fifteenth Amendment had been put at nought, the American Constitution was a fraud as far as Sherman was concerned. And justice! Sherman knew of every lynching, every violence that had happened in his time and before his time, and he felt every abuse in his own body, and therefore lived in his stasis of tension and fear. Otherwise he would have thought of the plans of the old Judge as the product of a senile mind. But as a Negro in the South, an orphan at that, he had been exposed to such real horror and degradation that the wildest phantasies of the old Judge seemed not only possible but, in Sherman's lawless land, almost inevitable. Facts combined to support his phantasies and fears. Sherman was convinced that all white Southerners were crazy. Lynching a Negro boy because a white woman said he had whistled at her. A Judge sentencing a Negro because a white woman said she didn't like the way he looked at her. Whistling! Looking! His prejudiced mind was inflamed and quivering like some tropical atmosphere that causes mirages.

At noon Sherman made the drinks and neither he nor the old Judge spoke. Then at dinnertime an hour later, Sherman was reaching for a can of lobster when Verily said:

'You don't need that, Sherman.'

'Why not, old woman?'

'Yestidy you opened a can of tuna fish and made yourself a tuna fish sandwich mess. There's ample plenty of the tuna fish to make a sandwich today.'

Sherman kept right on opening the lobster can. 'Besides,' Verily went on, 'you ought to be eating collards and corn-pones in the kitchen like anybody else.'

'Nigger doings!'

'Well, who do you think you are! The Queen of Sheba?'

Sherman was mashing the lobster with hunks of mayonnaise and chopped pickles. 'Anyway I'm not pure nigger like you are,' he said to Verily who was very dark. 'Look at my eyes.'

'I seen them.'

Sherman was busily spreading his lobster sandwich.

'That lobster was supposed to be for Sunday night supper when I'm off. I got a good mind to tell the Judge on you.'

But since Sherman was still the jewel, the treasure, the threat was an empty one and they both knew it.

'Go on and tell him,' Sherman said as he garnished his sandwich with bread and butter pickles.

'Just because you have them blue eyes is no reason to act so high and mighty. You nigger like the rest of us. You just had a white pappy who passed on them blue eyes to you, and that's nothin to put on airs about. You nigger like the rest of us.'

Sherman took his tray and stalked carefully through the hall to the library. But in spite of the party sandwiches he could not eat. He was thinking about what the Judge had said and his eyes were fixed and bleak in his dark face. His mind felt that most of the Judge's words were crazy, but Sherman, slanted by anxiety, could not think rationally; he could only feel. He remembered the campaign address of certain Southerners, cunning, violent, menacing. To Sherman the Judge talked no crazier than many another Southern politician. Crazy, crazy, crazy. All of them!

Sherman did not forget that the Judge had once been a congressman, thus holding one of the highest offices in the United States. And he knew people in high places. Just look at his answer from Senator Tip Thomas. The Judge was smart – mighty foxy – he could play a soft game of footsie. In dwelling on the power of the old Judge, he forgot his sicknesses; it did not even occur to Sherman that the brain of the old man who had once been a congressman could have deteriorated in old age. Zippo Mullins had a grandfather who had lost his mind in his old age. Old Mr Mullins ate with a towel around his neck, could not pick out the watermelon seeds but swallowed them whole; he had no teeth and would gum his fried chicken; at the end he had to go to the county home. The old Judge on the other hand carefully unfolded his napkin at the beginning of a meal and had beautiful table manners, asking Jester or Verily to cut up the food he couldn't manage. Those were the only two very old men that Sherman had actually known, and there was a world of difference between them. So Sherman never considered the possibility of brain-softening in the old Judge.

Sherman stared for a long time at the fancy lobster sandwich, but anxiety would not let him eat. He did eat one bread and butter pickle before going back to the kitchen. He wanted a drink. Some gin and tonic, half and half, would settle his spirits so that he could eat. He knew he faced another run-in with Verily, but he went straight to the kitchen and grasped the gin bottle.

'Look yonder,' she said, 'look what the Queen of Sheba is up to now.'

Sherman deliberately poured his gin and added cold tonic.

'I try to be kind and pleasant to you, Sherman, but I knew from the first it was no use. What makes you so cold and airy? Is it them blue eyes passed on from your pappy?'

Sherman walked stiffly from the kitchen, his drink in hand, and settled himself again at the library table. As he drank the gin his inward turbulence increased. In his search for his true mother, Sherman had seldom thought about his father. Sherman thought only that he was a white man, he imagined that the unknown white father had raped his mother. For every boy's mother is virtuous, especially if she is imaginary. Therefore, he hated his father, hated even to think about him. His father was a crazy white man who had raped his mother and left the evidence of bastardy in Sherman's blue and alien eyes. He had never sought his father as he sought his mother, the dreams of his mother had lulled and solaced him, but he thought of his father with pure hate.

After dinner when the Judge was taking his usual nap, Jester came into the library. Sherman was still sitting at the table, his tray of sandwiches untouched.

'What's the matter, Sherman?' Jester noticed the gin-drunk somnolence in the rapt eyes and he was uneasy.

'Go fuck,' Sherman said brutally, for Jester was the only white person to whom he could use words like that. But he was in a state where no words could relieve him now. I hate,

I hate, I hate, he thought as his unseeing eyes fixed, brooding and drunk, at the open window.

'I have often thought that if I had been born a Nigerian or coloured, I couldn't stand it. I admire you, Sherman, the way you stand up to it. I admire you more than I can say.'

'Well save your peanuts for the zoo.'

'I have thought often,' went on Jester who had read the idea somewhere, 'that if Christ was born now he would be coloured.'

'Well he wasn't.'

'I'm afraid –' Jester began and found it hard to finish.

'What are you afraid of, chicken-out sissy?'

'I'm afraid that if I were a Nigerian or coloured, I would be neurotic. Awfully neurotic.'

'No you wouldn't.' His right forefinger cut swiftly across his neck in a slashing gesture. 'A neurotic nigger is a dead nigger.'

Jester was wondering why it was so hard to make friends with Sherman. His grandfather had often said: 'Black is black and white is white and never the two shall meet if I can prevent it.' And the *Atlanta Constitution* wrote of Southerners of good will. How could he tell Sherman that he was not like his grandfather, but a Southerner of good will?

'I respect coloured people every whit as much as I do white people.'

'You're one for the birds all right.'

'Respect coloured people even more than I do white people on account of what they have gone through.'

'There's plenty of bad niggers around,' Sherman said as he finished his gin drink.

'Why do you say that to me?'

'Just warning the pop-eyed baby.'

'I'm trying to level with you about how I feel morally about the racial question. But you don't pay any mind to me.'

His depression and rage accented by alcohol, Sherman only said in a threatening voice, 'Bad niggers with police records and others without records like me.'

'Why is it so hard to be friends with you?'

'Because I don't want friends,' Sherman lied, because,

next to a mother, he wanted a friend the most. He admired and feared Zippo who was always insulting him, never washed a dish even when Sherman did the cooking, and treated him very much as he now treated Jester.

'Well, I'm going to the airport. Want to come along?'

'When I fly, I fly my own planes. None of those cheap, rented planes like you fly.'

So Jester had to leave it at that; and Sherman watched him, brooding and jealous, as he walked down the drive.

The Judge awoke from his nap at two o'clock, washed his sleep-wrinkled face, and felt joyful and refreshed. He did not remember any tensions of the morning and as he went downstairs he was humming. Sherman, hearing the ponderous tread and the tuneless voice, made a face toward the hall door.

'My boy.' said the Judge. 'Do you know why I would rather be Fox Clane than Shakespeare or Julius Caesar?'

Sherman's lips barely moved when he said, 'No.'

'Or Mark Twain or Abraham Lincoln or Babe Ruth?'

Sherman just nodded no without speaking, wondering what the tack was about now.

'I'd rather be Fox Clane than all these great and famous people. Can't you guess why?'

This time Sherman only looked at him.

'Because I'm alive. And when you consider the trillions and trillions of dead people you realize what a privilege it is to be alive.'

'Some people are dead from the neck up.'

The Judge ignored this and said, 'To me it is simply marvellous to be alive. Isn't it to you, Sherman?'

'Not particularly,' he said, as he wanted very much to go home and sleep off the gin.

'Consider the dawn. The moon, the stars and heavenly firmaments,' the Judge went on. 'Consider shortcake and liquor.'

Sherman's cold eyes considered the universe and the comforts of daily life with disdain and he did not answer.

'When I had that little seizure, Doc Tatum told me, frankly, if the seizure had affected the left part of the brain instead of the right, I should have been mentally and permanently afflicted.' The Judge's voice had dropped with awe and horror. 'Can you imagine living in such a condition?'

Sherman could: 'I knew a man who had a stroke and it left him blind and with a mind like a two-year-old baby. The country home wouldn't even accept him. Not even the asylum. I don't know what happened to him finally. Probably died.'

'Well, nothing like that happened to me. I was just left with a slight motor impairment . . . just the left arm and leg, ever so slightly damaged . . . but the mind intact. So I reasoned to myself: Fox Clane, ought you to cuss God, cuss the heavenly elements, cuss destiny, because of that little old impairment which didn't really bother me anyhow, or ought I to praise God, the elements, nature and destiny because I have nothing wrong with me, my mind being sound? For after all, what is a little arm, what's a leg, if the mind is sound and the spirit joyful. So I said to myself: Fox Clane, you better praise and keep on praising.'

Sherman looked at the shrunken left arm and the hand permanently clenched. He felt sorry for the old Judge and hated himself for feeling sorry.

'I knew a little boy who had polio and had to wear heavy iron braces on both legs and use iron crutches . . .crippled for life,' said Sherman who had seen a picture of such a boy in the newspapers.

The Judge was thinking that Sherman knew a whole galaxy of pitiful cases, and tears came to his eyes as he murmered, 'Poor child.' The Judge did not hate himself for pitying others; he did not pity himself, for by and large he was quite happy. Of course, he would love to eat forty baked Alaskas every day, but on the whole he was content. 'I'd rather stick to any diet than have to start shovelling coal or picking a harp. I never could manage even my own furnace and I'm not the least bit musical.'

'Yes, some people can't carry a tune in a basket.'

The Judge ignored this, as he was always singing and the tunes seemed all right to him. 'Let's proceed with the correspondence.'

'What letters do you want me to write now?'

'A whole slew of them, to every congressman and senator I know personally and very politician who might cotton to my ideas.'

'What kind of letters do you wish me to write?'

'In the general tenor of what I told you this morning. About the Confederate money and the general retribution of the South.'

The zip of gin had turned to dour anger. Although he was emotionally keyed up, Sherman yawned and kept on yawning just to be rude. He considered his soft, clean, bossy job and the shock of the morning's conversation. When Sherman loved, he loved, when he admired he admired, and there was no halfway emotional state. Until now he had both loved and admired the Judge. Who else had been a congressman, a judge; who else would give him a fine, dainty job as an amanuensis and let him eat party sandwiches at the library table? So Sherman was in a quandary and his mobile features quivered as he spoke, 'You mean that part even about slavery?'

The Judge knew now that something had gone wrong. 'Not slavery, Son, but restitution for slaves that the Yankees freed. Economic restitution.'

Sherman's nostrils and lips were quivering like butterflies. 'I won't do it, Judge.'

The Judge had seldom been said 'no' to, as his requests were usually reasonable. Now that his treasure, his jewel, had refused him, he sighed, 'I don't understand you, Son.'

And Sherman, who was always pleased with any term of affection, especially since they were so seldom addressed to him, basked for a moment and almost smiled.

'So you refuse to write this series of letters?'

'I do,' said Sherman, as the power of refusal was also sweet to him. 'I won't be a party to turning the clock back almost a century.'

'The clock won't be turned back, it will be turned forward for a century, Son.'

It was the third time he had so called him and the suspicion that was always dormant in Sherman's nature stirred wordlessly, inchoate.

'Great change always turns forward the clock. Wars

particularly. If it weren't for World War I, women would still be wearing ankle-length skirts. Now young females go around dressed like carpenters in overalls, even the prettiest, most well-bred girl.'

The Judge had noticed Ellen Malone going to her father's pharmacy in overalls and he had been shocked and embarassed on Malone's behalf.

'Poor J.T. Malone.'

'Why do you say that?' asked Sherman who was struck by the compassion and the tone of mystery in the Judge's voice.

'I'm afraid, my boy, that Mr Malone is not long for this world.'

Sherman, who didn't care about Mr Malone one way or the next and was in no mood to pretend to feelings he didn't truly feel, only said, 'Gonna die? Too bad.'

'Death is worse than too bad. In fact, no one on this earth knows what death is really about.'

'Are you awfully religious?'

'No, I'm not a bit religious. But I fear –'

'Why have you often referred to shovelling coal and picking harps?'

'Oh, that's just a figure of speech. If that's all I feared and if I was sent to the bad place, I would shovel coal along with the rest of the sinners, a lot of whom I would have already known beforehand. And in case I'm sent to heaven, by God I'd learn to be as musical as Blind Tom or Caruso. It's not that I fear.'

'What is it you do fear?' asked Sherman who had never thought much about death.

'Blankness,' said the old man. 'An infinite blankness and blackness where I'd be all by myself. Without loving or eating or nothing. Just lying in this infinite blankness and darkness.'

'I would hate that too,' said Sherman casually.

The Judge was remembering his stroke, and his thoughts were stark and clear. Although he minimized his illness to others as a 'little seizure' or 'slight case of polio', he was truthful to himself; it was a stroke and he had nearly died. He remembered the shock of falling. His right hand felt the

151

paralysed one and there was no feeling, just a weighty clamminess without motion or sensation. The left leg was just as weighty and without feeling, so in the hysteria of those long hours he had believed that half of his body was mysteriously dead. Unable to wake Jester, he had cried to Miss Missy, to his dead father, his brother Beau – not to join them, but for solace in his distress. He was found in the early morning and sent to the City Hospital where he began to live again. Day by day his paralysed limbs awakened, but shock had dulled him, and cutting off liquor and tobacco added to his misery. Unable to walk or even raise his left hand, he busied himself by working crossword puzzles, reading mysteries, and playing solitaire. There was nothing to look forward to but meals, and the hospital food also bored him although he ate every bite that was put on his tray. Then suddenly the idea of the Confederate money came to his mind. It just came; it happened like the song a child might sing that was suddenly made up. And one idea brought the next idea, so that he was thinking, creating, dreaming. It was October and a sweet chill fell upon the town in the early morning and at twilight. The sunlight was pure and clear as honey after the heat and glare of the Milan summer. The energy of thought brought further thoughts. The Judge explained to the dietitian how to make decent coffee, hospital or no, and soon he was able to lumber from the bed to the dresser and from there to the chair with the help of a nurse. His poker cronies came and they played poker, but the energy of his new life came from his thinking, his dream. He sheltered his ideas lovingly, telling them to no one. What would Poke Tatum or Bennie Weems know about the dreams of a great statesman? When he went home he could walk, use his left hand a little, and carry on almost as before. His dream remained dormant, for whom could he tell it to, and old age and shock had made his handwriting deteriorate.

'I would probably never have thought of those ideas if it hadn't been for that stroke that paralysed me so that I was half dead in the City Hospital for close on to two months.'

Sherman rooted in his nostrils with a Kleenex but said nothing.

'And paradoxically, if I hadn't gone through the shadow of death I might never have seen the light. Don't you understand why these ideas are precious beyond reason to me?'

Sherman looked at the Kleenex and put it slowly back in his pocket. Then he began to gaslight the Judge, cupping his chin in his right hand and looking into the pure blue eyes with his own creepy stare.

'Don't you see why it is important for you to write these letters I'm going to dictate?'

Sherman still did not answer, and his silence irritated the old Judge.

'Aren't you going to write these letters?'

'I told you "no" once and I'm telling you "no" again. You want me to tattoo "no" on my chest?'

'At first you were such an amenable amanuensis,' the Judge observed aloud. 'But now you're about as enthusiastic as a gravestone.'

'Yeah,' said Sherman.

'You are so contrary and secretive,' the Judge complained. 'So secretive you wouldn't give me the time of day if you were just in front of the town clock.'

'I don't blah-blah everything I know. I keep things to myself.'

'You young folks are secretive – downright devious to the mature mind.'

Sherman was thinking of the realities and dreams he had guarded. He had said nothing about what Mr Stevens had done until he had stuttered so much that his words seemed to make no sense. He had told no one about his search for his mother, no one about his dreams about Marian Anderson. No one, nobody knew his secret world.

'I don't "blah-blah" my ideas. You are the only person I've discussed them with,' said the Judge, 'except in a glancing way with my grandson.'

Secretly Sherman thought Jester was a smart cookie, although he would never have admitted it. 'What is his opinion?'

'He too is so self-centred and secretive he wouldn't give anyone the time of day even if he was just in front of the town clock. I had expected something better of you.'

Sherman was weighing his soft, bossy job against the letters he was asked to write. 'I will write other letters for you. Letters of acceptance, invitations, and so forth.'

'Those are insignificant,' said the Judge, who never went anywhere. 'A mere bagatelle.'

'I will write other letters.'

'No other letters interest me.'

'If you are so hipped on the subject you can write the letters yourself,' Sherman said, well knowing the condition of the Judge's handwriting.

'Sherman,' the old man pleaded, 'I have treated you as a son, and sharper than a serpent's tooth it is to have a thankless child.'

Often the Judge quoted this line to Jester, but with absolutely no effect. When the boy was small he had plugged his ears with his fingers, and when he was older he had cut up in one way or another to show his grandfather he didn't care. But Sherman was deeply affected; his grey-blue eyes fixed wonderingly on the blue eyes opposite him. Three times he had been called 'Son', and now the old Judge was speaking to him as though he was his own son. Never having had parents, Sherman had never heard the line that is the standard reproach of parents. Never had he sought his father, and now, as always, he kept the conjured image at a distance: blue-eyed Southerner, one among all the blue-eyed South. The Judge had blue eyes and so had Mr Malone. And so, as far as that goes, had Mr Breedlove at he bank, and Mr Taylor, and there were dozens of blue-eyed men in Milan he could think of offhand, hundreds in the country nearby, thousands in the South. Yet the Judge was the only white man who had singled out Sherman for kindness. And Sherman, being suspicious of kindness, wondered: Why had the Judge given him a watch with foreign words, engraved with his name, when he had hauled him out of that golf pond years ago? Why he had hired him for the cush job with the fancy eating arrangements haunted Sherman, although he kept his suspicions at arm's length.

Troubled, he could only skip to other troubles, so he said: 'I wrote Zippo's love letters. He can write, of course, but his letters don't have much zip, they never sent Vivian

Clay. Then I wrote "The dawn of love steals over me" and "I will love thee in the sunset of our passion as much as I do now." The letters were long on words like "dawn" or "sunset" and pretty colours. I would sprinkle in "I adore thee" often, and soon Vivian was not only sent but rolling in the aisles.'

'Then why won't you write my letters about the South?'

'Because the idea is queer and would turn back the clock.'

'I don't mind being called queer or reactionary either.'

'I just wrote myself out of a fine apartment, because after the love letters, Vivian herself popped the question and Zippo accepted very gladly. That means I will have to find another apartment; I wrote the very planks out of the floor.'

'You'll just have to find another apartment.'

'It's hard.'

'I don't think I could endure moving. Although my grandson and I racket around this big old house like two peas in a shoebox.'

The Judge, when he thought of his ornate Victorian house with the coloured windows and the stiff old furniture, sighed. It was a sigh of pride, although the people in Milan often referred to the house as 'The Judge's White Elephant'.

'I think I would rather be moved to the Milan Cemetery than have to move to another house.' The Judge considered what he had said and took it back quickly, vehemently: 'Pshaw, I didn't mean that, Son.' He touched wood carefully. 'What a foolish thing for a foolish old man to say. I was just thinking that I would find it mighty hard to live elsewhere on account of the memories.'

The Judge's voice was wavering, and Sherman said in a hard voice, 'Don't bawl about it. Nobody makin *you* move.'

'I dare say I'm sentimental about this house. A few people can't appreciate the architecture. But I love it, Miss Missy liked it, and my son Johnny was brought up in this house. My grandson, too. There are nights when I just lie in the bed and remember. Do you sometimes lie in the bed and remember?'

'Naw.'

'I remember things that actually happened and things that might have happened. I remember stories my mother told me about the War Between the States. I remember the years when I was a student at law school, and my youth, and my marriage to Miss Missy. Funny things. Sad things. I remember them all. In fact I remember the far-off past better than I recall yesterday.'

'I've heard that old people are like that. And I guess I heard right.'

'Not everyone can remember exactly and clear as a picture show.'

'Blah-blah,' said Sherman under his breath. But although he spoke toward the deaf ear, the old Judge heard and his feelings were hurt.

'I may be garrulous about the past, but to me it is just as real as the *Milan Courier*. And more interesting because it happened to me, or my relatives and friends. I know everything that has happened in the town of Milan since long before the day you were born.'

'Do you know about how I was born?'

The Judge hesitated, tempted to deny his knowledge; but since he found it difficult to lie, he said nothing.

'Did you know my mother? Did you know my father? Do you know where they are?'

But the old man, lost in the meditations of the past, refused to answer. 'You may think me an old man who tells everything, but as a jurist I keep my council and on some subjects I am as silent as a tomb.'

So Sherman pleaded and pleaded, but the old Judge prepared a cigar and smoked in silence.

'I have every right to know.'

As the Judge still smoked on in silence, Sherman again began to gaslight. They sat like mortal enemies.

After a long time, the Judge said, 'Why what's the matter with you, Sherman? You look almost sinister.'

'I feel sinister.'

'Well, stop looking at me in that peculiar way.'

Sherman kept right on gaslighting. 'Furthermore,' he said, 'I've got a good mind to give you quit notice. And how would you like that?'

And on these words, in the middle of the afternoon, he stomped away, pleased that he had punished the Judge and brushing aside the thought that he also punished himself.

Ten

Although the Judge seldom spoke about his son, he was with him often in his dreams. Only in the dream, that phoenix of remembrance and desire, could his memory live. And when he woke up he was always cross as two sticks.

As he lived very much in the here and now except for pleasant daydreams just before he went to sleep, the Judge seldom brooded over the past in which, as a judge, he had almost unlimited power – even the power of life and death. His decisions always were preceded by long cogitations; he never considered a death sentence without the aid of prayer. Not that he was religious, but it somehow siphoned the responsibility away from Fox Clane and dribbled it to God. Even so, he had sometimes made mistakes. He had sentenced a twenty-year-old Nigra to death for rape, and after his death another Nigra confessed to the crime. But how was he, as a judge, to be responsible? The jury after due consideration had found him guilty and had not recommended mercy; his decision just followed the law and the customs of the State. How could he know when the boy kept saying, 'I never done it,' that he was saying the God's truth? It was a mistake that might have put many a conscientious magistrate under the sod; but although the Judge regretted it deeply, he kept reminding himself that the boy had been tried by twelve good men and true and that he, himself, was only an instrument of the law. So, no matter how grave the miscarriage was, he could not pine forever.

The Nigra Jones was in another category. He had murdered a white man and his defence was self-defence. The witness of the murder was the white man's wife, Mrs Ossie Little. It had come about in this way: Jones and Ossie Little were sharecroppers on the Gentry farm, close to Sereno. Ossie Little was twenty years older than his wife, a part-time preacher who was able to make his Holy Roller congregation talk in strange tongues when the spirit came upon them. Otherwise he was a shambling, no-good tenant who let the farm rot. Trouble started as soon as he married a child-bride wife whose folks came up from around Jessup where their farm was in a ruined dust bowl area. They were travelling through Georgia in an old jalopy on the way to hope and California when they met up with Preacher Little and forced their daughter, Joy, to marry him. It was a simple, unsavoury story of the depression years and nothing good could reasonably be expected, and surely nothing good came of any part of the sorry affair. The twelve-year-old bride-child had character seldom met with in one so young. The Judge remembered her as a pretty little thing, at first playing dolls with a cigar box of doll's clothes, then having a little baby of her own to bear and care for when she was not yet thirteen. Then trouble, having started, compounded as trouble always does. First, it was rumoured that young Mrs Little was seeing more of the coloured tenant on the adjacent farm than was right and proper. Then Bill Gentry, provoked by Little's laziness, threatened to turn him off the farm and hand over his share to Jones.

The Judge pulled up a blanket on his bed as the night was very cold. And how did his fair-born, darling son get mixed up with Nigra murderers, shiftless preachers, child-brides? How? Oh how? And in what a mangled maw it was to lose his son!

Self-defence or not, the Nigra was doomed to die and Johnny knew it as well as anybody else. Why then did he persist in taking the case, which was a lost cause from the beginning? The Judge had argued to dissuade him. What would it fetch him? Nothing but failure. Yet, little had the Judge known that it would lead to more than a young man's hurt pride, more than a fledgling lawyer's failure – but that it would lead to obscure heartbreak and death. But how, oh how? The Judge groaned aloud.

Except for having to impose sentence, he had kept out of the case as much as possible. He knew that Johnny was all too deeply involved with the case, burned the midnight oil till daylight, and boned up on law as though in defending

Jones he was defending his own blood brother. During the six months Johnny was working on the case, the Judge reproached himself, he should have known. But how could he have known, not being a mind reader? In the courtroom Johnny was as nervous as any other fledgling lawyer at his first murder trial. The Judge had been distressed when Johnny agreed to take the case, was amazed at first at the way he handled it – hot potato that it was. Johnny was eloquent, just speaking the truth as he believed it. But how could you sway twelve good men and true like that? His voice did not rise and fall like most trial lawyers. He did not shout, then sink to a whisper at the incriminating point. Johnny just talked quietly as though he was not in court at all – how could that sway twelve good men and true? He was talking about justice with a voice that broke. He was also singing his swan song.

The Judge wanted to think of something else – to day-dream of Miss Missy and to go to sleep, but most of all he wanted to see Jester. In old age or invalidism, stories once remembered cast a spell on the mind. Useless to think about the time he had a box at the Opera; it was the first time the Atlanta Opera opened. He had invited his brother and sister-in-law as well as Miss Missy and her father for the gala occasion. The Judge had invited a whole box of friends. The first performance was *The Goose Girl,* and well did he remember Geraldine Farrar coming across the stage with two live geese on a kind of harness. The live geese said 'Quack, quack,' and old Mr Brown, Miss Missy's father, had said, 'First damned thing I've understood this evening.' How embarrassed Miss Missy was, and how pleased he had been. He had listened to the Germans squalling their heads off in German – the geese quacking – while he just sat there looking musical and learned. Useless to think of all these things. His mind came back to Ossie Little, the woman, and Jones – it would not let him rest. He struggled against it.

When was Jester ever coming home? He had never been hard on the boy. True, there was a peach switch in a vase on the diningroom mantelpiece, but he had never used it on Jester. Once when Johnny had been cutting up and throwing bread at the servant and his parents, he had lost his temper, taken down the peach switch, and dragged his young son to the library where, amid the wails of the entire household, he had cut him two or three times on his bare and jumping legs. After that, the switch remained stark in the vase on the mantelpiece as a threat but never once used from that day to this. Yet the Scripture itself said: 'Spare the rod and spoil the child.' If the peach switch had been used more often, would Johnny still be alive? He doubted it, but still he wondered. Johnny was too passionate; although it was not the passion he could readily recognize – the passion of the posse, the passion of the Southerner who defends his womankind against the black and alien invader – it was passion nonetheless, as strange as it had seemed to him and other Milan citizens.

Like a tedious tune that pounds in a fevered brain, the story insisted. The Judge turned mountainlike in his huge bed. When was Jester coming home? It was so late. Yet when he turned on the light he saw that it was still not nine o'clock. So Jester was not out so late after all. On the mantel to the left of the clock there was Johnny's photograph. The vigour of the young lost face seemed to blossom in the lamplight. On Johnny's left chin there was a small birthmark. This imperfection served only to sum up the beauty of Johnny's face, and when he noticed it the Judge felt closer to heartbreak.

Yet in spite of the spasm of grief that always came when he looked at the little birthmark, the Judge could not cry for his son. For underneath his emotions there was always resentment – a resentment that had been lulled at Jester's birth, softened a little by the passage of time, but always and forever there. It was as though his son had cheated him by depriving him of his beloved presence, the sweet and treacherous thief had plundered his heart. If Johnny had died in any other way, cancer or leukemia – the Judge knew more of Malone's illness than he let on – he could have grieved with a clear heart, cried also. But suicide seemed a deliberate act of spite which the Judge resented. In the photograph Johnny was faintly smiling and the little birthmark summed up the radiant face. The Judge folded back his twisted sheet and lumbered out of bed, steadying himself with his right hand as he crossed the room. He took down Johnny's photograph and put it in a bureau drawer. Then he steered himself into bed again.

There was the sound of Christmas chimes. For him, Christmas was the saddest season. The chimes, the Joy to the Worlds – so sad, so left, so lonesome. A flash of lightning lit up the dark sky. Was there a storm coming? If only Johnny had been struck by lightning. Yet one cannot choose. Either at birth or death one cannot choose. Only suicides could choose, disdaining the living quick of life for the nothing of the grave. Another flash of lightning was followed by thunder.

True, he had almost never used the peach switch, but he had counselled Johnny as a lad. He had been concerned about Johnny's admiration of Bolshevism, Samuel Liebowitz, and radicalism in general. He had always consoled himself by the fact that Johnny was young, was a quarterback on the University of Georgia football team, and that the fads and fancies of the young pass quickly when reality must be faced. True, Johnny's youth was so different from his father's waltzing, singing-and-dancing days when he was the beau of Flowering Branch and courted and won Miss Missy. He could only say to himself that 'Yond Cassius has a lean and hungry look; he thinks too much: such men are dangerous' – but he did not dwell on it, because in his wildest dreams he could not associate Johnny with danger.

Once he had said aloud that first year Johnny was in the firm, 'I have often noticed, Johnny, that when one is too much involved with the underdog, one is apt to go under oneself.'

Johnny had only shrugged his shoulders.

'When I first began to practise, I was a poor boy. Not a rich man's son like you.' Although he had noticed the embarrassment that flickered over Johnny's face, he had gone right on: 'I eschewed court charity cases which fall to the lot of a poor lawyer at first. My practice increased and soon I was able to defend the cases that brought in considerable financial returns. Financial returns or political prestige was, and always has been, a prime consideration.'

'I'm not that kind of lawyer,' Johnny said.

'I'm not trying to persuade you to emulate me,' the Judge said untruthfully. 'One thing – I have never taken a crooked case. I know when a client is lying and wouldn't touch the case with a ten-foot pole. I have a sixth sense in such matters. Remember the man who murdered his wife with a mashie on the golf course at the country club? The fee would have been princely, but I refused it.'

'As I remember it, there were witnesses.'

'Johnny, a lawyer of genius can bamboozle witnesses, convince the jury they were not where they swore they were, and could not possibly have seen the things they saw. However, I refused the case and many another like it. I have never committed myself to unsavoury cases, no matter how princely the fee.'

Johnny's smile was as ironical as the one in the photograph. 'Well, isn't that handsome of you!'

'Of course, when lucrative cases combine with a just cause, it is just sheer heaven for Fox Clane. Remember how I defended the Milan Power Company? Sheer heaven and a whopping fee.'

'The rates went way up.'

'You cannot sell your birthright for electricity and gas. I never had them as a child. Had to trim lamps and stoke stoves. But I was free.'

Johnny said nothing.

Often the Judge had taken down the photograph when paroxysms of emotion were caused by the little birthmark or when the smile seemed to mock him like a sneer. The photograph would be kept in the drawer until his mood changed or until he could no longer bear the absence of the likeness of his son. Then it would appear in the silver frame and he would gaze at the little blemish and even tolerate the remote and lovely smile.

'Don't misunderstand me,' he had counselled those years ago, 'I take lucrative cases but not out of self-interest.' The mature lawyer and ex-congressman had yearned for some word of appreciation from his young son. Had his honesty in saying home truths seemed like cynicism to Johnny?

After some time Johnny had said: 'Often this past year I have wondered how responsible you are.'

'Responsible!' The Judge flushed quickly, violently, 'I am the most responsible citizen in Milan, in Georgia, in all the South.'

To the tune of 'God Save The King', Johnny chanted, 'God help the South.'

'If it weren't for me, where do you think you would be?'

'A little scrap hanging out on the washline of heaven.' Johnny's voice changed. 'I never wanted to be your son.'

The Judge, still flushed with emotion, wanted to blurt, 'But I always wanted you to be my son.' Instead he asked, 'What kind of son do you think would be about right for the old man?'

'How about –' Johnny's mind turned over imaginary sons. 'Why, how about Alec Sisroe?' Johnny's light laugh blended with his father's bass guffaws. 'Motheromine, oh Motheromine,' the Judge quoted through his spittle and wild laughter. For Alex Sisroe quoted that poem every Mother's Day at the First Baptist Church. He was a prissy, weedy mother's boy, and Johnny would take off the performance to the delight of his father and disapproval of his mother.

The sudden, off-beat hilarity ended as quickly as it had begun. Often the father and son who responded to the ridiculous in the same manner were caught by such laughter. This side of their relationship had prompted the Judge to a further assumption, to a fallacy often common in fathers. 'Johnny and I are more like two brothers than father and son. The same love of fishing and hunting, same sterling sense of values – I have never known my son to tell a lie – same interests, same fun.' So the Judge would harp on such fraternal similarities to his audiences in Malone's pharmacy, in the courthouse, in the back room of the New York Café and in the barbershop. His listeners, seeing little relation between the shy young Johnny Clane and his town-character father, made no comment. When the Judge himself realized the widening difference between his son and himself, he harped on the father-son theme even more than ever, as though words could turn the wish into reality.

That last laugh about the 'Motheromine Boy' had been perhaps the last joke shared between them. And hacked about Johnny's reference to responsibility, the Judge had cut the laughter short and said: 'You seemed to criticize me for taking the case for the Milan Electric and Power Company. Am I right, Son?'

'Yes, sir. The rates went up.'

'Sometimes it is the painful choice of the mature mind to have to choose the lesser of two evils. And this was a case where politics were involved. Not that had any brief for Harry Breeze or the Milan Electric and Power, but the Federal Government was rearing its ugly head. Imagine when TVA and suchlike power plants control the entire nation. I could smell the stink of creeping paralysis.'

'Creeping paralysis doesn't stink,' Johnny had said.

'No, but socialism does to my nostrils. And when socialism takes away self-initiative and . . .' the Judge's voice meandered until he found a sudden image, 'puts people into cookie cutters, standardization,' the Judge said wildly. 'It might interest you to know, son, that I once had a scientific interest in socialism and even communism. Purely scientific, mind you, and for a very brief time. Then one day I saw a photograph of dozens of young Bolshevik women in identical gymnastic costumes, all doing the same exercise, all squatting. Dozens and dozens of them doing the same gymnastics, breasts the same, the hams the same, every posture, every rib, every behind the same, the same. And although I have no aversion to healthy womanflesh, whether Bolshevik or American, squatting or upright, the longer I studied the photograph the more I was revolted. Mind you, I might well have loved a single one among all those dozens of exuberant womanflesh – but seeing one after another, identical, I was revolted. And all my interest, however scientific, quite left me. Don't talk to me of standardization.'

'The last track I followed was that of the Milan Electric and Power raising the rates on utilities,' Johnny had said.

'What's a few pence to preserve our freedom and escape the creeping paralysis of socialism and the Federal Government? Should we sell our birthright for a mess of pottage?'

Old age and loneliness had not yet fixed the Judge's hostilities upon the Federal Government. He had spread his huffs of passing anger to his family, as he still had a family, or among his colleagues, as he was still an able, hard-working jurist who was not above correcting young trial lawyers when they misquoted Bartlett, Shakespeare, or the Bible, and his words were still weighed and heeded whether on the bench or not. It was the time when his chief concern had been the widening rift between Johnny and himself, but the concern had not yet changed to worry, and indeed he had mistaken it for youthful folly on the boy's part. He had not worried when Johnny had upped and got married after a dance, not worried that her father was a well-known rum runner – preferring in his secret heart a well-known rum runner to a preacher who might spoil the family feasting or try to crimp his style. Miss Missy had been brave about the matter, giving Mirabelle her second best string of pearls and a garnet brooch. Miss Missy had made much of the fact that Mirabelle had gone two years to Hollins College where she was a music major. Indeed, the two practised duets together, and memorized the 'Turkish March'.

The Judge's concern had not yet changed to worry until, after no more than a year of practice, Johnny had chosen to take the case of Jones *versus* the People. To what avail had Johnny graduated *magna cum laude* at the University, if he did not have a grain of common sense? To what avail had been Johnny's legal knowledge and education when he stepped on the bunions, corns, and callouses of every one of that jury of twelve good men and true?

Refraining from discussing the case with his son, he had cautioned him about a lawyer's sensitivity to jurors. He said, 'Talk on their own level and for God's sake don't try to lift them above it.' But would Johnny do that? He argued as if those Georgia crackers, millhands, and tenant farmers were trained jurors of the Supreme Court itself. Such talent. But not a grain of common sense.

It was nine-thirty when Jester came into the Judge's room. He was eating a double-decker sandwich which, after those hours of remembered anxiety and grief, the old man eyed hungrily. 'I counted on you for supper.'

'I took in a show and made myself a sandwich when I got home.'

The Judge put on his spectacles and peered at the thick sandwich. 'What's in it?'

'Peanut butter, tomatoes, and bacon and onions.'

Jester took a gaping bite of the sandwich and a chunk of onion fell to the carpet. To quell his appetite, the Judge shifted his eager gaze from the delicious sandwich to the onion which was stuck to the carpet with mayonnaise. His appetite still remained, and so he said: 'Peanut butter is loaded with calories.' Opening the liquor chest he poured some whisky. 'Just eighty calories an ounce. And more what I wanted anyhow.'

'Where is my father's picture?'

'In the drawer over there.'

Jester, who knew well his grandfather's habit of hiding the photograph when he was upset, asked, 'What's the matter?'

'Mad. Sad. Cheated. When I think of my son I often feel so.'

A certain stillness fell on Jester's heart, as it always did when his father was mentioned. The Christmas chimes were silvery in the frosty air. He stopped eating and silently placed the scallop-bitten sandwich on the end table beside the bed. 'You never talk about my father to me,' he said.

'We were more like brothers than father and son. Blood twin brothers.'

'I doubt it. Only introverts commit suicide. And you're no introvert.'

'My son was not an introvert I'll have you know, sir,' the Judge said with a voice that was shrill with rage. 'Same sense of fun, same mental calibre. Your father would have been a genius if he'd lived, and that's not a word I bandy about lightly.' (This was truer than anyone could have imagined, as the Judge used the word only when it applied to Fox Clane and William Shakespeare.) 'Like blood twin brothers we were until he got involved with the Jones case.'

'Is that the case where you always said my father was trying to break an axiom?'

'Laws, blood customs, axioms indeed!' Glaring at the bitten sandwich, he seized and ate it hungrily; but because his emptiness was not a hunger of the belly he remained uncomforted.

Since the Judge seldom talked about his son to Jester or satisfied his grandson's natural curiosity, Jester was used to asking angled questions, and so he asked: 'What was that case about?'

The Judge responded at so wide an angle that the answer and question did not directly meet. 'Johnny's adolescence was passed when communism was blaring wide and handsome in the grandstand. High muckety-mucks squatting in the very White House itself; the time of TVA, FHA, and FDR, all those muckety-muck letters. And one thing leading to another, a Negress singing at the Lincoln Memorial and my son –!' The Judge's voice soared with rage, 'and my son defending a Nigra in a murder case. Johnny tried to –' Hysteria overcame the old man, the hysteria of the fantastic incongruity which strikes upon the heart's chagrin. He could not finish for the painful cackles and flying spittle.

'Don't,' Jester said.

The rasping cackles and spittle continued while Jester watched soberly, his face white. 'I'm not,' the Judge managed to articulate until hysteria mounted again, 'not laughing.'

Jester sat upright in the chair, and his face was white. Alarmed, he began to wonder if his grandfather was having an apoplectic fit. Jester knew that apoplectic fits were queer and sudden. He wondered if people turned red as fire and laughed like that in an apoplectic fit. He knew, also, that people died from apoplectic fits. Was his grandfather, red as fire and choking, laughing himself to death? Jester tried to raise the old man so he could slap him on the back, but the weight was too heavy for him, and at last the laughter weakened and finally stopped.

Bewildered, Jester considered his grandfather. He knew that schizophrenia was a split personality. Was he acting crisscrossed in his old age, laughing fit to kill when he ought to be crying? He knew well that his grandfather loved his own son. A whole section of the attic was kept for his dead father: ten knives and an Indian dagger, a clown costume, the Rover Boy series, Tom Swift series, and stacks of child's books, a cow skull, roller skates, fishing tackle, football suits, catcher's mitts, trunks and trunks of fine things and junk. But Jester had learned that he must not play with the things in the trunks, fine things or junk, for once when he tacked the cow's skull to the wall of his own bedroom, his grandfather had been furious and threatened to switch him with the peach switch. His grandfather had loved his own and only son, so why did he laugh with hysterics?

The Judge, seeing the question in Jester's eyes, said quietly: 'Hysterics is not laughter, Son. It's a panic reaction of confusion when you cannot grieve. I was hysterical for four days and nights after my son's death. Doc Tatum helped Paul haul me into the bathtub for warm water baths and gave me sedatives and I kept on laughing – not laughing, that is – hysterical. Doc tried cold showers and more sedation. And there I was hysterical and the corpse of my son laid out in the parlour. The funeral had to be held over a day and I was so weak it took two big, strong men to hold me up when we went down to the church aisle. Tight fit we must have been,' he added soberly.

Jester asked in the same quiet voice: 'But why do you get hysterical now? It's over seventeen years since my father died.'

'And in all those years not a day has passed that I didn't think about my son. Sometimes for a glancing time, others for a brooding spell. I seldom ever trusted myself to speak of my son, but today most of the afternoon and the long evening I have been remembering – not only the skylarking times when we were young but the grown-up gravities that split and vanquished us. I was seeing my son at that last trial as plainly as I see you right now – plainer, in fact. And hearing his voice.'

Jester was holding the chair arms so tightly his knuckles whitened.

'His defence was masterly except for one fatal flaw. The fatal flaw was that the jurors never got the gist at all. My son argued the case as though he was talking to a panel of New York Jew lawyers instead of the panel of twelve men good and true of the Circuit Court in Peach County,

Georgia. Illiterate, one and all. Under the circumstances my son's opening move was a stroke of genius.'

Jester opened his mouth and breathed through it, so tense was his silence.

'My son's first motion was to request the jurors to rise and pledge allegiance to the American flag. The jurors shambled to their feet and Johnny read them through the rigmarole, the pledge. Both Nat Webber and I were caught flatfooted. When Nat objected, I rapped the gavel and ordered the words struck from the record. But that didn't matter. My son had already made his point.'

'What point?'

'At one stroke my son had joined those twelve men and prompted them to function at their highest level. They had been taught in school the pledge of allegiance and in speaking it, they were participating in some kind of holy exercise. I rapped the gavel!' The Judge grunted.

'Why did you strike it from the record?'

'Irrelevance. But my son, as defence lawyer, had made his point and lifted a sordid, cut-and-dried murder case to the level of constitutional law. My son went right on. "Fellow jurors and your honour –" My son looked hard at each juror as he spoke, and at me. "Each one of you twelve jurors has been lifted to an immense responsibility. Nothing takes precedence over you and your work at this hour."' Jester listened with his hand and forefinger propping up his chin, his wine-brown eyes wide and asking in his listening face.

'From the beginning, Rice Little maintained that Mrs Little had been raped by Jones, and his brother had every right to attempt to kill him. Rice Little just stood there like a little dirty feist dog guarding his brother's property line and nothing could shake him. When Johnny asked Mrs Little, she swore it wasn't so and that her husband had tried to kill Jones out of deliberate malice – and in the struggle for the gun her husband was killed – a strange thing for a wife to swear. Johnny asked if Jones had ever treated her in any way that was not right and proper and she said, "Never," that he had treated her always like a lady.'

The Judge added, 'I should have seen something. But then eyes had I, but saw not.'

'Plainer than yesterday I hear their words and see their faces. The accused had that peculiar colour of a Nigra who is deathly scared. Rice Little in his tight, Sunday suit and his face as hard and yellow as a cheese paring. Mrs Little just sat there, her eyes blue, blue and brazen, brazen. My son was trembling. After an hour my son shifted from the particular to the general. "If two white people or two Negro people were being tried for this same accident, there would have been no case at all, for it was an accident that the gun went off when Ossie Little was trying to kill the defendant."

'Johnny went on: "The fact is that the case involves a white man and a Negro man and the inequality that lies between the handling of such a situation. In fact, fellow jurors, in cases like this, the Constitution itself is on trial." Johnny quoted the preamble and the amendments freeing the slaves and giving them citizenship and equal rights. "These words I quote now were written a century and a half ago and spoken by a million voices. These words are the law of our country, I, as a citizen and lawyer, can neither add to nor subtract from them. My function in this court is to underscore and try to implement them." Then carried away, Johnny quoted "Four score and seven years ago –" I rapped.'

'What for?'

'These were just private words that Lincoln spoke, words that every law student memorizes, but I was not bound to hear them quoted in my courtroom.'

Jester said, 'My father wanted to quote them. Let me hear it now.' Jester did not know clearly what the quote would be, but he felt nearer to his father than he had ever been, and the riddling skeleton of suicide and the old glory hole trunks were being fleshed by a living image. In his excitement Jester rose and stood with one hand on the bedpost, one leg drawn up against the other, waiting. Since the Judge never needed a second invitation to sing or recite or otherwise exercise his voice for an audience, he gravely quoted the Gettysburg Address while Jester listened with tears of glory in his eyes, his foot drawn up and his mouth open.

At the end, the Judge seemed to be wondering why he

was quoting that. He said, 'One of the greatest pieces of oratory ever spoken, but a vicious rabble-rouser. Shut your mouth, boy.'

'I think it was terrible that you struck that from the record,' Jester said. 'What else did my father say?'

'His closing words, which should have been his most eloquent, petered out sadly after the high-flown impractical words of the Constitution and the Gettysburg Address. His own words drooped like a flag on a windless day. He pointed out that the amendments that followed the Civil War had not been implemented. But when he spoke of civil rights, he was so wrought up he pronounced it "thivil" which made a bad impression and naturally undercut his own confidence. He pointed out that the population of Peach County was almost equally balanced between the Nigra and white races. He said he noticed that there was no Nigra represented on the jury and the jurors looked quickly at each other, suspicious and puzzled.

'Johnny asked, "Is the defence being accused of murder, or of rape? The prosecution has tried to smear the defendant's honour and the honour of Mrs Little with sly and evil insinuations. But I am defending him against the accusation of murder."

'Johnny was trying to get to a climax. His right hand grabbed as though to conjure some word. "For more than a century these words of the Constitution have been the law of our land, but words are powerless unless they are enforced by law, and after this long century our courts are stately halls of prejudice and legalized persecution as far as the Negro is concerned. The words have been spoken. The ideas have been shaped. And how long will be the lag between the words and the idea and justice?"

'Johnny sat down,' the Judge added bitterly, "and I unscrooched my behind.'

'You what?' Jester asked.

'My behind, which had been scrooched up ever since that mistake about "thivil" instead of civil. I relaxed when Johnny's speech was finished.'

'I think it was a brilliant defence,' Jester said.

'It didn't work. I retired to my chambers to await the

verdict. They were out just twenty minutes. Just time enough to troop down to the courthouse basement and to check their decisions. I knew what the verdict would be.'

'How could you know?'

'When rape is even rumoured under such circumstances, the verdict is always guilty. And when Mrs Little was so quick to speak up for her husband's killer, it just looked downright strange. Meanwhile, I was as innocent as a newborn babe, and so was my son. But the jury smelled a rat and returned a guilty verdict.'

'But wasn't it a frame-up?' Jester said angrily.

'No. The jury had to decide who was telling the truth, and in this case they decided right, although little did I reck at the time. When the verdict was announced there was a great wail from Jones's mother in the courtroom, Johnny turned ghost pale, and Mrs Little swayed in her chair. Only Sherman Jones seemed to take it like a man.'

'Sherman?' Jester paled and flushed in quick succession. 'Was the Negro named Sherman?' Jester asked in a vacant voice.

'Yes, Sherman Jones.'

Jester looked puzzled and his next question was widely angled, tentative. 'Sherman is not a common name.'

'After Sherman marched through Georgia many a coloured boy was named for him. Personally I have known half a dozen in my lifetime.'

Jester was thinking about the only Sherman he knew, but he kept silent. He only said 'I don't see it.'

'Neither did I at the time. Eyes had I and did not see. Ears had I and did not hear. If I had just used my God-born sense in that courtroom, or if my son had confided in me.'

'Confided what?'

'That he was in love with that woman, or thought he was.'

Jester's eyes were suddenly still with shock. 'But he couldn't be! He was maried to my mother!'

'Like blood twin brothers we are, Son, instead of grand-father and grandson. Like two peas in a pod. Same innocence, same sense of honour.'

'I don't believe it.'

'I didn't either when he told me so.'

Jester had often heard about his mother so that his curiosity about her had been satisfied. She had been, as he knew, fond of ice cream, especially baked Alaskas, she played the piano, and was a music major at Hollins College. These scraps of information had been told him readily, casually, when he was a child, and his mother had not elicited the awe and mystery the boy felt for his father.

'What was Mrs Little like?' Jester asked finally.

'A hussy. She was very pale, very pregnant, very proud.'

'Pregnant?' Jester asked, repelled.

'Very. When she walked through the streets it was as though she expected the crowds to part for her and her baby like the Red Sea parted for the Israelites.'

'Then how could my father have fallen in love with her?'

'Falling in love is the easiest thing in the world. It's standing in love that matters. This was not real love. It was love like you are in love with a cause. Besides, your father never acted on it. Call it infatuation. My son was a Puritan and Puritans have more illusions than people who act out every love at first sight, every impulse.'

'How terrible for my father to be in love with another woman and be married to my mother, too.' Jester was thrilled with the drama of the situation and felt no loyalty to his baked-Alaska mother. 'Did my mother know?'

'Of course not. My son only told me the week before he killed himself, he was so upset, so shocked. Otherwise, he would never have told me.'

'Shocked about what?'

'To make an end to the story, after the verdict and execution, Mrs Little called for Johnny. She had had her baby and she was dying.'

Jester's ears had turned very red. 'Did she say she loved my father? Passionately, I mean?'

'She hated him and told him so. She cursed him for being a fumbling lawyer, for airing his own ideas of justice at the expense of his client. She cursed and accused Johnny, maintaining that if he had conducted the case as a cut-and-dried matter of self-defence Sherman Jones would be a free man now. A dying woman, ranting, wailing, grieving, cursing. She said that Sherman Jones was the cleanest, most decent man she had ever known and that she loved him. She showed Johnny the newborn baby, dark-skinned and with her own blue eyes. When Johnny came home he looked like that man who went over Niagara Falls in a barrel.

'I just let Johnny talk away, then I said, "Son, I hope you have learned a lesson. That woman couldn't possibly have loved Sherman Jones. He is black and she is white."'

'Grandfather, you talk like loving a Negro is like loving a giraffe or something.'

'Of course it wasn't love. It was lust. Lust is fascinated by the strange, the alien, the perverse and dangerous. That's what I told Johnny. Then I asked him why he took it so to heart. Johnny said: "Because I love Mrs Little, or would you have me call it lust?"'

'"Either lust or lunacy, Son, " I said.'

'What happened to the baby?' Jester asked.

'Evidently, Rice Little took the baby after Mrs Little died and left it on a pew of the Holy Ascension Church in Milan. It must have been Rice Little, he's the only one I can figure out.'

'It is our Sherman?'

'Yes, but don't tell him of any of this,' the Judge warned.

'Did my father kill himself the day Mrs Little showed him the baby and cursed him and accused him?'

'He waited until Christmas afternoon, a week later, after I thought I had knocked some sense into his head and it was all over and done with. That Christmas started like any other Christmas, opening presents in the morning, and piled up Christmas wrapping under the Christmas tree. His mother had given him a pearl stickpin and I had given him a box of cigars and a shockproof, waterproof watch. I remember Johnny banged the watch and put it in a cup of water to test it. Over and over I have reproached myself that I didn't notice anything in particular that day, since we were like blood twin brothers I should have felt the mood of his despair. Was it normal to horse around with the shockproof, waterproof watch like that? Tell me, Jester.'

'I don't know, but don't cry, Grandfather.'

For the Judge, who had not cried in all these years, was weeping for his son at last. The journey into the past which he had shared with his grandson had mysteriously unlocked his stubborn heart so that he sobbed aloud. A voluptuary in all things, he now sobbed with abandon and found it sweet.

'Don't, Grandfather,' Jester said. 'Don't, Grandy.'

After the hours of remembrance, the Judge was living in the here and now again. 'He's dead,' he said. 'My darling is dead but I'm alive. And life is so full of a number of things. Of ships and cabbages and kings. That's not quite right. Of ships and, and –'

'Sealing wax,' Jester prompted.

'That's right. Life is so full of a number of things, of ships and sealing wax and cabbages and kings. This reminds me, Son, I've got to get a new magnifying glass. The print of the *Milan Courier* gets wavier every day. And last month a straight was staring me straight in the face and I missed it – mistaking a seven for a nine. I was so vexed with myself I could have burst out bawling in the back room of the New York Café.

'And furthermore, I'm going to get a hearing aid although I've always maintained that they were oldladyish and did not work. Besides, one of these years I am going to get second senses. Improved eyesight, hearing, a vast improvement of all the senses.' How this would come about the old Judge did not explain, but living in the here and now and dreaming of a more vivid future, the Judge was content. After the emotions of the evening he slept peacefully all through the winter night, and did not wake up until six the next morning.

Eleven

Who am I! What am I? Where am I going? Those questions, the ghosts that haunt the adolescent heart, were finally answered for Jester. The uneasy dreams about Grown Boy, which had left him guilty and confused, no longer bothered him. And gone were the dreams of saving Sherman from a mob and losing his own life while Sherman looked on, broken with grief. Gone also were the dreams of saving Marilyn Monroe from an avalanche in Switzerland and riding through a hero's ticker tape parade in New York. That had been an interesting daydream, but after all, saving Marilyn Monroe was no career. He had saved so many people and died so many hero's deaths. His dreams were nearly always in foreign countries. Never in Milan, never in Georgia, but always in Switzerland or Bali or someplace. But now his dreams had strangely shifted. Both night dreams and daydreams. Night after night he dreamed of his father. And having found his father he was able to find himself. He was his father's son and he was going to be a lawyer. Once the bewilderment of too many choices was cleared away, Jester felt happy and free.

He was glad when the new term of school opened. Wearing brand new clothes he had got for Christmas (brand new shoes, brand new white shirt, brand new flannel pants), he was free, surehearted now that the 'Who am I? What am I? Where am I going?' was answered at last. He would study harder this term, especially English and history – reading the Constitution and memorizing the great speeches whether they were required in the course or not.

Now that the deliberate mystery of his father had been dispelled, his grandfather occasionally spoke of him; not often, not weeping, but just as though Jester had been initiated like a Mason or Elk or something. So Jester was able to tell his grandfather about his plans, to tell him that he was going to study law.

'The Lord knows I never encouraged it. But if that's what you want to do, Son, I will support you to the best of my ability.' Secretly the Judge was overjoyed. He could not help showing it. 'So you want to emulate your grandfather?'

Jester said, 'I want to be like my father.'

'Your father, your grandfather ... we were like blood twin brothers. You are just another Clane off the old block.'

'Oh, I'm so relieved,' said Jester. 'I had thought about so many things that I could do in life. Play the piano, fly a plane. But none of them exactly fitted. I was like a cat always climbing the wrong tree.'

In the beginning of the New Year the even tenor of the Judge's life was abruptly shattered. One morning when Verily came to work she put her hat on the back porch hatrack and did not go into the front of the house to start the day's house cleaning as usual. She just stood in the kitchen, dark, stubborn, implacable.

'Judge,' she said, 'I want them papers.'

'What papers?'

'The govment papers.'

To his outraged amazement and the ruin of his first cigar, Verily began to describe social security. 'I pays part of my salary to the govment and you supposed to pay a part.'

'Who's been talking all that stuff to you?' The old Judge thought probably this was another Reconstruction, but he was too scared to let on.

'Folks was talking.'

'Now, Verily, be reasonable. Why do you want to pay your money to the government?'

'Because it's the law and the govment is catching folks. Folks I knows. It's about this here income tax.'

'Merciful God, you don't want to pay income tax!'

'I does.'

The Judge prided himself on understanding the reasons of Nigras and said with soothing firmness, 'You have got this all mixed up. Forget it.' He added helplessly, 'Why, Verily, you have been with us close on to fifteen years.'

'I wants to stay in the law.'

'And a damn interfering law it is.'

The truth of what Verily wanted finally came out. 'I wants my old age pension when the time comes for it.'

'What do you need your old age pension for? I'll take care of you when you are too old to work.'

'Judge, you're far beyond your three score years and ten.'

That reference to his mortality angered the Judge. Indeed the whole situation made him fit to be tied. Moreover, he was puzzled. He had always felt he understood Nigras so well. He had never realized that every Sunday morning when at dinner time he had said, 'Ah, Verily, Verily, I say unto you, you will live in the Kingdom of Heaven . . .' he had not noticed how, Sunday after Sunday, that had irritated Verily. Nor had he noticed how much affected she had been since the death of Grown Boy. He thought he understood Nigras, but he was no noticer.

Verily would not be side-tracked. 'There's a lady will figure out them govment papers, pay me forty dollars a week, and give me Saturday and Sunday free.'

The Judge's heart was beating fast and his face changed colour. 'Well, go to her!'

'I can find somebody to work for you, Judge. Ellie Carpenter will take my place.'

'Ellie Carpenter! You know good and well she doesn't have the sense of a brass monkey!'

'Well, how about that worthless Sherman Pew?'

'Sherman is no servant.'

'Well, what do you think he is?'

'No trained servant.'

'There is a lady will figure out the govment papers, pay me forty dollars a week, and give me Saturday and Sunday free.'

The Judge grew angrier. In the old days a servant was paid three dollars a week and felt herself well paid. But each year, year after year, the price of servants had gone up so that the Judge was now paying Verily thirty dollars a week, and he had heard that well-trained servants were getting thirty-five and even forty. And even then they were scarce as hen's teeth these days. He had always been a servant-spoiler; indeed, he had always believed in humanity – did he have to believe in such high wages too? But, wanting peace and comfort, the old Judge tried to back down. 'I will pay the social security for you myself.'

'I don't trust you,' Verily said. He realized for the first time that Verily was a fierce woman. Her voice was no longer humble, but fierce. 'This woman will figure out my govment papers, pay me forty dollars a week . . .'

'Well, go to her!'

'Right now?'

Although the Judge had seldom raised his voice to a servant, he shouted, 'Now, God dammit! I'll be glad to be rid of you!'

Although Verily had a temper, she would not let herself speak. Her purplish, wrinkled lips just grimaced with anger. She went to the back porch and carefully put on her hat with the pink roses. She did not even glance around the kitchen where she had worked for nearly fifteen years, nor did she tell the Judge good-bye as she stomped away, through the back door.

The house was absolutely silent and the Judge was afraid. He was afraid that if he was left alone there in his own house he would have a stroke. Jester would not be back from school until afternoon and he could not be left alone. He remembered that as a little boy Jester would scream in the darkness, 'Somebody! Anybody!' The Judge felt like screaming that now. Until the house became silent, the Judge never knew how necessary the voice of the house was to him. So he went to the courthouse square to pick up a servant, but times had changed. No longer could one pick up a Nigra in the courthouse square. He asked three Nigras but they were all employed, and they looked at the Judge as though he was out of his mind. So he went to the barbershop. He had a haircut, a shampoo, a shave and, to kill time, a manicure. Then when everything had been done for him at the barbershop, he went to the Green Room at the Taylor Hotel to kill some more time. He took two hours over his lunch at the Cricket Tea Room and then he went around to see J. T. Malone at the pharmacy.

Rootless and dismal, the Judge passed three days in this way. Because he was afraid to be alone at home, the Judge was always on the streets of Milan or in the Green Room at the Taylor Hotel, at the barbershop, or sitting on one of the white benches of the courthouse square. At suppertime, he fried steaks for himself and Jester, and Jester washed the dishes.

As servants had always been available to him as a part of his way of life, it never occurred to him to go to an agency. The house got dirty. How long this sad state of affairs would have lasted is hard to say. One day he went to the pharmacy and asked J. T. Malone if Mrs Malone could help him out in finding a servant. J. T. promised to talk with Mrs Malone.

The January days were glossy blue and gold and there was a warm spell. In fact, it was a false spring. J. T. Malone, revived by the new turn of the weather, thought he was better and planned a journey. Alone and secretly he was going to Johns Hopkins. On that first fatal visit Dr Hayden had given him a year or fifteen months to live, and already ten months had passed. He felt so much better that he wondered if the Milan GPs hadn't been mistaken. He told his wife that he was going to Atlanta to attend a pharmaceutical convention, and the secrecy and deceit pleased him so that he was almost gay when he set out on his northward journey. With a feeling of guilt and recklessness he travelled pullman, killed time in the club car, ordered two whiskies before lunch and the seafood platter, although liver was the special on the menu.

The next morning it was raining in Baltimore and Malone was cold and damp as he stood in the waiting room explaining to the receptionist what he wanted. 'I want the best diagnostician in this hospital because the GPs in my hometown are so far behind the times I don't trust them.'

There followed the now familiar examinations, the wait for slides and tests, and finally the too-familiar verdict. Sick with rage, Malone took the day coach back to Milan.

The next day he went to Herman Klein and put his watch down on the counter. 'This watch loses about two minutes every week,' he said pettishly to the jeweller. 'I demand that my watch keep strict railroad time.' For in his limbo of waiting for death, Malone was obsessed with time. He was always deviling the jeweller, complaining that his watch was two minutes too slow or three minutes too fast.

'I overhauled this watch just two weeks ago. And where are you going that you have to be on strict railroad time!'

Rage made Malone clench his fists until the knuckles whitened and swear like a child. 'What the hell business is it of yours where I'm going! What the fuckin' hell!'

The jeweller looked at him, abashed by the senseless anger. 'If you can't give me proper service I'll take my trade elsewhere!' Taking his watch. Malone left the shop, leaving Herman Klein to stare after him with puzzled surprise. They had been mutually loyal customers for close on to twenty years.

Malone was going through a time when he was often subject to these fits of sudden rage. He could not think directly of his own death because it was unreal to him. But these rages, unprovoked and surprising even to himself, stormed frequently in his once calm heart. Once he was picking out pecans with Martha to decorate some cake or other when he hurled the nutcracker to the floor and jabbed himself viciously with the nut picker. On tripping over a ball that Tommy had left on the stairs, he threw it with such force that it broke a pane of the front door. These rages did not relieve him. When they were over, Malone was left with the feeling that something awful and incomprehensible was going to happen that he was powerless to prevent.

Mrs Malone found the Judge a servant, so he was rescued from the streets. She was nearly full Indian and very silent. But the Judge was no longer afraid to be alone in the house. He no longer wanted to call, 'Somebody! Anybody!' for the presence of another human being consoled him so that the house with the stained glass window, the pier table with the mirror, the familiar library and dining room and parlour was no longer silent. The cook was named Lee, and the meals were sloven, badly cooked and badly served. When she served soup at the beginning of dinner, her thumbs were stuck a half inch into the sloshing soup. But she had never heard of social security and could neither read nor write, which gave the Judge some subtle satisfaction. Why, he did not question.

Sherman did not altogether make good his threat of leaving the Judge, but the relation had much deteriorated. He came every day and gave him his injections. Then, sullen and looking put upon, he would idle in the library, sharpening pencils, reading immortal poetry to the Judge, fixing their noon toddies and so forth. He would not write any letters about the Confederate money. Although the Judge knew he was deliberately acting ugly and he was not getting a lick of work out of him, except for the injections, the Judge let him stay on, hoping things might change for the better. He would not even allow the old Judge the pleasure of bragging about his grandson and his decision to go into law. When he would mention the subject, Sherman would hum rudely or yawn like an alligator. The Judge often repeated, 'The devil has work for idle hands.' When the Judge said that, he looked directly at Sherman, but Sherman only looked directly back at him.

One day the Judge said, 'I want you to go to my office in the courthouse and look in the steel filing case under "Clippings". I want to read my clippings from the newspapers. Little as you know it, I am a great man.'

'The steel filing case under "C" for "Clippings"', Sherman repeated, for he was delighted with the errand. He had never been in the Judge's office and he had yearned to.

'Don't monkey around with my important papers. Just take the newspaper clippings.'

'I don't monkey around,' Sherman said.

'Give me a toddy before you go. It's twelve o'clock.'

Sherman did not share the noon toddy, but went straight to the courthouse. On the door of the office, there was printed on the frosted glass a sign saying: CLANE & SON, ATTORNEYS-AT-LAW. With a little thrill of pleasure, Sherman unlocked the door and went into the sunny room.

After taking out the file marked 'Clippings', he took his time to meddle with other papers in the steel cabinet. He was not looking for anything in particular, just a born meddler, and he was mad that the Judge had said 'Don't monkey around.' But at one o'clock that afternoon, while the Judge was eating his dinner, Sherman found the folder which held the papers from Johnny's brief. He saw the name Sherman. Sherman? Sherman? Except for this Sherman, I am the only one I know of who has that name. How many Shermans are there in town? As he read the papers, his head swayed. At one o'clock that afternoon he found out that there was a man of his own race whom the Judge had had executed, and his name was Sherman. And there was a white woman who was accused of fucking the Negro. He could not believe it. Could he ever be sure? But a white woman, blue eyes, was all so otherwise than he had dreamed. It was like some eerie, agonizing crossword puzzle. And he, Sherman . . . Who am I? What am I? All that he knew at that hour was that he was sick. His ears were waterfalls of disgrace and shame. No, Marian Anderson had not been his mother, nor Lena Horne, nor Bessie Smith, nor any of the honeyed ladies of his childhood. He had been tricked. He had been cheated. He wanted to die like the Negro man had died. But he would never fool around with a white person, that was for sure. Like Othello, that cuckoo Moor! Slowly he replaced the folder, and when he returned to the Judge's house he walked like a sick man.

The Judge had just waked from his nap; it was afternoon when Sherman came back. Not being a noticer, the Judge did not notice Sherman's shaken face and trembling hands. He asked Sherman to read the files aloud and Sherman was too broken not to obey.

The Judge would repeat phrases Sherman read, such as: *A fixed star in the galaxy of Southern statesmanship. A man of vision, duty and honour. A glory to this fair State and to the South.*

'See?' the old Judge said to Sherman.

Sherman, still shaken, said in a quavering voice, 'You have a slice of ham like a hog!'

The Judge, still wrapped up in his own greatness, thought it was some compliment and said. 'What's that, boy?' For although the Judge had bought a hearing aid and a new magnifying glass, his sight and hearing were failing rapidly and he had not got second sight and the improvement of all his senses.

Sherman did not answer, because having a slice of ham like a hog was one thing, but it was not insult enough for his life and the fucking blue eyes and who they came from. He was going to *do something, do something, do something*. But when he wanted to slam down the sheaf of papers he was so weak that he just put them limply on the table.

When Sherman had gone, the Judge was left alone. Putting his magnifying glass close to the clippings, he read out loud to himself, still wrapped up in his greatness.

Twelve

The green-gold of the early spring had darkened to the dense, bluish foliage of early May and the heat of summer began to settle over the town again. With the heat came violence and Milan got into the newspapers: *The Flowering Branch Ledger*, *The Atlanta Journal*, *The Atlanta Constitution*, and even *Time* Magazine. A Negro family moved into a house in a white neighbourhood and they were bombed. No one was killed, but three children were hurt and vicious feeling mounted in the town.

At the time of the bombing, Sherman was in trouble. He wanted to *do something, do something, do something,* but he did not know what he could do. The bombing went into his black book. And slowly he started to go out of line. First he drank water at the white fountain in the courthouse square. No one seemed to notice. He went to the white men's room at the bus station. But he went so hurriedly and furtively that again no one noticed. He sat on a back pew at the Baptist Church. Again, no one noticed except at the end of the service, and an usher directed him to a coloured church. He sat down in Whelan's drugstore. A clerk said, 'Get away, nigger, and never come back.' All these separate acts of going out of line terrified him. His hands were sweaty, his heart lurching. But terrified as he was, he was more disturbed by the fact that nobody seemed to notice him except the clerk at Whelan's. Harassed and suffering, *I've got to do something, do something, do something* beat like a drum in his head.

Finally he did something. When he gave the Judge his injections in the morning, he substituted water instead of insulin. For three days that went on and he waited. And again in that creepy way nothing seemed to happen. The Judge was as crickety as ever and did not seem sick at all.

But although he hated the Judge and thought he ought to be wiped from the face of the earth, he knew all along it should have been a political murder. He could not kill him. If it were a political murder, maybe with a dagger or with a pistol he could have, but not in that sneaky way of substituting water for insulin. It was not even noticed. The fourth day he went back to insulin. Urgent, unceasing the drum beat in his head.

Meanwhile the Judge, no noticer, was pleasant and unusually agreeable. This infuriated Sherman. It got to the point that with the Judge, as well as other white men, there was no motive for his hate, just compulsion. Wanting to go out of line and afraid, wanting to be noticed and afraid to be noticed. Sherman was obssessed those early May days. *I have got to do something, do something, do something.*

But when he did something it was so strange and zany that even he could not understand it. One glassy late afternoon while he was passing through the Judge's backyard going to the lane, Jester's dog, Tige, jumped on his shoulders and licked his face. Sherman would never know why he did what he did. But deliberately he picked up a clothesline, made a noose of it, and hanged the dog on an elm branch. The dog struggled only for a few minutes. The deaf old Judge did not hear his strangled yelps and Jester was away.

Yet, early as it was, Sherman went to sleep without supper and slept like the dead that night and only woke up when Jester pounded at the door at nine in the morning.

'Sherman!' Jester was calling in a voice that was shrill with shock. While Sherman took his time dressing, dabbling water on his face, Jester was still pounding at the door and screaming. When Sherman came out, Jester half dragged him to the Judge's yard. The dog, stiff in death, hung against the blue May sky. Jester was crying now. 'Tige, Tige. How? What?' Then he turned to Sherman who stood looking at the ground. A nightmare suspicion came to Jester which was suddenly affirmed by Sherman's downward-staring face.

'Why, Sherman? Why did you do this insane thing?' He stared at Sherman in the stun of not yet realized truth. He was hoping he would know the right thing to say, the right thing to do, and hoping he would not vomit. He did not vomit, but went to the shed to get a shovel to dig the grave. But as he lowered the body, cut the noose and placed Tige in the grave, he felt he was going to faint.

'How did you know right away I done it?'

'Your face, and I just knew.'

'I see you walking that white man's dog, getting all dressed up in them seersucker pants, going to the white man's school. Why don't nobody care about me? I do things, don't nobody notice. Good or mean, nobody notices. People pet that goddamned dog more than they notice me. And it's just a dog.'

Jester said, 'But I loved him. And Tige loved you too.'

'I don't love no white man's dog and I don't love nobody.'

'But the shock. I can't get over it.'

Sherman thought of the May sun on the courthouse papers. 'You're shocked. You ain't the only one who has been shocked.'

'A thing like this makes me think you ought to be in Milledgeville.'

'Milledgeville!' Sherman mocked. His limp hands waggled in an imitation of an idiot. 'I'm too smart, kid, to get in Milledgeville. Nobody else would have believed what I done about the dog. Even a crazy-doctor. If you think that is something crazy, you wait and see what else I am going to do.'

Arrested by the threat in his voice, Jester couldn't help but say, 'What?'

'I am going to do the craziest thing I have ever done in my life before, me or any other nigger.'

But Sherman would not tell Jester what he was planning to do, nor could Jester make Sherman feel guilty about Tige's death or even realize that he was acting creepy. Too upset to go to school that day, too restless to hang around the house, he told his grandfather that Tige was dead, had died in his sleep and that he had buried him, and the old Judge did not question further. Then for the first time in his life, Jester played hooky from school and went to the airport.

The old Judge waited in vain for Sherman, but Sherman was writing a letter with the 'calligraphy of an angel'. He was writing an Atlanta agency in order to rent a house in Milan in the white man's section. When the Judge called him, Sherman said that he was not going to come to work any longer and His Honour could get his injections somewhere else.

'You mean you're leaving me high and dry?'

'That's right. High and dry, Judge.'

The Judge was left on his own again without Sherman. Reading the *Milan Courier* with the new magnifying glass, with the silent half-Indian servant who never sang and Jester away at school, the Judge was tired and idle. It was a blessing when a veterinarians' convention was held in the town. Poke Tatum attended and he and a half-dozen other delegates stayed at the Judge's house. Mule doctors, pig doctors, dog doctors, they drank up a storm and slid down the banisters. The Judge felt that sliding down the banisters was going a bit too far, and he missed his wife's dainty church conventions when the preachers and church delegates sang hymns and minded their P's and Q's. When the veterinarians' convention was over and Poke gone, the house was lonelier than ever and the emptiness of the old Judge blanker, more dismal. He blamed Sherman for leaving him. He thought back to the times when there was not only one servant in the house, but two or three, so that the voices of the house were like mingling brown rivers.

Meanwhile, Sherman had got a reply from the agency and sent a money order for the rent. His race was not questioned. He began to move in two days later. The house was around the corner from Malone's house, next door to the three little houses that Mrs Malone had inherited. A store was beyond the house that Sherman had rented, and after that the neighbourhood was Negro. But shabby and beaten up as it was, his house was in a white section. Sammy Lank and the Lank brood lived next door. Sherman bought on time a baby grand piano and beautiful genuine antique-y furniture and had a mover move them to his new house.

He moved in the middle of May and at last he was

noticed. The news spread like wildfire through the town. Sammy Lank went to Malone to complain and Malone went to the Judge.

'He's left me high and dry. I am too furious to fool with him any longer.'

Sammy Lank, Bennie Weems and Max Gerhardt, the chemist, milled around the Judge's house. The Judge began to work on Malone, 'I don't hold with violence any more than you do, J. T., but when a thing like this comes up I feel it is my duty to act.'

Secretly the Judge was excited. In the old days the Judge had been a Ku Kluxer and he missed it when the Klan was suppressed and he could not go to those white-sheeted meetings at Pine Mountain and fill himself with a secret and invisible power.

Malone, no Ku Kluxer, was feeling unusually peaked these days. The house was not his wife's property, thank goodness, and besides, it was a sagging, waucome-sided house.

The Judge said, 'It's not people like you and me, J. T., who will be affected if things like this go on. I have my house here and you have your house on a very good street. We are not affected. Nigras are not likely to be moving in on us. But I am speaking as a chief citizen of this town. I am speaking for the poor, for the unprofited. We leading citizens have to be the spokesmen for the downtrodden. Did you notice Sammy Lank when he came to the house? I thought he was going to have apoplexy. All worked up, as what he should be since his house is the house next door. How would you like to be living next door to a Nigra?'

'I wouldn't like it.'

'Your property would depreciate, the property that old Mrs Greenlove left your wife would depreciate.'

Malone said, 'For years I have advised my wife to sell those three houses. They have turned into nothing but a slum.'

'You and I as foremost citizens of Milan . . .' Malone was meekly proud that he was bracketed with the Judge.

'Another thing,' the Judge went on, 'you and I have our property and our positions and our self-respect. But what does Sammy Lank have except those slews of children of his? Sammy Lank and poor whites like that have nothing but the colour of their skin. Having no property, no means, nobody to look down on – that is the clue to the whole thing. It is a sad commentary on human nature but every man has to have somebody to look down on. So the Sammy Lanks of this world only have the Nigra to look down on. You see, J. T., it is a matter of pride. You and I have our pride, the pride of our blood, the pride in our descendants. But what does Sammy Lank have except those slews of white-headed triplets and twins and a wife worn out with child-bearing sitting on the porch dipping snuff?'

It was arranged that a meeting would be held in Malone's pharmacy after hours, and that Jester should drive the Judge and Malone to the meeting. That night there was a moon serene in the May night. To Jester, to the old Judge, it was just a moon, but Malone looked at the moon with a hollow sadness. How many May nights had he seen the moon? And how many more moons like this would he ever see? Would this be the last one?

While Malone sat quiet and wondering in the car, Jester was wondering also. What was this meeting all about? He felt it had something to do with Sherman moving into the white section.

When Malone opened the side door to the compounding room, he and the Judge went inside. 'You go on home, son' the Judge said to Jester. 'Some of the boys will bring us back.'

Jester parked the car around the corner while Malone and the Judge went into the pharmacy. Malone turned on the fan so that the warm stale air was churned to a breeze. He did not fully light the drugstore and the half-light gave a sense of conspiracy.

Assuming that the arrivals would come through the side door, he was surprised when there was a loud knock at the front. It was Sheriff McGall, a man with dainty purplish hands and a broken nose.

Meanwhile, Jester had come back to the drugstore. The side door was closed but not locked and he entered very quietly. At the same moment, a group of new arrivals were knocking at the front and being admitted, and Jester's presence was unnoticed. Jester was very silent in the darkness of the compounding room, afraid of being discovered and sent away. What were they doing at this hour when the drugstore was closed?

Malone did not know what the meeting would be like. He had expected a group of leading citizens, but except for Hamilton Breedlove, the cashier at the Milan Bank & Trust Company, and Max Gerhardt, the chemist at the Nehi plant, there were no leading citizens. There were old poker cronies of the Judge, and there was Bennie Weems and Sport Lewis and Sammy Lank. Some of the other new arrivals Malone knew by sight, but they were nameless. A group of boys arrived in overalls. No, they were not leading citizens, but ragtag and bobtail for the most part. Moreover, on arrival they were halfway liquored up and there was the atmosphere of a carnival. A bottle was passed around and put on the counter of the fountain. Before the beginning of the meeting, Malone was already regretting that he had lent his pharmacy to it.

It may have been Malone's frame of mind, but he recalled something unpleasant about each of the men he met that night. Sheriff McCall had always sucked up to the old Judge so obviously that it had offended Malone. Besides, he had once seen the sheriff beat a Negro girl with his billy stick on the corner of Twelfth Street and Main. He looked hard at Sport Lewis. Sport had been divorced by his wife for extreme mental cruelty. A family man, Malone wondered what extreme mental cruelty could be. Mrs Lewis had got a Mexican divorce and later on she had married again. But what was that – extreme mental cruelty? He realized he himself was no saint and once he had even committed adultery. But no one was hurt and Martha never knew. An extreme mental cruelty? Bennie Weems was a deadbeat and his daughter was sickly so that he was always in debt to Malone and the bills were always unpaid. And it was said that Max Gerhardt was so smart that he could figure out how long it took a toot go get to the moon. But he was German, and Malone had never trusted Germans.

Those gathered in the drugstore were all ordinary people,

so ordinary that he usually didn't think of them one way or the other. But tonight he was seeing the weaknesses of these ordinary people, their little uglinesses. No, none of them were leading citizens.

The round yellow moon made Malone feel sad and chilly although the night was warm. The smell of whisky was strong in the drugstore and this faintly nauseated him. There were more than a dozen people there when he asked the Judge: 'Is everybody here that's coming?'

The Judge himself seemed a little disappointed when he said, 'It's ten o'clock; I guess so.'

The Judge began in his old grandiloquent speech voice. 'Fellow citizens, we are gathered here together as leading citizens of our community, as property owners and defenders of our race.' There was a hush in the room. 'Little by little we white citizens are being inconvenienced, even gravely put upon. Servants are scarce as hen's teeth and you have to pay them an arm and a leg to keep them.' The Judge listened to himself, looked at the people, and realized he was off on the wrong tack. Because by and large these were not the people who kept servants.

He started again. 'Fellow citizens, are there no zoning laws in this town? Do you want coal-black niggers moving in right next door to your house? Do you want your children crowded in the back of the bus while coal-black niggers sit in the front? Do you want your wife carrying on behind the back fence with nigger bucks?' The Judge posed all the rhetorical questions. The crowd muttered among themselves and from time to time there were shouts of 'No. Goddammit, no.'

'Are we going to let the zoning of our town be decided by niggers? I'm asking you, are we or are we not?' Balancing himself carefully, the Judge pounded his fist on the counter. 'This is the hour of decision. Who is running this town, us or the niggers?'

Whisky was freely passed around and there was in the room a fraternity of hate.

Malone looked at the moon through the plate-glass window. The sight of the moon made him feel sickish, but he had forgotten why. He wished he was picking out nuts with Martha, or at home with his feet on the banisters of the porch drinking beer.

'Who's going to bomb the bastard?' a hoarse voice called.

Malone realized that few in the crowd actually knew Sherman Pew, but that a fraternity of hate made them all act together. 'Should we draw lots, Judge?' Bennie Weems, who had done this sort of thing before, asked Malone for a pencil and paper and began to tear strips of paper. Then he marked an X on one strip. 'The X is the one.'

Cold, confused by the bustle, Malone still looked at the moon. He spoke in a dry voice: 'Can't we just talk with the Nigra? I never liked him, even when he was your houseboy, Judge. Just a biggity, disrespectful, and a thoroughly bad Nigra. But violence or bombing I don't hold with.'

'No more do I, J.T. And I am fully cognizant that we, as members of this citizens' committee, are taking the law into our own hands. But if the law does'nt protect our interests and the interests of our children and descendants, I am willing to go around the law if the cause is just and if the situation threatens the standards of our community.'

'Everybody ready?' Bennie Weems asked. 'The X mark is it.' At that moment Malone particularly loathed Bennie Weems. He was a weasel-faced garage man and a real liquorhead.

In the compounding room, Jester sat hugging the wall so closely that his face was pressed against a bottle of medicine. They were going to draw lots to bomb Sherman's house. He would have to warn Sherman, but he didn't know how to get out of the drugstore, so he listened to the meeting.

Sheriff McCall said, 'You can take my hat,' as he proffered his Stetson. The Judge drew first and the others followed. When Malone took the balled-up paper his hands were trembling. He was wishing he was home where he belonged. His upper lip was pressed against the lower. Everybody unrolled his paper under the dim light. Malone watched them and he saw, one after another, the slackened face of relief. Malone, in his fear and dread, was not surprised when his unrolled paper had an X mark on it.

'I guess it is supposed to be me,' he said in a deadened voice. Everybody looked at him. His voice rose. 'But if it's bombing or violence, I can't do it.'

'Gentlemen.' Looking around the drugstore, Malone realized there were few gentlemen there. But he went on. 'Gentlemen, I am too near death to sin, to murder.' He was excruciatingly embarrassed, talking about death in front of this crowd of people. He went on in a stronger voice, 'I don't want to endanger my soul.' Everybody looked at him as though he had gone stark raving crazy.

Somebody said in a low voice, 'Chicken.'

'Well, be durned,' Max Gerhardt said. 'Why did you come to the meeting?'

Malone was afraid that in public, in front of the crowd in the drugstore, he was going to cry. 'A year ago my doctor said I had less than a year or sixteen months to live, and I don't want to endanger my soul.'

'What is all this talk about soul?' asked Bennie Weems in a loud voice.

Pinioned by shame, Malone repeated, 'My immortal soul.' His temples were throbbing and his hands unnerved and shaking.

'What the fuck is an immortal soul?' Bennie Weems said.

'I don't know,' Malone said. 'But if I have one, I don't want to lose it.'

The Judge, seeing his friend's embarrassment, was embarrassed in turn. 'Buck up, Son,' he said in a low voice. Then in a loud voice he addressed the men. 'J.T. here doesn't think we ought to do it. But if we do do it, I think we ought to do it all together, because *then* it's not the same thing.'

Having made a fool and a spectacle of himself in public, Malone had no face to save, so he cried out, 'But it is the same thing. Whether one person does it or a dozen, it's the same thing if it's murder.'

Crouched in the compounding room, Jester was thinking that he never thought old Mr Malone had it in him.

Sammy Lank spat on the floor and said again, 'Chicken.' Then he added, 'I'll do it. Be glad to. It's right next to my house.'

All eyes were turned to Sammy Lank who was suddenly a hero.

Thirteen

Jester went immediately to Sherman's house to warn him. When he told about the meeting at the pharmacy, Sherman's face turned greyish, the pallor of dark skin in mortal fright.

Serves him right, Jester thought. Killing my dog. But as he saw Sherman trembling, suddenly the dog was forgotten and it was as though he was seeing Sherman again for the first time as he had seen him that summer evening almost a year ago. He, too, began to tremble, not with passion this time, but from fear for Sherman and from tension.

Suddenly Sherman began to laugh. Jester put his arms around the shaking shoulders. 'Don't act like that, Sherman. You've got to get out of here. You've got to leave this house.'

When Sherman looked around the room with the new furniture, the bought-on-time baby grand piano, bought-on-time genuine antique sofa and two chairs, he began to cry. There was a fire in the fireplace, for although the night was warm, Sherman was cold and the fire had looked cosy and homelike to him. In the firelight the tears were purple and gold on this greyish face.

Jester said again, 'You've got to leave this place.'

'Leave my furniture?' With one of the wild swings of mood that Jester knew so well, Sherman began to talk about the furniture. 'And you haven't even seen the bedroom suite, with the pink sheets and boudoir pillows. Or my clothes.' He opened the closet door. 'Four brand new Hart, Schaffner & Marx suits.'

Wheeling wildly to the kitchen, he said, 'And the kitchen with all modern conveniences. And all my own.' In an ecstacy of ownership, Sherman seemed to have forgotten all about the fear.

Jester said, 'But didn't you know this would happen?'

'I knew and I didn't know. But it's not going to happen! I have invited guests with RSVP invitations to a house-warming party. I bought a case of Lord Calvert's bottled-in-bond, six bottles of gin, six bottles of champagne. We are having caviar on crisp pieces of toast, fried chicken, Harvard beets, and greens.' Sherman looked around the room. 'It's not going to happen because, boy, you know how much this furniture cost? It's going to take me more than three years to pay for it and the liquor and clothes.' Sherman went to the piano and stroked it lovingly. 'All my life I have wanted an elegant baby grand.'

'Stop all this goofy talk about baby grands and parties. Don't you realize this is serious?'

'Serious? Why should they bomb me? Me who is not even noticed. I went to the dime store and sat down on one of those stools. That is the actual truth.' (Sherman *had* gone to the dime store and sat down on one of the stools. But when the clerk approached threateningly, Sherman said, 'I'm sick. Will you give me a glass of water, miss?')

'But now you've been noticed,' Jester said. 'Why can't you forget all this mania about black and white, and go North where people don't mind so much? I know that if I were a Negro, I'd certainly light out for the North.'

'But I can't,' Sherman said. 'I have rented this house with my good money and moved in this beautiful furniture. For the last two days I have been arranging everything. And if I do say so myself, it's elegant.'

The house was suddenly all of Sherman's world. He never thought consciously about his parentage these days, since his discovery in the Judge's office. There was just a sense of murk and desolation. He had to busy himself with furniture, with things, and there was always this ever present sense of danger and the ever present sense that he would never back down. His heart was saying, *I have done something, done something, done something*. And fear only buoyed his elation.

'You want to see my new green suit?' Sherman, wild with tension and excitement, went to the bedroom and put on his new Nile green silk suit. Jester, trying desperately to cope with the veering Sherman, watched while Sherman pranced through the room in the new green suit.

Jester could only say, 'I don't care about all this furniture and suits but I do care about you. Don't you realize this is serious?'

'Serious, man?' Sherman began to pound middle C on the piano. 'Me who has kept a black book all my life, and you talk about serious? Did I tell you about vibrations? I vibrate, vibrate, vibrate!'

'Stop pounding the piano like a lunatic and listen to me.'

'I have made my decision. So I am going to stay right here. Right here. Bombing or no. Besides, why the fucking hell do you care?'

'I don't know why I care so much, but I do.' Over and over Jester had asked himself why he cared for Sherman. When he was with him, there was a shafting feeling in the region of his belly or his heart. Not all the time, but just in spasms. Unable to explain it to himself, he said, 'I guess it's just a matter of cockles.'

'Cockles? What are cockles?'

'Haven't you ever heard the expression, cockles of your heart?'

'Fuck cockles. I don't know anything about cockles. All I know is, I have rented this house, paid my good money, and I am going to stay. I'm sorry.'

'Well you have got to do better than be sorry. You have got to move.'

'Sorry,' Sherman said, 'about your dog.'

As Sherman spoke, the little spasm of sweetness shafted in that region of Jester's heart. 'Forget the dog. The dog is dead. And I want for you to be living always.'

'Nobody lives for always, but when I live I like to live it up.' And Sherman began to laugh. Jester was reminded of another laughter. It was the laughter of his grandfather when he talked about his dead son. The senseless pounding on the piano, the senseless laughter, jangled his grief.

Yes, Jester tried to warn Sherman, but he would not be warned. It was up to Jester now. But who could he turn to? What could he do? He had to leave Sherman sitting there, laughing and pounding on middle C of the baby grand piano.

Sammy Lank had no idea how to make a bomb so he went to the smart Max Gerhardt who made him two. The explosive feelings of the last days, the shame, the outrage, the insult, the hurt and fearful pride had almost gone away, and when Sammy Lank stood with the bomb that soft May evening looking at Sherman through the open window, his passion had been almost spent. He stood numb of any feelings except a feeling of shallow pride that he was doing what had to be done. Sherman was playing the piano and Sammy watched him curiously, wondering how a nigger could learn how to play the piano. Then Sherman began to sing. His strong dark throat was thrown back, and it was at that throat that Sammy aimed the bomb. Since he was only a few yards away, the bomb was a direct hit. After the first bomb was thrown a feeling savage and sweet came back to Sammy Lank. He threw the second bomb and the house began to burn.

The crowd was already in the street and yard. Neighbours, customers at Mr Peak's, even Mr Malone himself. The fire trucks shrilled.

Sammy Lank knew he had got the nigger, but he waited until the ambulance came and he watched them cover the torn dead body.

The crowd outside the house stayed on to wait. The fire department put out the fire and the crowd moved in. They hauled the baby grand out in the yard. Why, they did not know. Soon a soft drizzling rain set in. Mr Peak who owned the grocery store adjoining the house had a very good business that night. The news reporter on the *Milan Courier* reported the bombing for the early edition of the paper.

Since the Judge's house was in another part of town Jester did not even hear the bombing, and only heard the news the next morning. The Judge, emotional in his old age, took the news emotionally. Uneasy and nostalgic, the soft-hearted, soft-brained old Judge visited the morgue at the hospital. He did not look at the body, but had it removed to an undertaking establishment where he handed over five hundred dollars in United States greenbacks for the funeral.

Jester did not weep. Carefully, mechanically, he wrapped the *Tristan* score he had inscribed to Sherman and placed it in one of his father's trunks up in the attic and locked it.

Rain had fallen all night but had now stopped, and the sky was the fresh and tender blue that follows a long rain. When Jester went to the bombed house, four of the Lank brood were playing 'Chopsticks' on the piano which was now ruined and out of tune. Jester stood in the sunlight hearing the dead and no-tune 'Chopsticks' and hatred was mingled with his grief.

'Is your father there?' he called to one of the Lank brood.

'No he ain't,' the child answered.

Jester went home. He took the pistol, the one that his father had used to shoot himself, and put it in the glove compartment of the car. Then cruising around town slowly, he first went to the mill and asked for Sammy Lank. He was not there. The nightmare feeling of out-of-tune 'Chopsticks', the little Lanks, added to his feeling of frustration that he could not find Sammy Lank and made him beat the steering wheel with his fists.

He had been afraid for Sherman but he never really felt it would ever happen. Not a real happening. It was all just a nightmare. 'Chopsticks' and ruined pianos and the determination to find Sammy Lank. Then when he started driving again, he saw Sammy Lank lounging before Mr Malone's drugstore. He opened the door and beckoned. 'Sammy. You want to come with me to the airport? I'll take you on an airplane ride.'

Sammy, sheepish and unaware, grinned with pride. He was thinking: Already I'm such a famous man in town that Jester Clane takes me for an airplane ride. He jumped in the car joyfully.

In the training Moth, Jester seated Sammy first, then scrambled around to the other side. He had put the pistol in his pocket. Before taking off, he asked, 'Ever been in an airplane before?'

'No, sir,' said Sammy, 'but I'm not scared.'

Jester made a perfect take-off. The blue sky, the fresh

windy atmosphere, quickened his numbed soul. The plane climbed.

'Was it you who killed Sherman Pew?'

Sammy only grinned and nodded.

At the sound of Sherman's name there was again the little cockles spasm.

'Do you have any life insurance?'

'Nope. Just younguns.'

'How many younguns are there?'

'Fourteen,' said Sammy. 'Five of them grown.'

Sammy, who was petrified of a plane, began to talk with nervous foolishness. 'Me and my wife almost had quints. There were three younguns and two things. It was right after the quints in Canada were born and they were our first younguns. Every time me and my wife used to think of the quints in Canada – rich, famous, mother and daddy rich and famous too – a little quinch came in us. We almost hit the jackpot, and every time we did it we thought that we were making quints. But we only had triplets and twins and little ole singles. Once me and my wife took all the younguns to Canada to see the quints in their little glass playhouse. Our younguns all got the measles.'

'So that's why you had so many children.'

'Yep. We wanted to hit the jackpot. And me and my wife were naturals for borning twins and triplets and such. But we never hit it. However, there was an article in the *Milan Courier* about our Milan triplets. It's framed and on our living room wall. We've had a hard time raising those younguns but we never gave up. And now that my wife has changed life, it's all over. I'll never be nothing but Sammy Lank.'

The grotesque pity of the story made Jester laugh that laughter of despair. And once having laughed and despaired and pitied, he knew he could not use the pistol. For in that instant the seed of compassion, forced by sorrow, had begun to blossom. Jester slipped the pistol from his pocket and dropped it out of the plane.

'What's that?' said Sammy, terrified.

'Nothing,' Jester said. He looked across at Sammy who had turned green. 'Do you want to go down?'

'No,' said Sammy. 'I ain't scared.'
So Jester circled on.

Looking downward from an altitude of two thousand feet, the earth assumes order. A town, even Milan, is symmetrical, exact as a small grey honeycomb, complete. The surrounding terrain seems designed by a law more just and mathematical than the laws of property and bigotry: a dark parallelogram of pine wood, square fields, rectangles of sward. On this cloudless day the sky on all sides and above the plane is a blind monotone of blue, impenetrable to the eye and the imagination. But down below the earth is round. The earth is finite. From this height you do not see man and the details of his humiliation. The earth from a great distance is perfect and whole.

But this is an order foreign to the heart, and to love the earth you must come closer. Gliding downward, low over the town and countryside, the whole breaks up into a multiplicity of impressions. The town is much the same in all its seasons, but the land changes. In early spring the fields here are like patches of worn grey corduroy, each one alike. Now you could begin to tell the crops apart: the grey-green of cotton, the dense and spidery tobacco land, the burning green of corn. As you circle inward, the town itself becomes crazy and complex. You see the secret corners of all the sad back yards. Grey fences, factories, the flat main street. From the air men are shrunken and they have an automatic look, like wound-up dolls. They seem to move mechanically among haphazard miseries. You do not see their eyes. And finally this is intolerable. The whole earth from a great distance means less than one long look into a pair of human eyes. Even the eyes of the enemy.

Jester looked into Sammy's eyes which were popped with terror.

His odyssey of passion, friendship, love, and revenge was now finished. Gently Jester landed the airplane and let Sammy Lank out – to brag to his family that he is such a well-known man now that even Jester Clane had taken him up on an airplane ride.

Fourteen

At first Malone cared. When he saw that Bennie Weems had taken his trade to Whelan's and that Sheriff McCall did not drink his customary cokes at the pharmacy, he cared. In the front of his mind he said, 'To hell with Bennie Weems; to hell with the sheriff.' But deep down he worried. Had that night at the drugstore jeopardized the goodwill of the pharmacy and a sale for the goodwill? Was it worth taking the stand he did at the meeting? Malone wondered and worried and still he did not know. Worry affected his health. He made mistakes – mistakes in book-keeping that were unusual with a good figuring book-keeper like Malone. He sent out inaccurate bills which customers complained about. He did not have the strength to push sales properly. He himself knew that he was failing. He wanted the shelter of his home, and often he would stay whole days in the double bed.

Malone, dying, was sensitive to sunrise. After the long, black night, he watched the false dawn and the first ivory and gold and orange of the eastern sky. If it were a fair and blossomy day, he sat up on the pillows and eagerly awaited breakfast. But if the day was gloomy with sour skies or rain, his own spirits were reflected in the weather so that he turned on the light and complained fretfully.

Martha tried to comfort him. 'It's just this first hot spell. When you get accustomed to the weather you will feel better.'

But no, it was not the weather. He no longer confused the end of life with the beginning of a new season. The wisteria trellis lake lavender waterfalls had come and gone. He did not have the strength to plant the vegetable garden. And the gold-green willows were turning darker now. Curious, he had always thought of willows in connexion with water.

But his willows had no water, although there was a spring across the street. Yes, the earth had revolved its seasons and spring had come again. But there was no longer a revulsion against nature, against things. A strange lightness had come upon his soul and he exalted. He looked at nature now and it was part of himself. He was no longer a man watching a clock without hands. He was not alone, he did not rebel, he did not suffer. He did not even think of death these days. He was not a man dying – nobody died, everybody died.

Martha would sit in the room knitting. She had taken up knitting and it soothed him to see her there. He no longer thought about the zones of loneliness that had so bewildered him. His life was strangely contracted. There was the bed, the window, a glass of water. Martha brought him meals on a tray and nearly always she had a vase of flowers on the bed table – roses, periwinkle, snapdragons.

The love for his wife that had so receded returned to him. As Martha thought of little dainty things to tempt his appetite or knitted in the sickroom, Malone felt a nearer value of her love. It touched him when she bought from Goody's Department Store a pink bedrest so he could sit propped up in bed without being supported by only the damp sliding pillows.

Since that meeting at the pharmacy, the old Judge treated Malone as an invalid. Their roles were now reversed; it was the Judge now who brought sacks of water-ground meal and turnip greens and fruit as one brings to a sick man.

On May fifteenth the doctor came twice, once in the morning and again in the afternoon. The current doctor was now Dr Wesley. On May fifteenth, Dr Wesley spoke with Martha alone in the living room. Malone did not care that they were talking about him in another room. He did not worry, he did not wonder. That night when Martha gave him his sponge bath, she bathed his feverished face and put cologne behind both his ears and poured more cologne in the basin. Then she washed his hairy chest and armpits in the scented water, and his legs and calloused feet. And finally, very gently, she washed his limp genitals.

Malone said, 'Darling, no man has ever had such a wife as you.' It was the first time he had called her darling since the year after they were married.

Mrs Malone went into the kitchen. When she came back, after having cried a little, she brought with her a hot water bottle. 'The nights and early dawns are chilly.' When she put the hot water bottle in the bed, she asked, 'Comfy, Hon?'

Malone scrounged down from his bedrest and touched his feet to the hot water bottle. 'Darling,' he said again, 'may I have some ice water?' But when Martha brought the ice water the cubes of ice bumped against his nose so he said, 'This ice tickles my nose. I just wanted plain cold water.' And having taken the ice from the water, Mrs Malone withdrew into the kitchen to cry again.

He did not suffer. But it seemed to him that his bones felt heavy and he complained.

'Hon, how can your bones feel heavy?' Martha said.

He said he was hungry for watermelon, and Martha bought shipped watermelon from Pizzalatti's, the leading fruit and candy store in town. But when the slice of melon, pink with silvery frost, was on his plate, it did not taste like he thought it would.

'You have to eat to keep up your strength, J.T.'

'What do I need strength for?' he said.

Martha made milkshakes and surreptitiously she put an egg in them. Two eggs in fact. It comforted her to see him drink it.

Ellen and Tommy came back and forth in the sickroom and their voices seemed loud to him, though they tried to talk softly.

'Don't bother your father,' Martha said. 'He is feeling pretty peaked now.'

On the sixteenth Malone felt better and even suggested that he shave himself and take a proper bath. So he insisted on going to the bathroom, but when he reached the washbasin he only grasped the basin with his hands and Martha had to lead him back to the bed.

Yet the last flush of life was with him. His spirit was strangely raw that day. In the *Milan Courier* he read that a man had saved a child from burning and had lost his own life. Although Malone did not know the child or the man, he began to cry, and kept on crying. Raw to anything he read, raw to the skies, raw to the world outside the window – it was a cloudless, fair day – he was possessed by a strange euphoria. If his bones weren't so heavy, he felt he could get up and go down to the pharmacy.

On the seventeenth he did not see the May sunrise for he was asleep. Slowly the flush of life he had felt the last day was leaving him. Voices seemed to come from far away. He could not eat his dinner, so Martha made a milkshake in the kitchen. She put in four eggs, and he complained of the taste. The thoughts of the past and this day were commingled.

After he refused to eat his chicken supper, there was an unexpected visitor. Judge Clane suddenly burst into the sickroom. Veins of anger pulsed in his temples. 'I came to get some Miltown, J.T. Have you heard the news on the radio?' Then he looked at Malone and was shocked by his sudden feebling. Sorrow battled with the old Judge's fury. 'Excuse me, dear J.T.,' he said in a voice that was suddenly humble. Then his voice rose: 'But have you heard?'

'Well, what is it, Judge? Heard what?' Martha asked.

Sputtering, incoherent with anger, the Judge told about the Supreme Court decision for school integration. Martha, flabbergasted and taken aback, could only say, 'Well! I vow!' as she had not quite taken it in.

'There are ways we can get around it,' cried the Judge. 'It will never happen. We will fight. All Southerners will fight to the last ditch. To the death. Writing it in laws is one thing but enforcing it is another. A car is waiting for me; I am going down to the radio station to make an address. I will rally the people. I want something terse and simple to say. Dramatic. Dignified and mad, if you know what I mean. Something like: "Four score and seven years ago –" I'll make it up on the way to the station. Don't forget to hear it. It will be a historic speech and will do you good, dear J.T.'

At first Malone hardly knew the old Judge was there. There was just his voice, his huge sweaty presence. Then the words, the sounds, ricocheted in his un-understanding ears: integration ... Supreme Court. Concepts and thought washed in his mind, but feebly. Finally Malone's love and friendship for the old Judge called him back from his dying. He looked at the radio and Martha turned it on, but since a dance band was playing, she turned it down very low. A newscast that announced again the Supreme Court decision preceded the speech by the Judge.

In the soundproof room of the radio station, the Judge had latched on the microphone like a professional. But although he had tried to make up a speech on the way to the station, he had not been able to. The ideas were so chaotic, so inconceivable, he could not formulate his protests. They were too passionate. So, angry, defiant – expecting at any moment a little seizure, or worse – the Judge stood with the microphone in his hand and no speech ready. Words – vile words, cuss words unsuitable for the radio – raged in his mind. But no historic speech. The only thing that came to him was the first speech he had memorized in law school. Knowing dimly somehow that what he was going to say was wrong, he plunged in.

'Four score and seven years ago,' he said, 'our fathers brought forth on this continent a new nation, conceived in liberty, and dedicated to the proposition that all men are created equal. Now we are engaged in a great civil war, testing whether that nation, or any nation so conceived and so dedicated can long endure.'

There was the sound of scuffling in the room and the Judge said in an outraged voice: 'Why are you poking me!' But once you get on the track of a monumental speech, it's hard to get off. He went on, louder:

'We are met on a great battlefield of that war. We have come to dedicate a portion of that field as a final resting place for those who here gave their lives that that nation might live. It is altogether fitting and proper that we should do this.'

'I said quit poking me,' the Judge shouted again.

'But, in a larger sense, we cannot dedicate – we cannot consecrate – we cannot hallow this ground. The brave men living and dead who struggled here have consecrated it far above our poor power to add or detract. The world will little note nor long remember what we say here –'

'For chrissakes!' somebody shouted, 'cut it!'

The old Judge stood at the microphone with the echo of his own words ringing in his ears and the memory of the sound of his own gavel rapping in his courtroom. The shock of recognition made him crumble, yet immediately he shouted: 'It's just the other way around! I mean it just the other way around! Don't cut me off!' pleaded the Judge in an urgent voice. 'Please don't cut me off.'

But another speaker began and Martha switched off the radio. 'I don't know what he was talking about,' she said. 'What happened?'

'Nothing, darling,' Malone said. 'Nothing that was not a long time in the making.'

But his livingness was leaving him, and in dying, living assumed order and a simplicity that Malone had never known before. The pulse, the vigour was not there and not wanted. The design alone emerged. What did it matter to him if the Supreme Court was integrating schools? Nothing mattered to him. If Martha had spread out all the Coca-Cola stocks on the foot of the bed and counted them, he wouldn't have lifted his head. But he did want something, for he said: 'I want some ice-cold water, without any ice.'

But before Martha could return with the water, slowly, gently, without struggle or fear, life was removed from J. T. Malone. His livingness was gone. And to Mrs Malone who stood with the full glass in her hand, it sounded like a sigh.